K.A. MERIKAN

ALL I WANT FOR CHRISTMAS IS

REVENGE

Contents

Chapter 1   1

Chapter 2   7

Chapter 3   15

Chapter 4   21

Chapter 5   31

Chapter 6   37

Chapter 7   47

Chapter 8   61

Chapter 9   69

Chapter 10   75

Chapter 11   83

Chapter 12   91

Chapter 13 99

Chapter 14 113

Chapter 15 123

Chapter 16 137

Chapter 17 143

Chapter 18 149

Chapter 19 161

Chapter 20 175

Chapter 21 187

Chapter 22 199

Chapter 23 209

Chapter 24 223

Chapter 25 229

Chapter 26 241

Chapter 27 249

Epilogue 259

CHAPTER 1

SAINT

MY UNCLE SHOULD HAVE warned me being a hitman is the loneliest of jobs. The only people who get to see the real me? My marks. And I never get to enjoy much time in their company.

But it is what it is.

"How do you like your steak? It's a pretty good cut, so I assume... rare?" I ask, basting the chunk of meat with herby butter while the gentleman sitting by the table grunts into the clean tea towel I stuffed into his mouth earlier.

Ugh, such an ugly sound.

"My thoughts exactly," I say, careful to not splash any of the fat on my white shirt.

After almost twenty years in this line of work, I should know better than to wear white, but it just looks so good against my tan I end up with it more often than not. What can I say? I like the finer things in life, and a crisp white shirt is my indulgence. I don't have a boyfriend to spoil so I might as well buy myself a new shirt after every job.

The scent of the meat fills the kitchen, making me salivate. I am always happy to give someone a proper sendoff rather than just end things with a quick jab of the needle or an unexpected twist to their neck. There is something poetic in a person getting to contemplate all the mistakes they made in life, as well as wonder about the good things that will never happen. And as I plate the steak alongside a serving of potatoes and a salad, I'm regretful I can't afford to let my victim have a final bite of delicious food.

Then again, he was the one who chose to reside in an apartment building in the middle of town, and I'm not letting him spoil my afternoon by shouting for help.

"I haven't dined in company for a while. Can you believe it?" I ask, taking a seat across from my mark, whose bloodshot eyes regard me frantically, as if he still believes there's a way out of this. Then again, civilians often do. They imagine themselves as action heroes capable of untangling my knots and then somehow escaping the clutches of a professional killer.

Obviously, if that kind of thing ever happened, I'd be out of a job.

Daryl, because that's the name of the guy who picked the meat I'm going to have for dinner tonight, huffs, and a bit of saliva dribbles down his chin, having soaked through the bundle of fabric.

I shrug, starting with the salad as I regard him. "Thank you for noticing. I am quite handsome. Tall, dark-haired, firm muscles, amazing eyes... Oh, I get laid, all right, but it's tough to date in my line of work. Suppose straight hitmen have it easier?" I ask.

The panic in his eyes makes me laugh, and he rattles in the chair as if he thinks I might want something sexual from him just because I'm gay.

"You're not even my type, so don't get ahead of yourself. It's just..." I glance at the snow falling outside the window. It shimmers like glitter in the glow of street lamps. "I don't know what it is about Christmas time, but it always makes loneliness feel more pronounced. People go pick trees together, drink hot chocolate in cafes, and frantically buy last-minute gifts. The irony, right? All this money I saved up over the years, and no one to buy a present for."

Even the delicious steak tastes somewhat bitter.

Daryl grunts into the gag, no doubt telling me something about 'having a family', and I shake my head, cutting into the steak. The juices make the meat look delectable, and I groan with pleasure as I bite in. "See, that's the problem. That dog you poisoned? It was Mrs. Walker's only family. She's right not to let that go. My uncle took out the people who killed our remaining family. And when *he* died, I avenged him too. It's what makes the world tick. Don't you think it's poetic that you'll also die by poison?"

Daryl's forehead shines with sweat but he tries breathing through his nose to calm down. That won't change his fate either.

"What? You're sorry?" I contemplate that for a while between one bite and another. "First of all, I don't think you are. Second, too little too late. That dog died in her arms. No apology can undo that. I don't even know why you have to make any of this about yourself when you'll be gone very soon, and I'll have no one to be honest with again."

Daryl thrashes, screaming into the gag, but I keep eating even as he falls over. That man couldn't unwind my knots if he dislocated each of his fingers, but I still peer his way. "On the way here, I was considering to maybe let you live until Christmas, but that would have been too much hassle. People like you aren't good companion material. I did my research, and there's a reason why you sleep alone and why you only have one steak in your fridge."

Once I'm done with the food, I get up promptly, because there's no point wasting any more time with my mark. I have to face the reality that he's not a suitable stand-in for a partner.

Daryl tries to crawl away, making jerky motions in the chair he's tied to, but even he must know it's hopeless.

I open the little case containing a syringe and the tiniest of needles, and then hold him still as the point goes into his ear. A moment of struggle, and then it's over. I leave him on the floor as he drifts out of consciousness, and take my time putting all the dishes into the washer, then clean every surface. By the time I'm done, he's gone, and I remove all the signs of his untimely death being anything but a sudden-onset medical issue.

It's not always the way I do things, I like my guns, and most of all, to make things personal with a knife, but Mrs. Walker "*didn't want to make a fuss*". Who am I to question her wishes when her money swells my bank account?

When I leave the apartment, a hollow feeling settles in my stomach despite the delicious meal I've just had. The person I revealed a bit of myself to is dead. And it's not like I wished *Daryl* in particular to be my new best friend, but the reality of being alone always hits harder when I pass brightly lit shop windows advertising gifts *for your loved ones.*

The only loved one I have is myself and treating myself to luxuries has long stopped feeling special.

The main street is something straight out of a Hall-mark movie, with small trees sitting in front of every shop and colorful lights stretched between lanterns. There's even a shimmery collection of elves for the kids to find as part of a month-long competition, but while one of them is peeking at me from the branch of a nearby tree, I don't plan to stay here long enough to see who gets the lifetime supply of chocolate offered to the winner.

A Christmas song streams from a clothing store nearby, but I ignore it, eager to reach my hotel room and call it a day when the door to one of the cute New England houses swings open, and a young man spills out.

He bumps into me, but it's him almost tripping in the process as his foot slides over the sidewalk.

"Watch it!" he snarls.

He uses a simple black cane to regain balance, but as he walks off, his limp is barely noticeable. He's wearing a dark gray camo jacket and heavy boots, along with a large, furry trapper hat, but it's his big dark eyes that catch my attention when our gazes meet for half a second. A few strands of black hair stick out from under the hat, getting in the way. A flush appears on his pale skin as he exhales a big cloud of vapor and mutters something to himself, but then he rushes past me as if this is a race.

He's upset about much more than almost tripping. I've spent years on my own, staring at people, reading them, so I know the signs. He takes a few more steps, crumpling an envelope in his hands along the way, and throws it at a trash can without checking if it reaches its goal. The paper bounces off the rim and onto the sidewalk, but he's already walking on as fast as the limp allows him.

There's no reason for me to care what made this stranger so angry, but maybe it's a bit early to stretch on the hotel bed and watch a cooking show? After all, it's only dark already because it's that time of the year.

My foot hovers above the asphalt, but curiosity gets the best of me and I step over a mound of snow to grab the envelope. The slush lingering in the gutter managed to get it a bit wet, but when I pull out the single piece of paper inside, the ink is sharp and clear, as are the jagged shapes of the letters.

As I read the first sentence, the melody of a new cover of 'All I want for Christmas is You' worms its way into my brain.

Dear Santa,

All I want for Christmas is revenge...

CHAPTER 2

ROWAN

I SCOOT DOWN BY the rat trap, cooing at the rodent desperately squeaking at me about its trapped tail.

"I know what it's like. Just let me help you," I whisper in frustration as the rat snaps at me.

I put on a pair of gloves and reach for the hinge of the ancient, cruel trap. This is no way to hunt. If Chuck wants to catch rats in the back of the store, he should either get one of those that kill on the spot, or humanely trap the animal and let it out later.

Or maybe I just feel a bit too much for the poor rat with its tail bent out of shape because I'm very much like him. A nuisance, scrambling to make a living, with a wonky knee that some days aches so much I need to use a cane. Trapped in Chuck's hunting and survival gear store. If I could find a different job, I would, but it's not easy in a small town when you're not always fit for work, and have barely any connections.

So it is what it is. I'm trapped, but the rat can still have another chance.

I lift the hinge, the rodent squeaks, but then rushes off behind a pile of boxes in the storeroom.

"What the hell?" comes from behind me so suddenly I lose balance and fall on my butt, looking back at Jas. She watches me from the open doorway, radiating hostility. Her small, upturned nose resembles a tiny pig snout when she makes one of her mean girl faces. "Wow. Just wow. This is sabotage."

I roll my eyes in frustration. "It's just one rat, okay? Can you keep it to yourself?"

Like it's not enough that I was late for work because I had a meltdown at therapy. I don't need my boss finding out I freed a rat from one of *his* traps because I felt sorry for it.

Jas's mouth stretches into a fake smile, and she cocks her hip, watching me as if it's my job to witness her new jeans, which, by the way, are identical to all her other jeans but are dark red rather than blue. At twenty, I'm not that much older than her, but I feel as if there's decades between us whenever I need to deal with all her petty teenage bullshit.

Maybe it's because I went through so much tragedy at her age, I'm surprised I'm not gray.

"Depends. What would you offer me in return?"

I stand and consider the contents of my backpack. "I've got a Snickers?" I try hopelessly, but when she spins on her heel and walks out, she doesn't need to say "*processed garbage*" for me to know I'm out of options. My transgression will be reported to our boss, who is also Jas's uncle, and there isn't a damn thing I can do about it, so I take my time pulling myself up without any more damage to my pride. I don't always need a cane, but the current cold, damp weather doesn't agree with my knee.

I barely manage to swipe the dust off my pants by the time Chuck marches in, thick gray beard first, and stares me down from under the visor of the camo baseball cap he wears all year round. "What in the fresh hell were you thinking?" he asks, spreading his arms as he regards me, with Jas hovering behind his back as if she's getting off seeing me suffer.

I'm like a spider getting its legs ripped out one by one. Some days I wish that girl would end my misery already. There are enough guns in this store.

I take a deep breath to give myself a few more seconds. I'm not tiny, but next to a guy like Chuck, my five-seven makes me feel like a cockroach under a giant's boot.

"Jas didn't see it all. I was trying to get the rat out of the trap, and into a box, so I could take it out." A smooth enough lie. *I'd* believe me.

Chuck flinches, as if smacked in the face. "The fuck is this tree-hugging garbage? There's enough of those pests already, and they breed like crazy. It would just come right back into my store. You one of those people who call *tracking* hunting, even when they don't shoot a single round once they find the animal?"

Why yes, I do consider myself a hunter. Just because I don't shoot the prey doesn't mean I didn't hunt it down. And what would I even do with a deer carcass? Bring it to my small apartment? Sell it? I don't have a truck to put it in, and frankly, I don't care to. I'm a good shot, but that doesn't mean I have to go around killing random animals for fun. Tracking is equally satisfying to me, if not more.

"No," I mumble.

I don't want to be a pushover. In my dreams, I tell Chuck exactly what I think of him, his buddies, my co-workers, and even the way *he* hunts. But I can't do that in real life when my rent is on the line.

"Then do your job. Or, whatever you can, since I'm not legally allowed to ask you to do plenty of things even Jas can do," Chuck says, once again hammering in the fact that my disability is a problem for him. He has no issue taking the tax break for employing me though. Of course.

Jas stares at me with a vacant, cruel expression. Some days I think she has a crush on me and wants attention, but other times, I'm pretty sure she's simply a bully.

"I'm sorry, I saw there was a new shipment of water filters, I'll go take that out to the shop floor." Anything to end this conversation. I'll need both hands to carry the box, so I won't be able to use the cane, but I can limp my way there. Worst case scenario, I'll fall face first and break my nose. It's not like I'm looking for dates.

Chuck stares me down, narrowing his eyes so intensely I'm starting to suspect he ought to wear glasses and is refusing to do so because that would be as good as admitting that he's no longer a fit young man. "Do that. And since you were late again, I'll deduct that first hour from your pay."

I nod and turn to the box.

My therapist should try having a conversation with Chuck. Maybe then she'd understand why I have violent fantasies. And they're not even so bad. I just sometimes wish he'd step into a snare I accidentally-on-purpose left on the floor.

My real anger is reserved for a few very particular people, but according to my therapist, it's not normal to want the men who murdered my family to suffer. I should *"heal"*, *"let go"*. Well, I won't. I'm permanently fucked up because of their actions, and I vomited all my rageful bile into the stupid letter to Santa she told me to write as a way to "*release my feelings*".

It's not my fault she didn't like what I wrote. It was too explicit for her to finish, apparently. Well, *maybe* my revenge fantasies are horrific because the things that happened to me were horrific. I can't even sleep peacefully, because almost every night I dream of a reality where I find out that one of those bastards got shanked in prison. But that's not going to happen, because none of them is doing time.

They all just... got away with it thanks to fake alibis, and my testimony was dismissed on account of age and the trauma I suffered. And yeah, it had been dark, the smoke obscured everything, but I will never forget the faces of the men who killed my mother, father and grandma. The bastard who shoved me down the stairs and then left me to die in a burning house is forever etched in my mind.

It was a miracle I survived, even though some days I regret that night didn't claim my life too.

I can't think about it too much or I might end up doing something stupid. It's enough that I keep tabs on those four monsters and casually collect details about them in a scrapbook like some psycho.

One day, if something happens to any of them, cops will knock on my door, find the photos, newspaper cuttings, my revenge plan, and arrest me. Neighbors will say *he kept to himself, didn't have any friends, but was a nice boy*. Textbook true crime drama. I might even get a Netflix series if the murders are particularly gruesome...

But I'm getting ahead of myself. My revenge fantasies are just that, and no justice will ever be given to my family or me.

That's reality.

Reality is also carrying a box and feeling stared at when it takes me far too much effort to put it on the floor. I look back to check who's spying on me, and when I can't spot a single customer, my gaze darts to the rounded mirror Chuck had installed in the corner of the ceiling, to catch shoplifters. I don't see anyone on there either.

A regular comes in, loudly greeting Chuck by the counter, but the strange sensation from before remains, as if I'm alone in the woods and can sense a predator stalking me in the shadows.

But it's most likely just Jas looking for another way to humiliate me. Or date me. I really don't know. It's not like I'm out, and that girl can be so fucking weird. I swear I sensed an innuendo in the way she asked for something in return for silence.

And I'm not being delusional. She once told me I have *"death in my eyes"*, and I didn't know if it was a dig or a compliment. I thanked her, confused, and she just smiled, so I've given up on trying to figure her out.

The sense of being watched persists, though by now, it could be my paranoia talking. The oppressive feeling of threat has never left me since the tragic home invasion that changed my life forever, and I can't be sure if I gained a sixth sense, or if I'm a skittish bug afraid of my own shadow.

By the end of the shift, my knee aches constantly, and I swallow some painkillers before venturing out after an unpleasant grumble from Chuck. But I do need this job, and the hunting store actually lets me utilize my skills and knowledge, so I'd rather stay, even with a boss like him.

As the cold bites my skin, I scoff at my decision not to take the car today. I do live very close to the store, right off the main street, but while at this point every step hurts, I don't have any alternative to making myself walk that distance.

By the time I leave the elevator in my apartment building, I'm drenched in sweat. At least it wasn't broken like last week.

I triple-check the locks on my door, have a look around the living room to make sure nothing's been rearranged, and only then turn on the TV. Silence unnerves me too much. It makes every squeak of the old floor sound like footsteps, so I'd rather fill it with white noise, because realistically, I know no one's out to get me. Aside from the car, I don't have any valuable belongings. What could a thief even take? The ancient TV? The heavy laptop that makes strange buzzing noises when it overheats? I do have a gun and a rifle, but those are strategically hidden.

I turn on the lamp just to be reminded that the light bulb is broken and I didn't buy a new one, so I have to settle on the small LEDs above the kitchen counter.

While the apartment is small, I feel more at ease with neighbors close by. I sometimes cat sit for Mrs. Treville, and in return, maybe she'll call the cops if she hears me scream. It's not like there's any other action going on at my place.

Still, I know that I stink after the long slog from the store, so I make myself move and drop my clothes into the laundry basket before rolling into the bathtub and turning on the water. The relief to my knee is almost instant as warmth envelops my chilled bones, and I slowly curl up on my side, listening to the noise of the cascading water, to the brush of my own toes against the side of the tub, the beating of my own heart. I never quite enjoyed the air bubbles escaping my ears, but it's a price I'm ready to pay for the sense of peace moments like this offer me.

I take my time, enjoying the nothingness in my head. There's a small window in the bathroom, and I watch snowflakes swirl in the wind as my skin warms. The colorful lights of the town's Christmas illumination dance on the wall outside as someone laughs in the street, utterly joyful.

Sometimes it's hard for me to remember that I used to have a normal life. That my dad took me hunting, that I always helped my grandma with baking, or even that I went to school. I was a bit of a morbid kid and didn't have many friends, but I had a family, a future.

I don't know how much time passes, but a growl in my stomach reminds me I need to eat something before dragging myself to bed.

I wrap a towel around my hips, feeling positively refreshed, and walk out into the dim living room. Maybe I can steal a light bulb from the store? A little sneaky fuck-you to Chuck?

But as I head into the kitchen, ready to put a TV dinner into the microwave and call it a day by passing out on the sofa, I catch movement in the corner of my eye, and my feet freeze to the carpet as a tall figure in black looms ever closer.

"Hello, Rowan," the stranger says, his voice muffled by a black fabric mask showing only his eyes in an opening above a print of wolf jaws.

CHAPTER 3

ROWAN

THE INTRUDER IS TALL, with broad shoulders, strong arms and thighs, and he moves with the confidence of someone who can twist my head off with his bare hands. He isn't yet pointing a gun at me, which makes him somehow even more terrifying, as if he didn't come here for valuables.

This could be one of my biggest nightmares come true, the one where one of the men who haunt my dreams decides to finish the job four years later. After all, I was supposed to die in that burning house, not crawl out through the basement like some rat.

I don't even think. The fact that he knows my name indicates he's here for *me*, not my things.

I grab a knife from a stand in the kitchen and throw it at him with a scream of pure terror and fury. For the blink of an eye, the invader freezes, as if this wasn't the reaction he expected. He evades the blade flying his way and inhales with a hiss.

"Rowan!"

Fuck. Fuck. Fuck.

He's here for me. He's here to break my legs again, but I'm not going to let that happen. This time, I will fight for myself.

"Get out! Get the fuck out! I've got a gun!" I yell, already moving to the door, even though it's painfully obvious I don't have a weapon on me, since my outfit consists of a towel and nothing more.

Afraid to turn my back on the intruder, I never look away from his imposing form as I paw at the door, but pulling on the handle is useless. All four locks are in place, of course. My muddled brain suggests the invader must have entered through here, but it's not the chill in my bones that's causing my goosebumps.

The window is open, and a gust of wind sends in a flurry of snow.

How? How the fuck did he get in here? I live on the third floor.

Everything happens all too fast. He's saying something about a wish, but I can barely hear him through the thudding of blood in my ears.

The gun. I need to get to the gun, because I don't have time to open all the locks before he descends on me. But as I turn and twist out of the assailant's grasp, my wonky knee gives out and I fall to the floor—or I thought I would, because the man in black grabs my arm, saving my face from hitting the carpet.

He's wearing leather gloves.

He's here to kill me.

He's gonna fucking *kill* me.

"Let me go!" I cry out, putting all my panic and determination into jabbing at him with my elbow.

I did hit *something*, and he moans in pain.

As soon as he lets go, I crawl toward my bedroom, not even caring that I lost my towel at some point. My heart is so frantic I'm getting dizzy, but I'd rather pass out than lie down and let him take my life.

"We need to talk!" he yells, but the sound of his voice tells me he's not as close as before and that's the only thing I care about.

I scramble to my feet and slam the bedroom door shut behind me as soon as I reach it. And lock it, because yes, I have a lock here too. And a latch.

I'm at my bedside table when I hear a slow, deliberate knock. "Rowan…"

But I don't care what he has to say. I grab my gun and take off the safety with blood thudding in my veins like a war drum.

"I'm going to shoot!" I yell, but that's my only warning. He's in my house. This is self-defense.

I shoot at the door three times, screaming my head off.

This is nothing like the well-aimed, deliberate practice at the range. This is survival, and I might not hit the jackpot, but I'm fine with that as long as it gets me the result I want.

There's a scramble in the corridor, as if his boots slipped on something, but then…nothing.

Pure silence, as if the world around me has stilled, awaiting my next move.

Is he… dead?

The deep breaths I'm taking won't help me calm down, but they give me enough self-control to step forward and put my ear against the door.

Nothing. No walking around, no wheezing or cries for help, zero sounds.

I slowly unlock the door with the gun in my sweaty grasp. "I'm coming out, but I *will* shoot again," I say as if I really have the confidence to be this cool-headed. My brain is a bowl of marbles hitting against each other as I walk. Some of them are definitely missing.

But as I walk out, hands trembling, there's no one in the apartment. No blood. No man dead on the floor. Even the window is closed.

I rush to it, and as I come close enough, there's no denying that the intruder broke the lock.

All I can think about is how badly I need to leave. There's some commotion in the corridor, but I pay it no mind as I put on a pair of sweatpants, a jacket over bare skin, and storm out as I am, since I don't have the brain capacity to grab shoes.

I need to be *somewhere else.*

One of the doors nearby shuts as I dash outside, not even bothering to lock my apartment behind me, because getting to the police station is my priority. I stumble toward the elevator, cradling the gun in my hands as it opens, letting me in. But while I keep watching the hallway for signs of the intruder or his accomplices, I see no movement until the door shuts behind me.

The muted wail of a siren is like a balm to my heart. Of course, one of my neighbors called the cops. I would have done it too.

The damp snow turns my feet into bits of ice, but I'm too frightened to care about the discomfort it's causing and run toward the promise of safety offered by the flashing red and blue lights. I don't realize I'm crying until the salty tears reach my lips.

I'm breathless by the time I reach the cop car.

"I—There was an i-intruder—" I utter, unable to make my tongue work right as a policeman I vaguely recognize from town leaves the car, watching me with narrowed eyes.

"Is that a gun, son? How about you hand that over first?" he says as his partner, a blonde woman with red blemishes on both cheeks, eyes me suspiciously.

I nod and put on the safety, carefully handing over the weapon as it strikes me that they could have treated *me* as the threat and dealt with it accordingly. But they're both small town cops, they know me from Chuck's shop, and they just watch the tears streaming down my face.

"A man... in a mask..." I try to explain with my feet freezing to the ground.

The female cop frowns. "I remember you came to the station to report an intruder last year. Is this... a similar situation?" she asks before glancing at the windows in the upper floor of my apartment building.

I hide my face in my hands as the cold invades my attention at last. "No, back then I... maybe I just thought I saw something. But tonight, there was a man in my apartment. He knew my name! I shot at him, but didn't get him."

The policeman flashes a light at me. "Have you been drinking? Drugs?"

"No! This is real. He broke in through my window! Please go see for yourself." I know it's pathetic of me to be this distraught, but being accosted in my safe place makes the terror of the night when I lost my whole family creep right back into my heart.

The woman leans toward her partner, but I can still hear her whisper. "He's had mental issues."

I sob as a black hole opens in my chest.

"Rowan, is it?" she says to me, gesturing at the back seat of the cop car. "Officer Huber will go to your apartment, just give him the keys. In the meantime, how about you wait here with me? I see you didn't have time to put on shoes."

What she really means is that she can see I'm crazy, but I appreciate her concern anyway. It's more kindness than I could hope for.

I hand over my keys, sit down, and the policewoman even hands me a blanket as I break down, ashamed of the people gathered in the street to watch me, but grateful that I'm still alive.

And yet even here, I don't feel safe. There's a chill crawling under my skin as the unexplainable sense of being *watched* refuses to go away.

CHAPTER 4

ROWAN

The week following the home invasion was like a return to hell.

I might not have ended up in the hospital this time, but the terror of the invasion tainted every breath I took, and whatever progress I made in therapy was now gone. I could barely get any sleep at night, woken up by each and every noise in the old apartment building, and while I ended up attaching new, firm locks to each window, nothing could help the sense of paranoia telling me that the guy who broke into my house—as the police ended up confirming—is still watching me and waiting for the perfect moment to strike.

Who was he?

Why did he come?

How did he know my name?

On one hand, I want to know, but on the other, I wish to never find out and put it all behind me. I can hear his muffled voice in my nightmares, and for once, I'm actually happy to leave my house and go to work, because being around people feels safer.

I grab my cane on the way out, and as I close all four of my door locks, I realize there's some commotion in the corridor. Two men are carrying a small sofa into the open door opposite mine, and I have to lean against the wall to let them pass.

I'm about to take a peek inside when Mrs. Treville waves at me. Bits of snow are scattered around her boots, so she must have just come in.

"How are you feeling?" she asks as I approach her on the way to the elevator. It isn't the first time she's asking me this, and I can't help but feel self-conscious. Normally, it's me who's concerned for *her*, because she's broken bones twice since I moved into this building, but when I see her warm smile, I know the concern is genuine and not meant to point out how weak I am.

"Much better, thank you. It's a walking stick kind of day though." I tap the floor with the cane I both hate and appreciate. It helps with my mobility, and yet makes me stand out more in ways I would rather not.

"Oh, I'm sorry to hear that, Rowan. Are you using those hot patches I told you about?"

I smile and I try not to think too much about how much she reminds me of my grandmother, a sweet woman who baked cookies with me at Christmas, and taught me how to swim. She deserved to live many more years than she got.

"I am actually. They're very helpful. Are we getting a new neighbor?" I ask, pointing at the open door. I do like to keep tabs on these things, to know who lives next to me in case something happens.

Her smile widens and she ushers her cat back into the apartment when the furball tries to sneak out. "Yes, and I have to tell you... he's really handsome. If I were your age, I'd be hanging out at the laundromat to *accidentally* bump into him."

I laugh. "Consider my curiosity piqued."

She leans closer to me and whispers. "I told him you're single. You know, to get that out of the way for you. He just thanked me but didn't say he *wasn't* gay. Or married."

I stiffen and my face flushes with heat. *She did not...* In moments like this, I regret coming out to her, but what can I do now that the cat's out of the bag?

"That's um... thanks." I *guess.*

It's only now that her face falls, as if she realized she might have overstepped. "Oh, I'm sorry. It's just that he's very... *very* good-looking, and polished. I kind of assumed he might be interested in men."

Which doesn't make any of this better, but I'm not going to scold a seventy-year-old for trying to save me from singlehood.

I clear my throat. "That's okay. Please say hi to Mr. Mittens from me," I say and limp off, trying to stop thinking about the fact that my elderly neighbor tried to awkwardly push another man at me. God, the poor guy will be running for the hills the moment he spots me.

The day gets even worse when I reach the elevator, and after pressing the button several times there's no reaction. I'm way more familiar with this kind of stuff than I'd like to be, but today this hurdle feels like too much to bear. Unfortunately, working isn't optional, so I approach the steep stairs with trepidation, and my mind instantly scrambles. It's not just that it will take me a lot of effort to go down them because of my knee.

When I look down the steps, all I can see is the stairs leading down to the basement of my old family house. I can almost hear the laughter that resonated in my ears after a man called Miles Brown shoved me off the landing with a bloodstained hand.

I hold on to the railing yet can't make myself move, as if something paralyzed both of my legs.

This isn't a day for a meltdown. Chuck will be pissed off if you're late again, the rational part of my brain reminds me, but I'm so damn tired after several sleepless nights in a row that willpower fails me. I find myself sitting down on the top step with my eyes closed, hoping that maybe I can force myself to slide down on my butt, like I used to do for fun when I was still a kid.

But first, I need to remind myself how to breathe again.

"Afternoon."

I glance back, sliding to the side when I realize I must be blocking the stairs. "Sorry," I say, but my lips stay parted, because this *has* to be the new neighbor, and Mrs. Treville wasn't lying.

He's so fucking gorgeous he doesn't belong to this ugly corridor with peeling paint and black mold in the corner of the ceiling. He's towering over me as I sit and looks like a classical statue come to life. His aquiline nose gives his face a regal aura befitting a Greek god, and his mid-length dark hair is swept back without a single strand out of place. I could be fooled into believing Orion himself came down to Earth to walk around mere mortals if I didn't know better. The finely knitted bottle green sweater he's wearing complements his hazel eyes, and as he leans against the banister and smiles at me, I'm left utterly baffled.

Because what could this guy be doing here?

I scramble up, helping myself with the cane to get out of the way faster. "You need space? For furniture?" I ask, pointing at the stairs I was blocking. No matter how hard I try, I can't look away from his eyes. They're such a striking blend of gold and greens they remind me of an autumn day in the forest, safe and away from anyone who might wish me ill. They're so piercing it's as if he's sent an arrow straight into my heart.

Or I've just bottled up my sexual frustration for too long.

He shrugs and offers me his hand. "No, we're done carrying everything in. I just wanted to introduce myself. The name's Saint."

I swallow and put on my best smile. One that doesn't scream stay away, he's not normal and tried to shoot a guy last week. "Rowan. I'm just across from you."

My heart skips a beat when he squeezes my hand. Am I this touch deprived? I really don't want to let go of his fingers, but the prerogative to not be weird wins out.

I make sure not to stare too much, but I clock the little things about him. The nice leather belt, the five o'clock shadow, how thick and nicely styled his hair is, and now that he's been standing here for a moment, I get a whiff of his cologne. The scent of lemongrass and something a bit musky. Expensive. Fresh.

I curl my toes in my boots when my mind tries to push my thoughts into territory they shouldn't enter about this perfectly polite man.

Now I wish I spent more time on my hair today. It's a tangled nest compared to his. At least it's clean.

"Rowan," the man repeats, watching me with sparks in his eyes. Is it just me or is he standing closer than a man ought to another? "The handsome gay neighbor?"

I stare at him, a deer in the headlights, and I have no doubt my face is starting to resemble a tomato. "Oh *God*. I'm so sorry. I promise I didn't set Mrs. Treville up to ask you about anything. She's just trying to be helpful."

Wait. Did he just call me handsome?

Saint laughs, and I can't help but admire his lips and even teeth. "No, I could see that. And I admit, that was a bit of an awkward conversation, but here I am, meeting my first gay man in this new town, and I didn't even need to go on Grindr."

My shoulders sag a little in relief, and my heart might be fluttering a bit too much. I know I'm not ugly, but he's probably just being friendly.

Or looking for a fuckbuddy.

Could I be his fuckbuddy?

Maybe. I don't know. I don't have any experience. If he offered, I'd probably end up being really shit at sex.

I smile back, daring to look into his eyes for a bit longer. God, they're beautiful. "You will have to cast your net wide. Rural Vermont isn't exactly a gay hotspot."

Saint laughs again and cocks his head. "No, unfortunately. But I always valued quality over quantity anyway. Maybe it will be easier to actually meet someone around here. What do you think?"

"I..." *Don't know how to make friends, but a guy like you will surely figure it out in no time.* "There's a few bars people like. And it depends on how you spend your days. Did you move here for a job? Or...?"

"I'm writing a book, and I needed a change of pace, you know?" Saint shrugs and nods at the cane in my hand. "Do you need any help? I know the elevator's stuck."

I try not to fixate on the fact that he just casually dropped that he's a writer on top of his whole city slicker aura. "No, I'm fine, I just... You're not meeting me on my best day, sorry. I was kind of hoping someone would come to fix the elevator in the next twenty minutes or so. Then I could avoid the stairs and still make it to work on time." *Sure, go on, just tell him your whole life story while you're at it.* "I *can* walk down the stairs, but these are quite steep and—" I take a deep breath. "Long story short, I hurt myself falling down the stairs and my brain really hates to even see them now, but I can't exactly make my way down without looking where I'm going."

"Look at me then. You seem compact enough. I could carry you. You know, strength training," Saint tells me, winking and flexes his bicep for my viewing pleasure as if he isn't amazing enough already.

I take another look at his arms. He's not a meathead, but yeah... tall, broad-shouldered, with thick arms.

I shake my head and laugh, because how is this interaction even happening to me? "You're not serious."

"You don't know me yet. Care for a ride?" Saint asks, stepping closer, close enough for his scent to make my head spin.

Even my ears get hot. Yeah, I'd fucking *ride* him in more ways than one. I think.

"What do I have to lose, right? My other knee?" I laugh nervously, but as soon as he gets the green light, Saint doesn't hesitate. He leans down, slides his arm behind my knees, and before I know it, I'm grabbing him around the neck.

When he offers me a proud smile, I know for sure that the stairs will be the last thing on my mind until he puts me down.

Saint weighs me in his arms, but his hands remain steady, and as he moves forward, taking me down the first step, our eyes meet. *Fuck.*

Yes. Yes, I do want to be his fuckbuddy, whatever that entails. The grassy scent he carries spins through my system as I float in his strong arms, hypnotized like a deer standing in the middle of the road as the truck of future heartbreak dashes straight at it.

By the time we reach the second floor, Saint's olive skin is tinted red, and he's breathing heavily, but his pride doesn't leave any room for complaints, and he only puts me down once we're at the very bottom of the stairs.

He's very careful about it too, making sure I'm leaning on the cane before he lets go.

During the time it took him to walk down two flights of stairs, I might have developed a crush. My heart is racing, my palms are getting sweaty, and it feels... good. Happy butterflies are fluttering in my chest as if I'm a teenager again.

"Wow. You're... really strong," I utter, desperately trying to keep my composure. I'm not even embarrassed over being such a weakling, because it got me a moment in this hunk's arms.

Saint stretches. "No. I need to up my game. I think I've had too many bagels last month. But let me know if you need another ride," he says and pulls out his phone. "What's your number?"

Damn, he's so smooth. If he's *trying* to get into my pants, he's going about it the right way. I can't stop thinking about the tense muscles of his arms as I dictate my number. "I wish I could treat you to coffee or something? For the help. But I really need to get to work, or my boss will kill me." *Look at me, world. I'm flirting.*

Saint's smile is so blinding it warms my loins. I hope to never say that out loud.

"Sounds good. Maybe you could pop in to my place for dinner later?"

And this is when words jam in my mouth, blocked by my messy brain. Half of it is screaming yes and not wanting to question Saint's intentions, while the other half suggests that maybe Saint is some kind of sex addict who needs his next hit.

But most of all, I can't get over the hurdle of being invited to his place. Not dating has meant I really haven't had to face being inside someone's home, nor having them over at mine. Just the thought of it makes me so irrationally nervous my tongue swells until I'm unable to communicate.

I need to try to be normal though, I really do. So I laugh it off. "How do I know you're not a serial killer?"

"Depends on how you define a *serial* killer."

It passes from his mouth like many other offhand comments he could have made, yet my paranoia tells me to see a glimpse of truth in that handsome face.

I take him in from head to toe. "You're gonna have to kill me another night, because I finish work late. But thanks. We really need to do that." There. Smooth...ish.

"I'll text you," Saint says, offering me a nod.

So that was... surprisingly pleasant.

I walk off with a spring to my step, and even my knee seems to hurt less. I can't get over it. He carried me down the stairs. *Carried* me. Like some knight in shining armor.

When I glance over my shoulder, he's still there. Watching me. Then winks.

I grin and keep walking on clouds.

Chapter 5

Saint

Snowflakes create glinting flurries, set alight by the Christmas illuminations in the town center, and whenever I tune into the cheerful seasonal music playing in the cafe, the sense of nostalgia rushing through me becomes almost unbearable. 'It's the Most Wonderful Time of the Year' was my mother's favorite song, and while I used to detest it as a kid, now it never fails to bring back memories of her making copious amounts of cookies. The whole house smelled of vanilla and cinnamon, and every sip of the flavored coffee I'm nursing brings it all back.

A time when December wasn't the loneliest of months.

But tonight feels different. Rowan might not be aware he's being watched, but seeing him work behind the counter of the hunting store across the street eases my loneliness as if I'm there with him, chatting for real rather than just imagining it. Something about him intrigued me from the moment he passed me in the street. I don't know what grabbed my attention more, the long legs or the big dark eyes filled with boiling fury. In the end, it was the letter he discarded that revealed the truth of his soul and pulled me to him as if he were a feral cat I could befriend. And I can never pass a cat in the street and not pet it or at least attempt to.

Thirst for revenge oozed out of every letter on the page so intensely I could feel blood on my tongue as I read the words over and over, drinking up his righteous anger.

It got me so excited I lost my cool. So much so that I may have gotten ahead of myself breaking into his home. I should have done my due diligence first. Obviously, had I known he'd lost his whole family during a home invasion and house fire, I wouldn't have let myself in, I'm not a psycho.

I could hardly believe it when he shot at me through the door. The excitement of finding out he had the guts to do that was a close second to seeing him naked. So much passion lay dormant in that compact body raked with scars, and I now long to unearth it all. So. Damn. Much.

I won't let his initial reaction discourage me, because it's not like I have anything planned for the rest of the month. So I've decided to take my time. Stalk him as if he's the juiciest deer in the herd and I'm just waiting for him to reach his peak before I sink my teeth into his flesh. After all, he longs for the closure of seeing his family's tormentors die, and he would take the bait if I go about it right this time. Once he knows what I can offer him, he will step into my snares out of his own free will.

That was the extent of my plan until yesterday. When I first arrived at his place, all I wanted was a companion, someone who might understand me, maybe even a future apprentice, if I played my cards right. But then the elderly neighbor dropped the bomb of him being gay, and I haven't been able to think of anything else since. He can become more than just a work buddy. If Rowan is gay, he can become my *lover*. A lover I don't have to hide my true self from, and who doesn't need to be left behind whenever work dries out or the heat intensifies. I've never had anything like it. And so, with the offhand comment of a gray-haired lady, the stakes of the game became sky-high.

Because now I'm determined to make him mine, and I will grant him the kind of revenge he's never even dreamed of. But my prey is skittish and needs to become acquainted with me first. By the time we develop enough trust for me to reveal my true self, he will be ready to accept me as I am.

He doesn't need to know that he's mine already.

I managed to (literally) sweep him off his feet earlier, and the air between us sizzled as if his body were a volcano. Maybe I pushed a bit too hard by inviting him over, since that's trapping him rather than hunting him down, but nobody's perfect.

It's just so hard to contain myself when he's at my fingertips. His gaze burns with a thirst for blood that matches mine, cruel fantasies lurk behind the deep dark eyes, and I just want to let him know he can tell me everything. That I'll understand.

I'm usually good at waiting. In my line of work, a man needs to sometimes stay hidden for hours on end, but he makes me feel an urgency that tingles in my gums and makes me want to close my fingers around his neck. Gently. But firmly, so he knows who he belongs to.

I wish to stand closer to him again, inhale the minty scent he carried on him this morning. Does he like biting?

Being grabbed and fucked? He does seem to be on the shy side, but that only thrills me more.

I want to see his black hair sticking to his sweaty forehead as he spreads his legs, begging for my dick. Or would he be shy and unsure about it? I can go either way as long as he's under me, gasping and moaning—

Fuck.

Getting ahead of myself again.

First, I need to squeeze a date out of him.

I like that he's made it a chase, forcing me to work for it. Hunting him down will make devouring him all the more delicious. A proper gourmet meal.

My back is covered in goosebumps as I see him wave at someone, then walk away from the counter at closing time. I toss a bill onto my table, put on my thick woolen turtleneck and the elegant coat that doesn't keep me adequately warm without layering, and walk out into the frosty air. My head spins as I watch Rowan's boss flip the sign on the front door of the store to *Closed*, and I dash across the street, heating up from the excitement of this hunt.

Will he smile once he sees me? Or will he be flustered, like when I approached him earlier? Maybe he already has a secret lover his neighbor doesn't know about? He could have flirted with me for fun.

The very idea that there could be someone else makes me want to take a knife to the throat of this shadow man. But there's no need for drastic measures. I'll take this slow. If there is someone, I'll make sure to show Rowan that I'm *better*, and only take out the other guy if need be.

The urgency rises within me again, even though I've stalked him for a week and never seen him share physical intimacy with anyone. In fact, I haven't even seen him meet up with friends either.

He's alone.

Oh, we're so alike.

I get closer, and as he leaves his workplace in that cute fur-lined hat, I dash along the sidewalk, making sure to bump him with my shoulder just hard enough to tip him off balance.

As predicted, he wobbles, and I, the culprit, swoop in to steady him.

"Are you oka—oh, it's you," I say as if I haven't waited for this moment for hours. "I'm so sorry. My mind was somewhere else."

He doesn't back off even though he glances inside the shop, probably to check if his boss isn't looking. He has such a pretty profile with those pouty lips, shapely nose, and the long black eyelashes.

A smile surfaces on his lips when our eyes meet again. "S-Saint? What are you doing here? Researching for your novel?" he asks, handing me the answer on a platter.

"Yes, it's my first evening in town, so I went out for coffee, to soak up the atmosphere, you know. I want to make the setting of my next book feel like a character in its own right," I say, and since he isn't pulling back, my hands stay on his waist. What do I have to lose?

"That place is really nice," he points to the cafe I've just been at. "I can't imagine getting a lot of inspiration in this boring town though." As soon as there's movement in the shop, Rowan pulls out of my grip.

I'm guessing he's not out then.

Doesn't matter. We'll get there.

"You'd be surprised," I say with a smirk, and seeing he's still close, still looking my way, has my heart beating faster. "It's all about perspective. I was planning to check out the Italian place down the street. Care to join me?"

He stares at me for a prolonged moment, giving me time to admire his slender neck. I should get him a scarf.

"I... Sorry, that place is a bit out of my budget," he says, and his pale cheeks flush.

How adorable. He thinks I'd let him pay.

"Oh, no, it's my treat! To apologize for walking into you," I say and rub his arm as the wind blows around us, creating a spiraling cloud of snow, as if we're inside a Christmas snow globe.

It's as if the universe is telling me he's the one.

Rowan bites his pale lip, already smiling, and pushes his hands into his pockets. After observing him for a week, I know that he doesn't always need his cane. I hope the fact that he isn't holding it now means he's feeling better.

"I mean... I am hungry."

No surprise there. I've seen his shopping, and he eats like he's trying to ruin his health. His last food haul was particularly bad. Microwave meals, hardly a vegetable in sight, two bananas, and a discounted, broken chocolate Santa.

"Well, then let me treat you. In exchange, you tell me everything there is to know about Rosehill Pines."

And about you.

That's what I truly care about.

He nods with a widening smile and makes a little gesture toward the store he works at. "Okay. I can tell you all about the hunting season."

There's only one type of prey I'm hunting, though. And I don't care if it's in season.

CHAPTER 6

ROWAN

THE HUNTING TROPHIES, OLD guns, and pictures of people long gone from this world don't scream *Italy*, but the food is still excellent. Even the tomatoes making up a simple salad appetizer are so flavorful they might just be the best I had in a long time, if not ever. I usually buy the cheapest products I can get, always fighting to keep my head above water as the cost of living mounts up, but if Saint wants to treat me, I'm not going to stop him.

I asked him some questions about his book, and apparently he's writing a murder mystery but is still waiting for the details to come to him. As we share a plate of pasta, which apparently is meant to be eaten as the first course, not the main dish, I find myself getting more and more nervous. He's gay. I'm gay. And now we're eating out of the same bowl, sharing smiles at a cozy, candlelit table in a restaurant I could never afford.

And *he* is paying.

Does this mean we're... that he... that this is a date?

I've never been on a date. Not since my life stopped being normal, and before that, I've only taken girls out on perfectly innocent outings before I realized they didn't do anything for me. But if this *is* a date, it's my first with another man, and I fear that I might lose the ground under my feet at any moment, sinking into the dark waters of... whatever this is.

He is handsome, charming, asks me a lot of questions and actually listens to answers. I find him so attractive he's all I've been thinking about at work, but it's one thing to imagine a man kissing me, and doing it—quite another.

The attack on my family not only left me alone in the world but also with scars on my mind and body. Saint might not find my physical disability off-putting, but there's only so much patience a man can have for a virgin who's afraid to be alone with a stranger.

I'm spoiled goods. And no matter how intensely I lie to myself sometimes, nobody wants to deal with the aftermath of the shit I've been through. We're just getting to know each other, and while my baggage is such a big part of me, I can't spring it on him on the day we met.

How would I even do that? '*Hey, and by the way, I'm messed up because my family was brutally murdered in a house invasion, and I almost lost my life, but let's just enjoy pasta*'.

No, I'm determined to enjoy this evening.

"I don't like to go hunting with the guys from the shop though," I go on after he inquires about my hobbies. "There's this whole macho banter around it, and it's not just that I'm smaller and can't keep up. They're loud and kind of obnoxious, and while I don't have much time off, going to the woods on my own, only focusing on tracking, is very calming to me. Especially in winter. I like the snow, dressing warm, the chill in the air. Is that weird?"

Saint licks a bit of sauce from his lips and smiles. The candlelight adds a golden sheen to his hazel gaze, and I find myself so painfully smitten, my inadequacies feel even more obvious.

"No, not at all. Tracking is often way more enjoyable than the kill itself. It's almost... meditative," he adds with a thoughtful frown.

My heart skips a beat when I realize we have a hobby that connects us. "You hunt too?"

Then again, he's a writer doing research. He's probably just interested in finding out about the area from me. Unless he's not against slumming it with a local for a month or two. Would I be okay with that? Probably. Even if I end up with my heart broken, at least I would have *lived* for those few weeks. If I manage to accept his presence in my apartment without freaking out, that is.

I laugh a bit too loudly when we stick our forks in the same piece of pasta, and he pulls his hand away, letting me have it. "I do. But not as intensely as you must have to get all this experience. Did you start early?"

I stall, because his innocent question stabs into me like a javelin. But the sharp blade only exists in my head so I clear my throat and speak. "Y-yes. I used to go hunting with my dad. He taught me a lot. I had some teenage growing pains, and it helped us reconnect. I think that was more important for him than the hunting itself. Sometimes we would even camp out in the woods and learn all about survival skills." That was before I became afraid of my own shadow.

"Oh! Are you still into that? Wild camping?"

"Yes and no. I have... don't laugh! I've got a bit of a survivalist interest. I know some basic foraging, how to filter water, and I've got one of those bug-out bags with everything I might need if I had to leave within minutes."

Saint smirks. "Of course. In case of a nuclear disaster."

I bump his foot with mine. "I told you not to laugh!"

"No, no, this is very serious." But we're both laughing by now. "I hope you practice skinning a deer at least once a month."

"I don't usually kill the animals, maybe apart from the odd rabbit I know how to prepare myself. But I like to know I *could*. Does that make sense?" It probably doesn't, and before I can even consider inviting Saint over, I'd have to make sure he doesn't accidentally find my serial killer mood board.

If this is even a date.

"I'm assuming you don't have the space for a lot of meat in your apartment. It would have been a waste."

"I only have a small freezer, and it's usually stuffed with frozen TV dinners." I have the last piece of pasta from the plate with a smile. "This is already the best meal I've had this year. Maybe I have been missing out."

Saint grins. "My invitation still stands. Don't want to brag, but I'm a pretty good cook. I had to learn quickly after I moved in with my uncle. He couldn't even boil an egg."

That piques my interest. He's still a bit of a mystery to me, as I've been foolishly talking a lot about myself. I haven't even asked him about his pen name.

"When was that?" I ask before I can bite my tongue. If I ask about personal matters, it will only be fair for him to prod me about mine. Something I want to avoid.

"I was in my early teens," Saint tells me, sipping the wine he picked for us with such elegance I feel like I'm in the company of a prince, not a normal guy. The title of our Hallmark movie? *A Christmas Prince for Rowan.*

"He—uh, needed to unexpectedly take care of me, or I'd have ended up in the system. I had no other family left."

I take a big sip of wine to gather my thoughts, because I don't want to say anything insensitive, or too forward, but he's been so open, I feel ready to tell him a bit more about myself.

"I'm so sorry. I'm glad someone was there for you," I say, not wanting to pry into how he became an orphan. He looks so elegant. Maybe his parents died in a private jet crash and he got taken in by his rich uncle to grow up in a big mansion with marble stairs. "I... I lost my family too. I was sixteen, badly injured and recovering. After a few months in the hospital, I had a family technically sign up to take care of me, but I turned eighteen not long after, and a few months later I was on my own. I actually came here, to Rosehill Pines to start fresh with some insurance money to tide me over. Sorry. That's a total trauma dump on you." I gulp down the wine to hide my awkwardness, but when his warm hand closes over mine on the table, I freeze as my heart starts a race deep in my chest. Because is this an attempt to comfort me, or an escalation of touch? I still don't know if this is a date or him being friendly.

"Damn. That's tough. I didn't know... that we were alike that way. It's so difficult to be on your own, especially after such a loss, and injury on top of that... That takes a lot of strength."

Don't cry. Don't cry. Don't cry. Don't cry.

I have to take a deep breath but manage to keep my emotions under control. We're in a cozy booth in a far corner, so I'm pretty sure no one can see our hands and let the touch linger, soothed by his warmth. What are the odds of me meeting someone like him? Someone who knows loss?

And to be appreciated as strong on top of that? It rarely crosses my mind, as I usually see myself as a weakling who can't even stand up to his boss.

"It's just going through the motions, you know? I have to come up with a way to live, because I don't want the alternative." I won't be letting go of my life while those murderous fucks are still out there, enjoying theirs when they should rot in the ground, eaten by maggots.

The smile is gone from Saint's face, and that's when I know I've said too much. Nobody wants the truth about my feelings, not even my therapist, who'd rather have me write them in a letter to a fictional character than engage with them herself.

But just as I'm about to stand up and apologize for spoiling his evening, Saint's thumb strokes the inside of my hand so very gently. "It can get so lonely, and seeing others celebrate Christmas time makes it somehow worse, right?"

He gets it.

I nod, and, gossip be damned, when the waiter brings our main dishes, I don't pull my hand away. It feels too good to be held.

I speak only when the server leaves, but I'm glad his presence offered me a moment to gather my thoughts and take a deep breath, because I really can't be crying on this maybe-date.

"People come to the shop to buy gifts. Everyone talks about their family plans... It's hard. But last year, I got to spend time in Mrs. Treville's apartment, taking care of her cat while she visited friends in Florida, so that was something different at least. Is that why you're here this month? To distract yourself? Sorry, that was rude. I bet you have a lot of friends, and then there's your uncle too."

Saint shakes his head, glancing at the aubergine on his plate. He's so unbearably handsome in the turtleneck that emphasizes his wide shoulders. "He's gone too. It's just me now. And... yeah, maybe you're right. Maybe choosing to set a book at Christmas time is my excuse to work throughout December and not think too much about all the things I'm missing."

I reluctantly pull my fingers away so I can eat, but I only do that because it's the reasonable thing. If I had my way, I'd let the chicken go cold just so I can hold his hand for a bit longer.

"You did come to the right place then," I say, trying to lighten the mood. "Rosehill Pines is trying to win some kind of Christmas town award, so they always go all out. We could... go see the Christmas market next week if you'd like?"

Saint's eyes light up as if I've promised to suck his dick once we leave the restaurant. "I would like that. I used to really love this time of year. But now it's... spoiled," he says, digging into his food.

"Maybe you just need to make new memories?" I say, half convincing myself. Because maybe that's what I need to climb out my own hole, and I've been reluctant to admit it.

Saint exhales and catches my gaze for long enough to get my body as hot as a radiator in the middle of winter. "Maybe this year I can do that. Who knows?"

With me? I hope it's with me. I hope that if this *isn't* a date, then maybe we could have one as the days pass. If I'm frugal with my spending, maybe I could treat him to something at the Christmas market. Or take him hunting and wow him with my marksmanship?

The conversation flows, as does the wine, and by the time we get dessert, it feels as though I've known him for weeks not a day. He urges me to try the cheesecake off his plate, and I end up feeding him a spoonful of ice cream.

This is either a date, or something gay men do with friends, which I wouldn't know since I don't have any friends, gay or otherwise.

It's late when we leave the restaurant, but we're both tipsy, and the Christmas lights somehow become even more fun when he points out how some of the lamp poles look uncannily like dicks from certain angles. This is already the best night I've had all year, and it's not yet over.

"How can you walk around with your neck bare like that?" Saint asks as we stroll down the empty street, toward our apartment building. I want this date or non-date to last forever so I keep my pace slow.

I shrug, smiling at the massive glittery snowflakes hanging across the street. They don't even seem so tacky right now. "I was in a hurry in the morning and forgot. It's fine."

Saint frowns and pulls on his dark brown scarf, freeing it from under his coat. I stall, because a part of me already knows what he intends, but when he faces me and puts the silky-smooth wool around my neck, I'm still too shocked to speak.

"There. Can't have you losing your voice. I like how it sounds," he adds with a little smirk.

Behind him, snow dances around a streetlight, and there are white flakes on his shoulders and uncovered hair, shimmering like silver dust. When something in his gaze changes, I lean in without thinking. Or is it the gentle tug of the scarf that pulls me closer?

It doesn't matter, because all I can think of are his lips on mine. Soft, warm, inviting.

The kiss is only a peck on the mouth, but before he pulls back, he gives my top lip a quick lick that sends sparks all the way down my body. I'm half hard just from that gesture, and I find it hard to breathe, hard to focus.

He kisses me, and now wraps the scarf around my neck for good measure.

This is a date. This is most definitely a date.

Saint chuckles, looking around, but it's late, and we're the only ones out here, as if the whole town is a diorama depicting our first day together—*Stop!* Once again, I'm letting my imagination run rampant. For all I know, this might be our *only* day together but I'm going to treasure it in my mind forever.

"Well... I guess I should walk you home now," Saint tells me, his hands so warm I can feel them even through my thick jacket.

My home? His home? To the door? Will I be brave enough to invite him in?

Those are questions for when we get there. For now, I smile and savor the magical moment.

Chapter 7

Rowan

I have never expected to experience the butterflies I've so often read about, but despite it being December, and the snow falling all around us, butterflies come to life deep inside me, dancing at every word from Saint's mouth.

We talk about the TV show I've been watching, about Saint experimenting with a new type of tomato in his pasta sauce, even about tomorrow's weather, and the conversation flows with ease like waves in the sea, back and forth. I can't remember feeling this comfortable with anyone. This must be what people mean when they say they clicked with someone.

Every now and then, our hands brush, and it sends a shiver down my spine. The scarf wrapped around my neck smells fresh, like newly cut grass, yet with a dark, masculine undertone that makes my senses overreact to every sensation.

But as easy as I find talking to him, when we step into the elevator and get stuck in its small, closed interior, words die at the back of my throat as a sense of expectation falls over us, nudging at me.

What are the rules of this date? Should I invite him to my place? I desperately want his hands on me, yet the very idea of another person in my home, especially someone I don't know well, makes my throat constrict.

I wish I was normal. I wish I wasn't scared of things people do all the time.

But I think back to the freaky situation from last week and know I won't be able to gather enough courage to challenge myself tonight. A dark shadow settles on my mind as I think about the masked intruder who knew my name. He almost feels like a figment of my imagination at this point, but the police confirmed my window lock was broken, so I didn't dream him up after all.

Saint clicks on the timed light button as we stop on our floor and goes out first, offering me a small smile. "I wish I came here last month. I'm starting to feel I might not have as much time for writing as I anticipated."

I realize I've been ignoring this absolute *stud* at my side, too stuck in my own head. "Why? You're not leaving soon, are you? You just moved in." I hope that didn't sound too desperate as I follow him into the dim corridor.

He's tall, broad shouldered, with an elegant, sturdy figure that makes my mind wander, but in truth I wouldn't even know how to go about unpacking such a fine man. Or any man for that matter.

Saint shrugs. "I can stay if there's a reason to."

I walk a bit slower, to extend our time together. "Rosehill Pines is beautiful in the spring... There's a hot air balloon festival in March." I push my nose into the scarf when he's not looking my way, and try to remember the fresh scent clinging to it, so I can remember it later, in bed. Whatever happens, this evening has already been the best one in forever. For once, I'm not thinking about bashing Otto Grass's head open with a nail-studded baseball bat, but about warm skin and the weight of a man on top of me. It feels illegal to have such thoughts about someone I know in person, but Saint keeps close, sliding the backs of his fingers against my hand as we face our respective doors in the quiet of the evening.

"I had something else in mind, actually," he says, capturing my gaze with his tempting hazel eyes.

My heart beats faster, and I can't look away from his handsome features. An intrusive thought tells me he might be hypnotizing me, or that he drugged me, but I shake it off, melting in the warmth of his attention.

"What is it?" I ask, but then the light in the corridor goes off.

The twinkling lamps outside illuminate him faintly, and as their color changes from green and yellow to red, he seems even more handsome. He's my Christmas miracle.

But the darkness means I've already prolonged the time needed to get from the elevator to our doors beyond reason.

Saint clears his throat, the faint glow from outside making his smile appear soft, almost shy. "I really enjoyed myself tonight, and...well, I was thinking maybe you'd like to continue this evening at my place?"

Anxiety wraps its cold fingers around my throat, preventing me from speaking. This is my dream come true. Saint, this absolutely stunning man, is interested in me. And I'm standing there like an idiot instead of jumping his bones.

It's as if he can sense my hesitation, and he slides his fingers over my hand. The warm touch thaws my nerves, and the tightness in my throat finally eases.

"I... I want to. So much. But... I have this thing. About being in someone's house, or inviting them to mine. It's not about you," I say quickly and squeeze his hand because it's hard for me to find the right words. "Especially at night. I've experienced a... break-in, and I get nervous about these things. I know it's unreasonable. Sorry."

Saint's features turn grim, and he pulls me close, wrapping his firm arms around me. Oh, it's been so long since I've been held. And *never* quite like this. Heat floods my face as I bury my nose in the folds of his coat, but I let him hug me, so content for him to be the barrier between me and the world.

We only met earlier today, yet I already crave him like I crave revenge on those who wronged me.

"That's awful," he whispers.

I hug him back, basking in how safe he makes me feel. He's bigger than me, and strong enough to carry me down the stairs. I always liked men who were a bit older than me but never realized how much I actually desire knowing that someone's taking care of me. Maybe because the big guys I interact with at the hunting store make me walk on pins and needles. But Saint feels... safe.

"If you just give me some time..." I whisper pressing into him, helpless against my fears. "Oh, God, I want you so much." I can hardly believe I said that out loud, but it feels so natural to be honest about it.

His breath is raspy as we simultaneously take a step toward the wall and my back flattens against its cool surface. His forehead feels warm against mine, and when our lips meet, the kiss is no longer just a light smooch. He opens my mouth with his, and the very tip of his tongue teases me so gently my knees soften.

I've kissed a total of two girls all the way back in high school, but never like this. His tongue caresses mine, and I open to him, sliding my hands to those sturdy arms. I won't lose my balance when I'm in Saint's embrace. I don't even care that we're in the corridor outside the apartment. It's dark. It's night. And I want it too much.

All the worries about being bad at kissing disperse like marshmallows melting into hot chocolate, because he leads the way with ease. All I have to do is give in. My heart beats in a frantic rhythm against his chest, and I'm afraid he will soon *feel* how much I want him.

Reality and time splinters as we hold one another in the dark, and while our clothes are thick and start getting uncomfortably hot now that we're indoors, I can't bring myself to pull away. Because what if he calls this a mistake and excuses himself, leaving me in the dark?

His hands are gentle, if passionate, and they're everywhere, rubbing and squeezing my shoulders, arms, and—oh—trailing down my sides so sensually I rise to my toes.

I'm so hard it's excruciating, but I don't have the words to tell him.

Until he takes my hand and guides it between our bodies, down his stomach.

I moan into the kiss when I feel his rock-hard erection. Instincts take over. Breathless from the kiss I want to never end, I press my palm against him harder, dizzy from excitement. I now realize I've been repressing my desires, letting them lie dormant because I was too afraid to act on them, but they're there. In the dark, they're free to crawl out as I hold Saint close.

His breath catches, and he nips my lip, triggering a jolt that goes straight to my balls. Our eyes meet, and there's nothing that can stop me from giving him what he wants. I wish to be touched by him too, but what I need most is to become an object of desire, for the feelings of inferiority to disappear as I bask in Saint's lust.

The slightest push on my shoulders tells me exactly what he expects.

I steal one more kiss and slide down the wall, then to my knees. I don't even care my leg aches after all that walking, or that someone could turn on the light at any point. For him, I'd kneel on this hard floor all day, as long as I got to inhale the leathery scent of his belt and the warm musk of his arousal.

He towers over me so beautifully, one arm resting against the wall while the other pulls off my hat. He makes quick work of opening the buttons on his coat. At least this means I'm not the only one overheating. "You're so damn hot, Rowan," Saint whispers, watching me with eyes so intense they might just start burning.

His words are like rocket fuel to my confidence. While I don't consider myself unattractive, I rarely get complimented on my looks in any way. The guys at the shop consider me a skinny weakling worthy of their pity. It doesn't matter that they're not my target audience, because their comments still chip away at my confidence.

Old ladies will sometimes say I'm a *"nice-looking boy"*. But 'hot'? To hear that from a man like Saint? Fuck... I'll give him the best head I can.

When I pull his pants and underwear down just enough to let his cock out, I don't wonder about my confidence anymore. My brain is flooded with pure lust and as I close my hand around his shaft, I can hardly believe how good that makes me feel. His scent is so rich and warm as I lean in, pressing my face to the warm flesh revealed by the open pants. His pubes are trimmed and feel so delicious against my nose as I give Saint the first, tentative pump.

A grunt escapes his throat, and his hand rests on my nape in either reassurance or a claiming gesture. I don't know, maybe it's both. I can take both.

His dick is so perfect I don't have the words to describe it, and yes, I'm worried that I won't be able to satisfy him but I'm sure gonna try. The shaft throbs in my grip, hard as steel, and I can't wait any longer. Arousal replaces my blood as I wrap my lips around the head, and as it flows through me, my body rocks, desperate for release.

I had no idea if sex would ever even be something to happen in my life, and now here I am, on my knees, going down on the hottest man in this damn town. I want to make him come, I want to hear those sexy grunts, and I want to see the face he makes when I swallow his spunk.

A salty flavor spreads across my tongue as I bob my head, trying to take in more of him, and if his cum tastes anything like this, I want him to call me whenever he needs to get off.

A shiver of delight and embarrassment courses through me at those thoughts, but I can't help it. He's perfection, and I want to be the vessel for his lust. I want him to get addicted to me and suffer sleepless nights just because I'm not in his bed.

"Yeah, suck it, take it deeper," Saint whispers, swallowing as I clutch his pants, holding him in place, already hooked on the warmth of his hard dick, on its weight on my tongue.

His wish is my command. I may have zero experience, but at the moment, my desire is enough to guide me. Saint squeezes the hair at the back of my head a bit tighter, and drives his cock in deeper with a slow thrust of hips. His dick is so hot on my tongue as it pulses to the rhythm of his heartbeat, and I can only hope to give him an experience he'll be coming back for.

My own arousal is on the backburner when I focus on allowing him deeper into my mouth, but I still gag a little when his cockhead prods at my throat, a sensation that is so confusingly hot I reach down and squeeze myself through my pants.

It should be an uncomfortable sensation, and it is, but something about it speaks to my lizard brain and makes me want more. I want to drive him mad.

At this point, I'm steaming up in my winter jacket, so I quickly unzip and push it off, with that hard dick moving up and down my palate, prodding for entrance yet withdrawing as soon as I choke. My cock is so stiff it might rip a hole in my pants, so I rub it a bit more while Saint fucks my lips. There's something illicit about the smacking noises my mouth makes as I suck on him, but I don't give a damn about it being lewd or embarrassing. Maybe I'm a pervert who likes getting it in a public place?

I'm pretty sure I just heard someone turn on the TV in their apartment, and I don't even care that it might be an attempt to block out the two dudes fucking in the hallway, because all I can think of is sucking Saint dry. On my knees in front of him, I'm no longer a pathetic victim unable to keep himself safe. I am someone worthy of desire. Someone attractive enough to lure a hunk like Saint, even if just this one time.

"Oh fuck... Such... pretty lips," he huffs, making me look up, hungry for praise.

I've been so engrossed in his dick, its scent and flavor, that I've forgotten about anything else, but meeting his eyes is exhilarating. Only half his face is visible thanks to the colorful ambience outside, but the dark flush covering his skin is unmistakable. When he bites his lip to hold in a moan while driving into my mouth faster, he's a fucking *vision*. I slide my hand under his sweater, and he feels just as I expected. Rock hard with a dusting of hair. My favorite kind of man, in theory at least, and reality is outperforming my fantasies in every way.

Need has me whimpering softly as we work together for his pleasure. Even drunk on arousal, I can sense him getting harder, his movements becoming more erratic, and then, he pulls my head back by the hair. I stick out my tongue, desperate for another taste of him, but he steadies himself, working his dick at a frantic pace. "You want to swallow?" he rasps, touching my tongue with his cockhead.

"I want to taste you," I mumble. My lips caress his cock as I speak, and I don't know whether I should focus on the way it drips pre-cum, or at the handsome face above. Saint's eyebrows are drawn, and there's a new intensity in his eyes now, a darkness I'm more than happy to embrace.

He nods, but his face stiffens as he stares at me like a hawk about to hunt down a mouse. The little hiss he makes warns me moments before the first jet of cum splashes on my tongue, and as it's followed by several more, I shiver, swallowing the thick spunk. I'll need to get used to the taste, but that doesn't matter. I still want him to do this again. I want him to *ravish* me over and over.

He rests his forehead against the wall once he's done, and I close my lips around his cockhead, holding it in my warm mouth while he recovers. My excitement is still a raw, throbbing need, but I'm happy to wait, enjoying everything this moment has to offer. His scent is so intense I could get off just smelling him. He's such a beautiful man, and the taste of his cum makes my whole body vibrate with glee, because I did that. I made him come.

When I look up, our eyes meet, and I smile as widely as his dick allows me.

"You look so pretty like this, with my cock in your mouth," Saint murmurs, stroking my cheek. "But I want to see you come too."

Before I know it, one of his hands is at my nape, the other on my arm, and he's pulling me up as if I weigh nothing. Within half a second, he has me facing the wall, and before I can make a peep, he's opening my pants while molding his body to mine from behind. I shiver, overcome with a new kind of excitement, but time rushes forward when my new lover claims me with a bite on the nape.

Every muscle in my body yields, and I barely keep in a moan as he sucks on my flesh while pumping my dick.

I shamelessly push my ass against him, overwhelmed with a thousand different dirty scenarios in which he fucks my brains out. His fingers are thicker than mine, his grip is strong, but it's the way he presses me into the wall and the next bite to my neck that sends me over the edge.

No one has ever touched my dick, but I don't even have time to analyze that, too busy painting the wall with my cum.

When I moan too loudly, he puts his other hand over my mouth, but it only makes my orgasm intensify. I fight for air through my nose, pressing my forehead to the wall, happy to be his feast.

We both still, listening to each other's breathing as our bodies cool, but delicious moments aren't meant to last forever, and he finally pulls away after kissing my nape a final time. "Okay, I didn't expect this would happen. Here out of all places," he adds with a chuckle.

I turn around, using the wall to keep myself steady. I'm still panting, strands of hair are stuck to my hot face, and in a sudden onslaught of shyness, I pull up my pants, but I can't help smiling anyway.

"I didn't even know if we were on a date or not until you kissed me," I confess.

Saint grins, and for the first time since we've met, his perfect hair is a bit out of place. "Really? After I tried inviting you twice on the same day?"

I try not to stare as he lazily zips his pants and buckles up his belt. Unsuccessfully. His hands are so big, and veiny, and beautiful I could just lick every finger.

I rub some cum off my face. "I guess I just... This is new to me."

Saint cocks his head with a small smile and kisses me again, his eyes soft like two hazel clouds. "You did suggest there's not that many suitable guys here."

I stroke his side, amazed that I'm allowed to touch him. "For you? Only one," I dare tease him, but instantly look away, shocked by my own boldness. Then again, I did just have his dick in my mouth, so I think I'm allowed to be playful.

Saint grins and nuzzles my nose as he finishes arranging his clothes. "I'm thinking that too. You're like no one I've ever dated."

I kiss him once more, reveling in the softness of his lips. "I wish this night would never end. Thank you for the *best* date."

Saint shrugs, stepping away, toward his door. "I had a great time too. We have to repeat this very soon."

I turn to my door with a smile, but keep looking back at him, so I fail at getting my key into the hole. "Stop distracting me!" I end up laughing.

Saint opens *his* door with flawless perfection. "You know I will even when you can no longer see me," he says before disappearing into his apartment.

He's so right it doesn't even seem smug of him to say it.

My mind is floating on love endorphins as I meticulously close the locks on my door without urgency. I still walk over to the windows to make sure they're secured, but it gives me an unexpected sense of safety to know Saint is next door. He would have come if I screamed. I just know it. And if he couldn't force the locks open, he would have used an axe to get in.

I wash my face and, for once, smile at my reflection.

"*You're so hot, Rowan,*" I whisper to myself with glee, but as I'm about to undress, my phone pings, and I grin at the sight of Saint's name in the message.

[*Do you have work tomorrow? - Saint*]

Really? He can't get enough of me so much he wants another date tomorrow? I might just have to put my hair in pigtails, because I'm feeling like a schoolgirl with her first crush.

[*I'm free. You?*] I write back.

[*Join me outside?*] Saint answers, and my cheeks burn as I spin on my heel and head for the door. When I peek out into the corridor, he's sitting on a blanket in front of my apartment, and there's a tray of crackers, and wine resting right next to him. He even lit a few tiny candles to illuminate the space for us.

I'm speechless when he offers me a smile. "I don't really want this date to be over yet, and you did say you don't want the night to end..."

This is not only sweet and thoughtful, but also shows that he's okay with my weird-ass phobia. He's willing to lean into what I need, and even make it fun. I grab my jacket, because the corridor is a bit chilly, and with my heart fluttering out of control, I sit down next to him.

But if he's leaning into me, I need to put in the effort too. Maybe we could actually have another date in the hallway of his apartment and gradually move farther from the safety of the public space, until I start feeling comfortable being with him behind closed doors? Because I'm not losing my virginity in a corridor.

"This is... amazing." I'm a dumbass. I met him today, and I'm already falling for him. "Who needs sleep, right?"

His hand closes on mine. "Not me."

CHAPTER 8

ROWAN

I BARELY SLEPT LAST night yet couldn't be happier. I'm walking on clouds, wrapped in Saint's scarf, and I never felt more special. It's as if finally something good is happening in my life. Making out in the corridor by candlelight has to be the most romantic thing that's ever happened to anyone.

I refuse to question why Saint chose me. He might be more classically handsome than me, but that doesn't mean he can't take interest in me! Our connection feels strong even though we've just met, but things like that happen sometimes, so why not to me? Our conversations flow, the sexual tension is off the charts, and it turns out we have more similarities than I would have ever imagined.

He also likes horror movies, he wants to go hunting with me, he's been on his own since his uncle died, and he isn't tied down anywhere, so he could stay in Rosehill Pines as long as he wants. Or I could leave, because nothing's keeping me here.

I haven't considered my future in a while, but today, I feel as though the world is my oyster.

Many would say I'm getting ahead of myself, but our connection feels right, and I would be an idiot if I didn't give it a fair chance. We've already kind-of planned to spend Christmas together, since neither of us has any family, and for the first time in years, I'm actually excited for the twenty-fifth.

I'm running a few errands since it's my day off, but I can't wait to be back home in the hope that he's available to meet up, since his job allows so much flexibility. He teased me that he's not ready to reveal his pen name, but it only makes me wonder if he isn't some big name author.

It's slowly getting darker as I pass a French bakery, which is far too fancy for my wallet. I stop by the window, because Saint told me how much he loves gingerbread and there's gingerbread cheesecake on offer. I wouldn't buy it for myself, but to hell with budgeting. That beautiful man deserves the best, and since he's such a foodie, he'll appreciate fancy dessert.

I leave the shop shocked by the amount of money I needed to part with to get just three pieces of cake, but it would be worth it, and by the time I reach my floor, a smile sits firmly on my face. I'm tempted to knock on Saint's door and surprise him, but there's someone else I want to pay a brief visit to, so I make my way to Mrs. Treville's apartment and ring her bell.

I shake my head when I hear the chain rattle on the other side, because it would be safer for her to first ask who is at the door. Otherwise, what is the chain for?

But I won't be chastising a woman in her seventies and smile as soon as I see her. "Hello, hope I'm not interrupting anything?"

The scent of stew invites me in, but I have no intention of crossing the threshold when she's also there, as unreasonable as that is. "I was just making lunch. How are you, Rowan?" she asks, adjusting her red apron.

I offer her one of the pretty pink boxes. "I'm very good, actually. I came with this little thank you gift. You must have a sixth sense, because... me and Saint," I point to our new neighbor's door. "Really hit it off."

She opens the door more widely, revealing her pink home full of old-timey pictures on each wall. "Oh that's wonderful! I had a sense about that one," she says with pride and accepts my offering "But you didn't have to bring me anything, honey."

"No, I really did. I've not been feeling great lately, and a new friend might be exactly what I need, so thank you."

Friend. More like man to climb like a tree.

"That is so sweet! I will tell my grandson all about it," she says, but just as she retreats into her flat, her cat makes a dash into the hallway.

I block him with my foot at the last moment, and the fluffball makes an unhappy hiss, but then Mrs. Treville manages to scoop him up with one hand.

"Maybe he wants to meet Saint too. He's a very good cook, apparently."

Mrs. Treville shakes her head. "He's got enough food at home, but the grass is always greener on the other side."

We say our goodbyes, and I whip up my phone as soon as I'm on my own again. I know it's stereotypically lesbians whose dates last seventy-two hours, but I just can't get enough of Saint and I'll use any excuse to be around him. I've also made up my mind. I will challenge myself to enter his home.

[*Are you working?*] I text Saint.

I only have to wait a moment for his response. [*Just started whipping up lunch. You?*]

I decide to surprise him and knock on the door with a stupid grin on my face. It's not like me to smile this much, but he does that to me. Ants crawl up my back when I hear footsteps on the other side, and then he's there, greeting me with a wide smile. "Rowan! Come on—" He stalls, mid-way through the gesture meant to invite me. He must have remembered what I told him yesterday, and I want to kiss away the torn expression passing through his face.

I take a deep breath and show off the boxes with cake. "I got us gingerbread cheesecake, and... if you're ready to bear with my anxiety, I'd like to try coming in. Unless it's a bad time?"

Saint blinks, taken aback, but just as my inadequacy smashes into me with the might of a thousand suns, he opens the door wide and steps aside, revealing a bare corridor and three doors. "Of course! I didn't know you'd want to, that's all."

I look at him with the smile frozen to my lips, but now that reality slams into me, my mind screams *Danger! Danger!* at being alone with a stranger—No. Saint isn't a stranger. He's the first man who kissed me. The first man with whom I had sex. The first man I went on a date with, and he is amazing.

"Smells nice, what are you cooking?" I ask to distract him from the fact that my feet refused to move inside right away.

"Oh, I just put the pie in the oven. It's roasted butternut squash and feta. And, I was about to make a salad to go with it," he says, gesturing inside. He grabs my trembling hand in a gesture so reassuring my shoulders sag a bit.

There's nothing to be afraid of.

Saint is handsome, funny, oh so sexy, *and* cooks. I need to get my shit together.

"It's like with the stairs," I say softly, squeezing his hand. He's so patient with me I could cry. "I didn't actually fall. I was pushed. During a house invasion. It's like my body remembers." There's a relief to telling someone about it, and I step inside with one foot.

I freeze when Saint leans in to hug me, but the moment his warm arms settle around me, the anxiety I've lived with for so long seems more bearable. Even his scent is soothing.

"I'm so sorry."

Maybe it's his thing to be the white knight to broken bugs like me. I don't have to feel guilty about him saving me if it gives him pleasure, so I hug him back with a sigh.

"I should say it's okay, but it's not. I still have nightmares about it and triple-check the locks in my house. You... you're making it easier though." I kiss his shoulder, and when I glance down, I see that I didn't even notice when both my feet landed beyond the threshold of his home.

Maybe I can do this if someone who actually gives a shit about me holds me by the hand?

"We could... eat in the corridor, with the door open. So you know it's safe," Saint proposes, pulling back to look at my face. He's so handsome yet, unlike many beautiful people, doesn't act like the whole world is beneath him.

He makes me feel so safe already. The cake is not enough, but it's a start. I want to give him everything. Saint is... unreal. He makes the effort most people don't.

"Let's do that if I don't manage, but I want to try and see how I feel with the door closed, if that's okay with you."

One deep breath later, I take another step inside with him holding my hand, and take in the bare-bones apartment that's eerily similar to mine but way blander. No wonder, he only arrived yesterday and surely he keeps his stuff where his real home is.

"Sure! Test out whatever you need," he says and presses a kiss to my forehead.

I could melt. He's so kind to me. I'd say I don't deserve it, but after all the miserable times I've been through, don't I deserve some kindness?

"The setup of this place is a mirror of mine. My bedroom is on the other side. But you have a nicer kitchen," I point out the granite countertops. Maybe being in Saint's space won't be so frightening after all? Maybe I've just wound myself up over the years?

I remember this one girl telling me she was extremely afraid of spiders, yet one day she posted a photo of herself holding a tarantula in her hand, just like that. Apparently, it was a spur-of-the-moment decision for her, so maybe it could work the same way for me? Maybe I was more terrified of the *idea* of being in an apartment with someone else, and could actually convince myself that it isn't reasonable?

Saint's mouth quirks, and he shows me the cutting board surrounded by several vegetables, including one I have never seen.

"I hope you like fennel," he says with a mysterious smile and returns to his work as I glance at the sofa I saw carried in yesterday. There are two books resting next to it on the floor, and Saint doesn't even have a TV. If I were him, I'd have stayed in a hotel, but maybe he doesn't care much about conveniences beyond the kitchen?

"I'm not sure. I don't know vegetables all that well, but on the other hand, I don't exactly check the ingredients of the meals I buy, so maybe I had it and don't even know. That must sound very uncultured to you." I laugh, more at ease by the minute. "Is it okay to leave the door open?" I ask as I make it all the way to a small dining table with two chairs and put the cheesecake in the middle.

"Sure, whatever's most comfortable. And fennel has this particular taste not everyone likes, but if you hate the salad, I can just cut up some tomatoes for you instead," Saint says and places a white vegetable on the chopping board. He uses a massive knife to cut it in half, and then proceeds to slam it down at lightning speed, without ever fully taking the blade off the board.

My eyebrows rise and for a moment, the fact that I'm alone with someone else retreats to the very back of my mind. "Oh, my God! You're so good with the knife. You sure you're not a chef?"

Hazel eyes meet mine, and he grins, shaking his head. "I am sure. It's just a matter of practice. I really like cooking and food. It got me through some really bad times, and when I feed myself well, I feel like I'm taking care of myself," he says and starts chopping the vegetable lengthwise.

What is this guy *not* good at?

"Are you a rule follower or can we have dessert first?" I wink at him and point at the pink box, more at ease. Even my heart is slowing its crazy pace.

Saint snorts and raises his knife, wiggling it as if it were a finger meant to call out bad behavior. "Lunch first. We're gonna be civilized about this and take our time savoring the dessert!"

I raise my palms and shake my head with a smile. "Okay, okay, we do it your way. Can I use your bathroom?"

When Saint nods, I head down the corridor without even limping too much. After yesterday's kneeling my knee should be aching like hell, yet here I am, spared by my faulty body. I can't help but take a good look at his bed, because a part of me hopes that I might end up resting in those black sheets eventually, but I don't want to be a creep, and head straight for the bathroom. I'm only washing my hands, so there's no need to shut the door, but as I grab the hand towel, facing a small drying rack attached to the radiator, my gaze stops on a black item with a white print on one side.

My stomach clenches as I pull it off the drying rack. Deep down, I already know what I'm looking at, but my mind doesn't want to accept it.

It's the black balaclava with the print of a wolf skull with teeth bared in a silent threat. The mask worn by the intruder who tried to do fuck knows what to me just a week ago.

The intruder who knew my name.

With panic choking me, I put the mask back on the rack, aiming for the same position it was in. The man who broke into my house is in the other room, and he had a knife.

All the hairs on my body bristle and I feel like I'm gonna throw up.

What. The. Fuck?

CHAPTER 9

SAINT

I CAN ALREADY SENSE the warmth of his body against mine. I'm in my kitchen, pulling the savory pie I made for lunch out of the oven, but my mind is traveling to the soon-to-be future, where Rowan is my companion, my partner, my lover, and he's next to me when I wake up each morning.

Wouldn't that be something? To finally have someone to share my life with, both in and out of work? I'd get him the best medical care there is, and take him places he's never imagined visiting. We'd go on thrill rides in amusement parks, to fancy restaurants, and see all the sights the world has to offer. Together. It's never been as fun on my own.

As I plate the salad and cut two pieces of the pie, all I can think about is the way he smiled at me when he came over, and I want to see it again. He even bought us cake. How cute is that?

"Lunch is ready," I call out, placing both plates on the table.

He comes out of the bathroom looking pale, but I think he's beautiful like that. With the black hair and dark eyes, he's like Snow White. I wish I could tell him the truth already, so we can be honest with each other at last, but I don't want to spook him. It's not the right time.

Rowan glances toward the open door as if he forgot something, but then sits at the table. "Oh… Looks delicious," he says, but doesn't meet my eyes.

Does he secretly hate vegetables but feels the need to lie not to hurt my feelings? That is so him. But while I value how considerate he is, I want to be that for him too, and I give his hand a gentle stroke.

"Don't worry if you don't like it. I won't be offended if you try both and decide to just have the cake for lunch."

"It's fine, I'm sure it's great." Rowan says and grabs a fork but hesitates over the knife for some reason. "Do you… I realized you told me about some of the places you traveled to, but never where you actually live."

"I'm from Brooklyn," I tell him, digging in. The pie is still very hot, so I cover my mouth and suck in air to cool the morsel down. But it's delicious. Creamy, rich. Perfection. "I have an apartment there, but I spend most of my time somewhere else. You know, ever since my uncle took me in. He moved around a lot for his job."

"And what did he do?"

Rowan takes a bite of the pie and tells me it's delicious, yet there's a stiffness to his shoulders. Something is off, and I can't work it out. Maybe he's not comfortable in my house because of his phobia. I'm proud of him though that he's challenging himself. Maybe if we do this a couple of times, he'll understand that he's perfectly safe at my side.

"A private detective." It's only a half-lie, since there is a lot of investigative work involved in being a professional killer, but I can't wait to tell Rowan everything. About my past, our future, and about the gift I'm already crafting for him.

He looks up for half a second, poking at his salad. "Oh. So, like a policeman?"

I shake my head. "He wasn't afraid to get his hands dirty. And he made me the man I am. I don't know where I'd be if he hadn't decided to take care of me."

He taught me everything I know.

And I still miss him, even though he was quiet, grumpy, and never stopped trying to lure me into dating a girl. But when a guy broke my heart, my uncle broke his hand, so he was supportive of my dating life in his own way.

Rowan finally eats a bit of salad, slouching over the table. It reminds me of how he fell asleep against my shoulder last night. I would have carried him to bed, but that could have been a violation of his boundaries, and I didn't want to freak him out. I learned my lesson the first time I visited his home.

"And there's no boyfriend in Brooklyn I should know about?" He smiles stiffly. "You're so handsome it's hard for me to believe you're single."

Oh, so this is it. Sweetie's getting into his own head about our relationship. But I have nothing to hide. Well, at least when it comes to that aspect of my life.

I swallow and stroke his hand in reassurance. "Look, there's a lot of gay men in New York City, but you know what happens at a buffet? People can't pick just one thing. They've already overeaten, but they're still coming back for seconds. I don't want that. I want something real. Someone who wants to invest their time into me only."

I take a sip of water. It's not often that I bare my soul like this, but here we go. Those are special circumstances. *He* is special.

And one day, hopefully sooner rather than later, I'll make his Christmas wish come true. He won't have to fear his revenge plan going wrong, or being caught by the cops. I'll show him how to clean the scene, and which poisons are least likely to be recognized with standard lab tests.

And since he's here, in my apartment, maybe I can show him my bedroom after dessert? He didn't have any hangups about sex last night, so why wait?

"And you chose *me* off the menu?" Rowan asks, meeting my gaze. He's searching for something, but I don't know what exactly. Reassurance?

I smile, and the truth about the beginning of our relationship scratches the back of my throat, begging to be told, but it's too early. Rowan isn't ready for it yet. So I offer him another half-truth. "I wanted to talk to you because you're hot. But then we clicked, and... I don't know, when something feels right, I believe in following my heart. And what's on *your* mind?"

He looks so troubled I'm itching to kiss away his worries.

Or maybe that's just my need to have him under me talking.

"I... I think this was a bad idea. Not you," he adds. "You've been great, and I want to keep seeing you. I just don't think I was ready to come to your place."

It's hard to hide my disappointment when Rowan gets up.

"Oh, would you like to eat at your place? Or in the hallway?" I ask, getting to my feet too.

"No, but thank you. Sorry, I think I need to be alone for a bit," he says and walks toward the door. I might be a bit disgruntled to see him leave, but I'm happy that he's limping a bit less today. "Maybe we can have the cake later, if you can hold off eating it all." He's joking, but when he smiles, his lips are stiff.

Either I'm missing something or being in my place really proved too much for him. In any case, it's time to throw in the towel. I raise my hands and follow him to the open door, because there's nothing to gain from pressuring him. "All right. Can we maybe go for a walk later, if you feel better? I was thinking about getting hot chocolate at that Sweet Heaven place."

He nods and I kiss the sweet lips that gave me so much pleasure last night. Unable to help myself, I stroke his side, prolonging the connection, but I have to let go eventually.

I admire the shape of his legs and ass as he enters his home, but he's gone from view much sooner than I would have liked. Oh well, I'll be seeing him later. My uncle always called me impatient, and I'm starting to see his point.

I come back to the table to finish my lunch, but as I have my first bite, I notice the knife on the other side of the table is gone.

Did he... steal my knife?

What?

I rise, about to knock on his door, but what is the point? I can always ask for it later. Still, feeling overheated and somewhat annoyed by the way he baited me into a date only to leave, I rush to the bathroom to splash my face with cold water. It feels soothing, and I enjoy the sensation of cold droplets rolling down my neck as I lean against the sink, gathering my thoughts. But when I open my eyes and spot the balaclava on the drying rack, they scatter in a violent swarm.

"Fuck..." I utter, heating up all over again.

I hardly could have expected him to gather the courage to come into my apartment so soon and didn't bother hiding anything. What a fucking blunder.

He might have not noticed the mask though. It's just a black piece of fabric among black socks.

Then again, not only did his demeanor change after the bathroom visit, but he went as far as stealing my knife. He might have done that expecting me to attack. As if I would ever hurt him.

I take a deep breath and walk to the door.

This can be salvaged.

I glance through the peephole, still on the fence about what I should do. For a while, there is no movement in the corridor, but then Rowan's door opens by a few inches, and he glances toward my apartment through the gap. A moment later, he steps out, looking around as if there was someone after him, and he's not only dressed in his camo jacket, boots and gloves, but also wears a massive backpack, and holds a duffel bag in his hand.

Fuck. He did see the mask and recognized it. And now he's making a run for it.

It seems I won't get to finish my lunch after all.

CHAPTER 10

ROWAN

EVERYTHING WAS A LIE, and this... stranger, this fucking monster who broke into my home a week ago, found his way in through the back door for reasons known only to him. Is he even really gay, or did he simply woo me because it was the easiest way to get to me?

God, I can't believe I sucked him off last night, and while I've been riding a high at the time, I now feel disgusted with myself.

I'm so stupid. So naive. I'd clutched at the first crumb of affection thrown my way when I should have known he was too good to be true.

What if he's friends with the fuckers who murdered my family and killing me is a sick test of loyalty? Well, whatever motivates him, I'm not going down without a fight.

Though an *actual* fight is my last resort because the first one, the most reasonable one, is to *run*.

With my survival bag in the backseat, a gun in my pocket, and a lump in my throat, I drive off, hoping the growing darkness will help, not hinder, my efforts to get away.

It's not snowing, thank fuck, but I can't risk him finding me, so instead of going down the most obvious route out of town, I take a small road that will take me to a motel I have long planned to stay at in a situation like this one. I hoped to never need my bug-out plan, but the past seems to have caught up with me, and I'm not taking any chances. The cops didn't put the people who murdered my family behind bars, and I don't trust them to keep me safe. Not when Saint—or whatever the hell his real name is—hasn't yet done anything I can prove.

It's all on me, and while I only have so much money, I'm planning to make it count.

In a bout of fury, I slam my fist against the steering wheel and scream into the emptiness in my car. I feel sick when I think about last night. Was he getting off on the power he held over me? Does he enjoy toying with me like a cat would with a mouse?

I know this road well, but I'm still wary, because it's covered with a thin layer of snow and I don't want to hit any unfortunate animal.

I take several deep breaths that don't help. What the fuck am I supposed to do? I thought I actually connected with someone for once, but turns out I'm all alone and in more trouble than ever I could have imagined. A raspy voice asks me if Mrs. Treville is Saint's accomplice, but I dismiss that thought, since she's been nothing but kind to me in the two years I've been her neighbor.

But it no longer matters, because I'm never going back to that town. Okay, maybe I will. Somehow. Eventually. I can't afford to replace every single necessity I own or pay rent for two apartments. I'm so fucked.

The farmland gives way to a forest I often spend my days off in, but while this means I'm getting farther away from the man who now occupies both my dreams and nightmares, I remain tense, and my thoughts are scattered.

A faint light in the rearview mirror makes the hair on my nape bristle, but just as I'm about to dismiss my worries, this is a public road after all, the car starts gaining on me. In itself, that wouldn't be so strange, since people have different ideas about road safety, but the closer he is, the harder my grip on the steering wheel becomes.

I can no longer deny it.

That's Saint's car.

Air gets stuck in my throat. My hands creak as they tighten on the steering wheel and despite knowing these are not the conditions for street racing, I hit the gas, praying to anyone who might hear me. God might have ignored my calls for help when my family was being butchered, but maybe this time he would intervene? But I can only go so fast on this dark, winding road, and if I hit a tree or roll, Saint could mete out whatever torture he sees fit.

I can't fucking think.

I'm so scared.

Who the hell is this guy?

I have to make a split-second decision when my car speeds toward a fork in the road. The right turn will take me to a road similar to this one, but I'm over twenty miles from the next town. The left turn will take me into the forest where the road might be covered in snow.

I turn left at the last second. I'll take my chances in the forest. It's getting dark and I can hide there, whereas on the road, Saint could gain on me and push me into a ditch.

I speed up more, to leave him as far behind as possible before stopping. I know the exact spot where I want to park, but by the time I burst out of the car, stepping into deep snow, this whole idea no longer seems so great. Snow. Fucking snow. I was so preoccupied by the chase itself that I forgot that I'd be leaving very clear tracks. And I have no means to hide my vehicle either.

For a moment, I consider getting back into my car and driving off, but that might end up with me getting stuck farther along. My fate was decided when I chose the wrong turn, and while I need to accept everything it now throws my way, I'm not dead yet.

I grunt when my knee twists uncomfortably after a few steps in the snow, but I don't have time to overthink why it's hurting. I need to move. The backpack contains only so much food and water, but despite putting myself in this precarious position, I'm determined to survive. The roar of the other car makes me tremble, and I choose not to switch on my flashlight as I move faster, trudging through the snow, ever farther from the road.

In the dark, every naked tree, every bush seems to hide a monster about to take me out before Saint can even catch up, but I swallow down the irrational fear and even out my breathing.

It's only when I hear an engine stop not far behind me that the inadequacy of my escape becomes painfully obvious. Despite the air feeling like shards of ice in my throat, I speed up, braving the ache in my knee, but it's dark, and I end up losing precious seconds tangled into a small bush hidden beneath the dense snow. I can't even swear in frustration, too afraid the bastard who's been stalking me for God-knows how long might hear me.

My life might be pathetic, maybe even worthless, but I still want to live, and like a deer fleeing a wolf, I intend to run until I can't anymore.

A chill goes down my spine when my name echoes between the trees in Saint's silky voice. A tiny part of me wants to turn back and walk right into his arms. I felt so safe with him last night, and now even that happy memory is tainted. I don't know what kind of monster he is, but I won't just roll over and find out.

The trees whisper above me, sending clumps of wet snow down as the wind intensifies, and I feel as though I'm in a war zone, trying to avoid missiles. Despite the predator on my tail, I manage to reach a large fallen tree without being spotted. Or so I hope.

I slide over the thick, snow-covered trunk, and land a few feet below, as the ground drops just behind it, but while I'm no longer in sight, my tracks are, so I still and listen. In this freezing weather, my fingers will soon turn into icicles, but if push comes to shove, I'll shoot, and he should damn well remember that I'm more than capable of pulling the trigger.

He stops calling out for me, which gives me time to take a breather, but my heartbeat speeds up when I hear the snow creak close by.

I imagine his feet sinking into the hardened shell of snow, his tall, strong form stalking my way, ready to strike, but at this point I can either stay hidden and hope he walks on, or reveal myself and confront him.

Unwanted images of his smiling face and phantom kisses to my neck fill my head with doubts. Now that he's not an anonymous masked man, the thought of killing him feels unbearable. I try to reignite the flame of fury inside me, but it's so damn hard. He was touching me last night under false pretenses, seduced me with his lies, and I still hesitate like some lovesick puppy.

I need to end this.

I shoot to my feet, gun in both hands, but as I turn to face him, my knees tremble, because he's right in front of me, on the other side of the log. The moon is shining on us through the leafless trees, revealing the somber expression on the handsome face I wanted to kiss only an hour back.

If I pull the trigger now, I will get him in the chest and won't need to fear for my life any longer.

But I can't bring myself to do it when he's looking straight at me, without even a shadow of fear.

"I'm sorry I scared you," Saint says, breaking the silence.

My teeth chatter, and I panic as the muzzle of my gun shakes, revealing how uncertain I am. "Don't come any closer!"

Terrible memories of my parents being killed rush to the forefront of my mind, as if to warn me that I might share their fate if I don't choose myself over this stranger.

"I read your letter. The one you threw away when leaving your therapist's office last week," he says as if this isn't fucking insane.

My brain can't handle it, and I stutter out, "What?"

He moves fast like a cobra, ducking to one side and grabbing my handgun as I pull the trigger. The bullet tears through the air, but he wrestles the pistol out of my hand before I can defend myself.

Struck by nauseating panic, I grab the hunting knife from my pocket and slash at him, but he's so much faster than me. I did catch *something* with the blade, but it might have been his coat. He smacks my hand so hard I drop the knife, and by the time I try to run off again, he's closing a handcuff around my wrist.

"Let me go!" I whimper, struggling like a wounded animal, but only manage to slip in the wet snow, falling to my knees as frightening thoughts cloud my mind with promises of a painful end.

"Careful!" Saint shouts and shoves me face-first into the snow. Cold steel closes on my other wrist, and as I try to pull away, I *can't*, because he's on top of me. What next? Is he going to strap me to a tree and gore me?

But he stills, straddling the backs of my thighs, and just as I expect him to punch the back of my head, he shoves his hand into the pristine snow next to my face. "Oh, this is such an interesting texture, with the shell of melted ice over the snow. Like a good meringue. You know they have meringue with fruit and cream for Christmas in Australia and New Zealand? It's called a pavlova. Maybe we could have that this year. You know, to change things up a bit?"

My brain stops, crashing into his words without understanding. "'We'? For Christmas? What—"

What the hell is he on about? There's no *us*. And the upcoming holidays couldn't have been farther from my mind when he's pushing me down like prey he isn't yet ready to consume. But when he gets off me and rolls me to my back in a single move that feels frighteningly practiced, questions lock in my throat as I meet his dark gaze.

The wind whistles in the trees and rustles Saint's hair when he smiles. "You look quite delicious like that. But I don't think this is the best place to have a chat. I know somewhere quiet and comfortable. Just righ—"

I lash out when the meaning of his words gets through to me at last. He's going to drag me to some hole where he can torment me for as long as he wants, and I'd rather die than see it happen. My leg flies up as I try to kick him, but he must have anticipated that, and his shins block my knees from moving. I scream for help when his fingers dig into the sides of my face.

I try to bite his fingers when he stuffs a rubber fucking ball into my mouth, but he seems to expect that too, and none of my efforts phase him one bit. Before I can even attempt to push the gag out, he closes it at the back of my head, as if he's done it a hundred times.

That's it. A deranged psycho has captured me, and there's nothing I can do but cry in sheer terror.

Pathetic.

Shame flushes through me when tears drizzle down my cheeks, warming cold skin.

And yet, I continue struggling as he uses two straps to bind my legs together. "There, all ready," he tells me with a wide grin. "We can't have you hurting yourself or screaming your head off. Unless you're ready to cry out my name," he says and... winks at me as if this is a play fight between lovers.

I scowl at him, but wiggling around like a fish out of water won't help, so I give up when he picks me up and throws me over his shoulder as if it's something that requires very little effort. He pats my ass, making me stiffen.

Why? Why me? He said something about my letter. What the fuck was that about? Is he a friend of those four bastards and has decided to silence me forever? Why am I not dead yet then?

He starts walking through the snow, back to the car. "Now let's go where no one can hear you scream—No. That didn't come out right." He laughs. Fucking *laughs*. "You know what I mean."

Do I?

CHAPTER 11

ROWAN

SHAME SHOULD BE THE least of my worries in the current circumstances, but I burn with it when Saint makes me sit on a thick sheet of plastic, since my pants are soaked through, and he doesn't want to get his seat wet. I'm unable to do anything, gagged and strapped in with a seatbelt, yet I still worry why he even has large sheets of plastic in his trunk. But that makes me think too much about the torture he could inflict on me, and as tears streak down my face, I make myself breathe through my nose.

I should have shot him when I had the chance. But no. I hesitated. He felt too familiar, I gave him the benefit of the doubt, and now here I am, approaching his murder cabin deep in the woods.

"You have good instincts," he tells me as the vehicle rolls down the narrow road with snow piled on both sides. "You drove toward my place. This way we won't need to waste much time. I didn't get to eat earlier," he said. The *because of you* is silent.

I curl my shoulders, helplessly trying to make myself smaller. Why would someone like him even focus on me in a sexual way? Is it the power play? Did he enjoy lying to me? Is this why he's put in a gag that makes me dribble down my chin? To show me how powerless I am?

I grunt at him, but stare ahead, trying to remember landmarks in case I do manage to escape, but it's all trees, and they all look the same in the cold glow of the LED headlights.

But then, a wooden cabin emerges from the darkness like some pioneer fever dream, with a small porch and a stone chimney on one side. He parks with a soft sigh and turns toward me. I can't see his face when it's shadowed, but my nape tingles, reminding me that I'm in the clutches of a predator, strapped in with a safety belt, cuffed, gagged, and with my legs bound. There's no fucking way for me to escape in this state, so I need to be smart about it and hope for an opening in the future.

"Wait here," Saint tells me and gets out of the car, slamming it shut behind him as he rushes for the door.

I'd laugh if I wasn't so terrified. How the fuck would I *not* wait?

I hit the back of my head against the headrest. I should have known a guy like Saint was too good to be true, but what point is there to contemplating my hurt feelings when he might be about to disembowel me, or put me in a cage and make me eat dog food? How the fuck would I even know what he wants?

My thoughts come to a sudden halt when in a flash of lights, the house in front of me comes alive. Strings of colorful LEDs make the thick layer of snow on the roof look like a cozy comforter, and a reindeer figure twinkles at me from the front porch.

What kind of festive torture is this supposed to be?

Have I become a character in one of those Christmas horror movies? Will he split me in two in a Santa costume and use my skin as gift wrap?

I flinch when Saint opens the door and reaches in, pulling my legs out first before dragging the rest of me into the cold. "Here we are! No one for miles, but we have everything we need," he says and throws me across his shoulder again, as if any of this was perfectly normal.

Christmas abduction. Yay.

My brain can't quite comprehend the eerie clash between the reality of my situation and the warm, cozy glow transforming the cabin and its surroundings into a scene straight from those cheesy Christmas commercials that always rang so false since I lost my family. I shake my head and shout into the gag, but Saint ignores me and enters the warm interior smelling of pine and wood.

"There's no need for this. Just calm down, and we can talk in peace," he tells me, carrying me across the wooden floor. With my face against his back, I can't see much, but colorful lights flash at me from every corner, and I swear I spot decorated stockings hanging above the fireplace.

Seeing all of this Christmas cheer upside down is very fitting, because I feel like I've entered a different dimension altogether. One in which it's normal to hunt someone down in the woods, like he's just game, and enjoy eggnog by the fire while your victim writhes on the bearskin rug.

We pass an opulent Christmas tree adorned with a set of baubles in the classic red, gold, and green colors. Boxes wrapped in red tartan lay under it, adorned with massive silk bows, and I arch my neck to check if—yep, a big-ass fucking glittery star sits on top of the tree.

What. The. Fuck.

We go down a hallway, and when the light comes on in the next room, I stiffen at the sight of white tiles. Of course he's not gonna kill me just like that. Why make cleanup difficult when a massive bathtub is right there!

I should be more scared, but the irony of my situation replaces raw fear with an odd mixture of amusement and anger. I can't be certain of anything, and it's breaking my mind as if it's a glass bauble hitting stone tiles.

He puts me down so fast I lose my balance.

He steadies me against the wall. "Sorry. I forgot what hanging with one's head down can do to people." He sounds apologetic, as if *that* is the biggest issue with his treatment of me!

And how does he even know what hanging upside down does? How many times has he done this? Maybe him appearing in my life has nothing to do with the murder of my family? After all, it would be just my luck to become the victim of one horrific crime, only to be abducted by a serial killer later in life. If the universe is to be in balance, someone has to be unlucky, so that someone else can win the lottery.

He looks into my eyes, and for a second I get a glimpse of the hazel softness I started falling for, but I now recognize Saint for the wolf he is, and I shall not be fooled again. "I will take the gag out, but don't scream. There's no one around. Not in the house, not in the forest. And don't try to bite me. It won't end well."

Resigned, I lean against the wall and nod, ready to speak the moment he takes out the ball. "Please don't eat me. Or if you have to, don't cut off my leg, then keep me alive, eat the leg, and then cut off my other leg. If you *have to* eat me, just kill me quickly. Please." I sniff as tears streak down my face once more.

The gag drops to the floor as Saint leans in, wiping away my tears. "What are you talking about?" His eyes are so soft, so gentle as he strokes my face that I sob even harder, unable to control my own body. It's so pathetic. I am pathetic, and the worst thing is no matter what I say, my fate rests in his beautiful hands.

"Look, will you feel better if I uncuff you? I don't even like pork very much, and I heard human meat is more intense. Not really the right flavor profile for me, if you catch my drift," he adds, winking.

I don't. I don't know what he wants from me, but I'll take any opportunity to survive this. "Please. I just... I'm... very confused," I utter, trying to calm down and play his game as I glance around for potential weapons.

Saint inhales and opens his coat before placing it on a hanger meant for towels. He then pushes up the sleeves of his turtleneck and leans into the tub, first closing the drain and then starting the water.

"You need to calm down. My intentions are perfectly harmless—" He stalls, considering what he just said, and smiles at me. "Toward you, that is. I just want us to have a nice long chat."

I don't trust him for a second, but it does give me some hope. "Okay... I'll try. I'll listen," I say even though my voice trembles.

The bubbling of the water becomes a constant whoosh in my ears as Saint leans down to remove the straps from around my legs. I could use this moment to my advantage. To maybe slide on top of him and then attempt slamming his head against the floor with my weight, but I'm under no illusion about the difference in our physical strength and prowess, especially when my hands are still cuffed back. So I calm my frantic mind and focus on breathing until the moment he unbuckles my belt, and then casually pulls down my fly.

I stare at him, wide-eyed as blood rushes to my head, setting even my ears on fire. "You... what? What are you doing?" I whimper in panic, but my messy brain reminds me of how he pushed me against the corridor wall last night, and how hard I came with his fingers wrapped around my dick.

This is wrong. So wrong.

Yet I don't move as he shoves my pants down and kneels to help me out of my boots. It's a bizarre situation, yet I fear any wrong move might shatter the frail truce we've established.

"You need a warm bath. We can talk while you have a nice, long soak," he says and pulls on my underwear, exposing me completely. If this had happened a few hours earlier, I would be hard as a rock and begging for more, but fear makes me feel beyond naked and vulnerable.

I'm too afraid to voice my objection, because at this point, he seems capable of anything. "Thank... you?" I mumble, trying not to overthink the fact that this will be the first time he sees me fully naked.

It shouldn't matter, but I'm self-conscious of the scars on my legs. Even though years have passed, some are still big and pink. I shouldn't care, since he's some psycho, but I do. Because I still like him. He's the first man I kissed, and I don't want him to scowl at my naked body,

"You're welcome," Saint tells me and spins me around as if I'm a puppet.

There's a click, and then, one of the cuffs opens, setting me free. A voice whispers that this is the opportunity I've been waiting for, but the rest of me knows I have no chance against this man. Not right now and not like this. So I raise both my arms when Saint pulls off my top, leaving me naked next to his dressed self.

He scans me from head to toe, which makes me feel smaller than I am. I awkwardly cover my crotch, hoping my body doesn't betray me, because a part of me appreciates that he's bigger, stronger, that he knows what he wants. And since he hasn't yet attempted to punch me or cut me up, I relax enough to be open to that feeling. I don't like what that says about me, but is it such a surprise that I am messed up sexually too?

I await his verdict with my heart beating furiously, glad my hair is long enough to just about cover my eyes, but he takes away my one protection by brushing the sweaty strands aside.

I shiver, hunching my shoulders, but when Saint lifts my chin with one finger so our eyes can meet, he's smiling. "God, you're pretty. It's okay. All of this is for you. This cabin, the bath," he adds, dipping his hand in to check the temperature of the water. "Me."

I gather the courage to hold his gaze, and when I speak my voice remains steady. "Who are you?"

Saint holds my forearm and directs me into the water. It's hot, but not unpleasantly so when I step into the tub, then sit, holding on to a metal rail attached to the wall. I'm not at all surprised when he grabs the open cuff and closes it on the steel bar, securing me to it.

"What are you really asking?" Saint inquires as he opens a bottle and pours some of its contents into the water, filling the bathroom with the scent of gingerbread and vanilla.

"Why did you break into my house? Why did you seduce me? Why are you doing this?" I gently rattle the cuff to make my point, but as the tub fills, I can't help but relax into the warm, fragrant bath.

Saint crosses his arms on his chest, then reaches into his pocket and pulls out a folded piece of paper. He unwraps it with care, as if it's a historical artifact, but when he presents it to me, my stomach drops at the sight of my own, anger-jagged writing.

I barely remember it through the haze of fear but he did mention a letter back in the woods. At once, the water around me feels cold.

"What the hell?"

Saint exhales and puts the letter on a shelf with little decorative jars. "Why are you like this? I'm here to give you what you want."

I stare at him as my brain fogs up with fear. "You're... Santa?"

Saints mouth spreads in a grin, and he clicks his fingers. "No, better yet, I am your *personal* Santa. I deal in revenge, and that's what you wished for, right? Wait here," he adds as if I have any choice in the matter, and darts out, jogging down the corridor.

I'm slowly adjusting to this new reality. As freaky as this is, as betrayed as I feel... at least it doesn't look like he intends to kill me, so that counts for something.

I glance toward the letter filled with my gory revenge fantasies. I never imagined anyone other than my therapist would be reading it, but I'm willing to roll with this insanity for now and see if it leads me to safety. After all, there have been people who avoided death by playing to a psycho's tune. Maybe I'll be one of them?

But when Saint steps back inside, and a second pair of eyes stares at me from an open trash bag he's holding, terror sinks its claws back into my flesh.

I scream so loudly it makes even my own ears ring.

CHAPTER 12

ROWAN

A HEAD. HE'S GOT a fucking human *head* in a bag and he's showing it off like a cat bringing me a dead mouse.

"What the fuck?" I yell, backing away as far as the cuff will allow me.

I'm torn between terror and morbid curiosity, but in the end, I stare at the bluish skin of the man whose head Saint is holding. And as I take my time looking at his features instead of seeing the head merely as a disembodied body part, recognition sets in.

My jaw drops. I've been keeping tabs on this man for so long I'd almost became desensitized to seeing his ugly mug, but while he looks different with his features slack, there's no doubt that this is the same guy who opened my parents' wedding whisky and then smashed the empty bottle on my dad's head.

"It's Ted," I mumble, shaking while my heartbeat speeds up with either fear or… elation?

What. The. Fuck.

Saint exhales, closing his eyes. "Oh, damn. When you made that face, I worried for a moment that I got the wrong guy. But it's him, right? The first man you want dead? I considered putting him in a box, letting you unpack it, but it didn't fit in the fridge that way, and I figured it would be overkill."

The dry blood on Ted's nose and beard tells me his death was far from peaceful. I should be terrified, and sure, I'm freaking out that this is actually happening, but I don't feel sorry for him.

Maybe that makes me a bad person, but this human waste deserved whatever he got.

I look back up at Saint's face, breathless in both terror and wonder. He's a fucking killer. No doubt about that.

"*You* did this?" I ask to confirm the obvious.

Saint huffs, pulls up the edges of the bag, and then spins it, to seal the head back inside before placing it under the sink. "I already told you. I saw you dropping the letter, and… it really spoke to me. Reading it felt like meeting an old friend, even though I only learned your name when I saw your signature at the bottom."

I watch him, stunned, yet feel myself gradually relax in the warm water. A normal person would say 'yeah, but I didn't *actually* want to kill anyone!', but that wouldn't be the truth. While I didn't have any concrete plans on how to get rid of the four men I hate with all my heart, I did want them dead.

I still do.

"So you killed him… for me?"

"That's what I wanted to propose when I broke into your place. Which I am sorry for, big mistake. I should have done my research first, but I got too excited and wasn't thinking straight," Saint tells me, dragging a plastic stool closer to the tub. He sits on it and turns off the water before resting his elbows on the rim and staring into my eyes, like a puppy expecting belly rubs.

I'm trying to organize it all in my head. A killer found my letter and decided to make my Christmas wish come true. Did I miss something?

"So you decided to lie to me instead? *Date* me? What the fuck?" I have to bite my tongue before I say something worse, because I am cuffed to the wall by a man who just proved how desensitized he is to violence.

Saint blows a raspberry, resting his cheek on one hand. "You weren't supposed to find out like that. I figured I could ease you into it, get friendly, but then I found out you're gay too, and it all clicked in my head. We are alike," he says, waving his other hand between us.

"Except I don't *kill people*," I say through gritted teeth.

He squints at me, and somehow it makes him even more beautiful, like a panther ready to strike. "But you want to."

It's more of a statement than a question, and it hangs between us like the last morsel of food on a shared plate. I don't know how to answer, because he might just be right.

Saint continues with a smirk. "You have the same desires I have, and I've been alone for so long. We could be a really good match."

I suck on my lip, taking it all in. In some ways, Saint *is* cutting me open. Not with a knife, but with his words. He's pulling out the ugly side I never show anyone.

I deflect by glancing at the bag under the sink. "Did he suffer? Did he know why he was dying?" my voice gets a raspy undertone I don't recognize.

Saint's eyes glint like liquid gold as he leans toward me. "Oh yes. He was terrified. I cut his head off with a saw while he was alive. I don't enjoy torture, but I figured you wouldn't want him to go fast. If you have any specific instructions for the other three, we can deal with them your way."

My therapist worked on helping me 'let go', on forgiving and moving on. She said revenge doesn't solve anything, and that it wouldn't make me feel better. So why does this gruesome news make me slide neck-deep into fragrant water with a sense of relief?

I look at the handsome monster in front of me and find it hard to hate him, even though I resent being lied to and seduced under false pretenses. I'm also aware he's some sort of psycho and might turn on me at any point, but when I imagine the man who killed my father terrified and begging for his life only to be laughed at and tortured, it feels right.

I float closer to the edge of the tub.

"What's the catch?" I whisper, my breath going shallow as Saint reaches out and strokes his finger down my neck.

Fuck, he's gorgeous. Tempting. Charming, too. And while he's just shown me his deranged side, I still can't deny that my body reacts to his presence with much more than fear.

Maybe the attack from years ago has fucked me up in more ways than one?

"I want an apprentice. And a partner. And since I know we are a good match, I offer to give you your revenge if you agree to be mine."

The last word is heavy with implications I'm not sure I understand. It sounds so delicious and tempting coming off his tongue, but I have to remember I'm dealing with a man capable of anything. I shouldn't be fooled by the pretty packaging. There's a finality to "mine", and the cuff on my wrist suggests what that might truly mean.

But I'd make a deal with the Devil for revenge. That is how much I want to see those bastards suffer. "And what would that entail?" I ask, feeling as though I'm sealing my fate already.

Saint takes a deep breath and exhales as his hand drifts down my chest, caressing my pecs, then the muscles of my stomach. It's an exhilarating moment, but I need to keep my head on straight if I'm not to fall into a trap, so I harden my gaze, settling it on him.

Saint shrugs. "I want to have a man in my bed. But not just any man. Someone who knows what I am and doesn't run to the cops. I want company. I want someone I can take on jobs and teach my craft. As I said, I want a partner."

"A partner or a sex slave?" I mumble.

He squints and his long fingers slide back to my neck as he assesses me. "I want a partner who won't leave." '*Whatever I do*' seems to be the rest of that sentence. "I want access to you, be it for a cuddle, or to fuck your brains out."

A shiver goes down my spine, and I clench my ass even though my dick hardens. How the hell am I getting aroused when there's a motherfucking *head* with us in the bathroom?

"And we'll kill the other three?" I whisper, out of my depth. I'm asking, but it feels as though I'm already agreeing to his dangerous bargain, and he knows it. I can see it in the flush of his skin, in the way he swallows. I shouldn't find it hot, but he's offering me something I thought I could never achieve, and on top of that, he desires me so much he wants my body as payment.

"Exactly. And just so we're clear, there will be no other people and no weird shit. Just normal sex between the two of us," he says, touching my cock as he dips his hand into the water.

I'm falling into his web, and it won't be easy to untangle myself.

"And... you won't break off the deal if it turns out I'm not good at it?" I curl my toes when his thumb brushes the slit at the tip of my cockhead.

Saint's hand closes on my half-hard dick, and he swirls his finger over its head very slowly as his features sharpen. Dark eyes drill into me as he licks his lips, hyper focused on me as if I were the last man alive. "Are you saying you're not experienced?"

"Yeah, I... spent a lot of time in the hospital, and didn't really have a chance to date." Am I really explaining the reasons behind my virginity to a murderer? Yes, yes I am.

"You were pretty good so far," Saint chuckles, pumping my dick. His touch is firm and so intense my skin feels too tight around my body, prompting me to thrust my hips up. "I can teach you everything. And I won't hurt you. Promise."

If I were a good person, I wouldn't be so tempted. But Saint might be right. We might be more alike than anyone could imagine. I want this revenge with every cell in my body.

Instead of giving in, I try to salvage some kind of balance by making my own demand. "We kill them all before Christmas Day, and I'm yours." I say, but it feels like I'm writing a contract with my own blood as ink.

The truth is that he doesn't have to honor our agreement. For all I know, he might just keep me in a cage and then dispose of me once he gets bored, but the relief in his eyes isn't a lie, as if he really expected that I might as well say no. I don't know what he planned to do in that eventuality, considering he showed me the head of a dead man and confessed to his crime, but as long as I do what he wants, he has no reason to break his promise.

Can I go through with this?

"A challenge. I like it," Saint tells me with a predatory smile that's only missing sharp teeth and pulls his hand away from my cock to offer it to me. "Do we have an understanding? Our deal *will* start now."

What am I getting myself into?

But when I think about the justice system failing me, about my parents and grandmother, about the bastards who killed them walking free, about all the time I spent in hospital, it's easy to swallow my fear and shake Saint's hand.

CHAPTER 13

ROWAN

I SWITCH OFF THE showerhead and touch my hole, paranoid I've done something wrong and that Saint will be dissatisfied with me. I did know basics about how to prepare for bottoming, and Saint instructed me before I told him to wait for me in the bedroom, but I'm still worried about what's about to happen. Much more so than I am about the head in the fridge.

I considered the small window a few times, even though Saint showed his trust in me by uncuffing me before he left. But he did take my clothes to the washing machine, so it's not like I have the means to survive a trek through the snow in the middle of nowhere.

And I don't want to.

As scared as I am, I want to see this through. Revenge seemed like a pipe dream, but now that it might become reality, I do think I'm capable of it.

The man waiting for me is the key to fulfilling my destiny.

One deep breath later, I step out of the bathroom without even a towel around my hips, since I'll be naked soon anyway. I still smell of the vanilla and gingerbread oil Saint poured into the bath, and every step I take toward the open door to the bedroom makes more goosebumps erupt on my skin.

Truth is, I want to see him naked too. His cock is perfect, and the glimpse of stomach I got that time I gave him head turns me on every time I think about the tense muscles under my fingers.

Maybe I'm just as delusional as he is, believing this agreement we made can end on a good note for me, but what do I have to lose? A miserable life of celibacy, penny-pinching and impotent rage? Maybe it's better to risk going out with a bang rather than rot on the inside.

Still, when I push the door and see him naked, standing by the window and looking out into the snowy landscape while a bedside lamp reveals his toned legs, back, and ass, I'm struck into silence. Because *fuck*, he is the most gorgeous man I've ever seen, and for reasons I can't quite grasp, he set his eyes on me. Broken me with scars all over my body and a bad knee.

Smiling, he steps toward me and calls me over with a gesture. "You look so hot like that."

Do I? I force myself not to slouch as I walk over to him. The bedframe is dark wood, the bedding has a green plaid pattern, and the many pillows make the setting hotel perfect.

Awkwardness steams off me, but as soon as he is within reach, I wrap my arms around his waist and hug him. I can't explain it, but I feel safest in the eye of the storm. I sigh in relief, then inhale the scent of his skin, and when he embraces me too and rests his chin on my head, I'm ready to lie down and take whatever he intends to unleash on me.

He might be a killer, but he's not planning *my* death. Not yet at least.

"Are you hiding from me?" Saint asks, amused.

"I'm just a little nervous," I whisper and kiss his neck. Not too nervous to explore his back with my fingers though. He's muscular, fit, but not a meathead. I remember the graceful movement in which he ducked away from my gun, then disarmed me. It turns me on that he's *proficient*. That he knows what he wants and how to deal with things, even if his methods might be questionable.

His hum is like warm syrup rolling down my tongue, but when his lips press to the side of my neck, the shock of pleasure has me rising to my toes. Nobody else has touched me like this. Ever. And I hunger for his attention despite knowing what he's capable of.

"Your cheeks are so flushed, and your lips too. It makes me remember last night, when I came on your tongue. You looked drunk on my cum."

My breath quickens when I remember what a frenzy I was in. Our new arrangement is *wrong*. Technically, I can't say no to him anymore. But the truth is that I don't want to.

"I wanted to taste you so badly," I confess, closing my eyes. There's no room for lying anymore. He's shown me his true face, so I might as well show mine. Horny to the point of desperation, and bloodthirsty with no outlet for violent urges.

And here he is, the man to satiate both those needs. My very own devil.

"Then I think you should do it again," Saint tells me, and as he brushes his face against mine, his teeth nip the apple of my cheek, making me whimper. His hand is back on my cock, then it opens and touches my balls too, claiming me without words.

I like him calling the shots, since he clearly knows what he's doing better than me. Both in sex and in murder. Where I had fantasies, jerking off, and a revenge scrapbook, he was out there living life to the fullest and taking no prisoners.

I gasp and I'm about to go to my knees like a good boy when Saint picks me up by the waist. I grab his nape for balance, but two steps later, he drops me into the soft bedding.

I watch him climb in right next to me, like a predator on the prowl.

"I'll train your throat in the future," he teases, running his fingers over my Adam's apple. "But tonight we have other pleasures to explore."

It sounds so illicit. He'll "*train*" me. As though it will be my job to open my mouth for his dick whenever he wants to come. It shouldn't excite me, but it does.

He slaps my ass as he rolls onto his back, stretching out his delicious body in front of me. "Come here, I want to taste your cock too, pretty thing."

My body explodes with heat, but he doesn't wait for my move and grabs my hips, pulling me into the position he wants me to be in. Air gets trapped in my throat when I feel his breath on my balls, but I'm facing his stiffening dick, on all fours above him, and he's told me exactly what he wants me to do.

I drift off, for a second just admiring his shaft, which rests on his stomach, stiff and dark. I lean down to kiss it, but when his fingers tease my taint, I'm reminded that my legs are shamelessly spread, and he's getting to see *everything*.

He lets out a happy grunt as he weighs my nuts in his hand. "You're pretty everywhere. I can't wait to be balls-deep in this tight little hole."

I hear a click and my face is on fire. He's getting lube. That has to be lube. I distract myself by licking his cock from head to base, and then rest my chin on the soft, trimmed bed of hair, already high on sensation. His shaft grows harder against my cheek but there's so much to take in—the washboard-hard stomach, the toned legs peppered with dark hair, even his feet are attractive somehow. I can't believe I get to touch him so freely, undecided like a kid at a buffet. But then, a soft, warm tongue teases my own cock and I shiver, tense in the best possible way.

I moan, falling to my elbows and burying my face against his hard dick.

He chuckles and slides a slippery finger all the way down my crack, stopping to circle my hole. And while I tighten at the touch, his fingertip prods at my entrance. This is his right. That's what I agreed to.

"Go on, suck me, lazy boy," Saint says, brushing his lips against my cock. "I want to feel your tongue work its magic." His other hand slides up my stomach, and it turns me on so much that my legs are spread for him, and that I'm now starring in his personal porn video.

No one ever wanted me like this, and while I know that he's been lying to me with frightening ease, the erection throbbing in my mouth as I hollow my cheeks isn't fake, and neither is the new, searing sensation deep inside me.

We didn't need to discuss whether anal sex was going to work for us. He knows what he wants, and I know where my fantasies have always led me. Now that my body senses what's going to happen, it's aroused in a whole new way.

There's an ache inside me, and only he can soothe it. Despite my inexperience, I know this with absolute certainty, and when one of his fingers slips in, I'm torn between shock and delight.

I have heard people's first times can be uncomfortable, and the unfamiliar sensation definitely feels odd, but I throb with the need to explore this more, for him to unleash his worst—or maybe his best—on me. Take me for a ride I never expected.

Saint strokes the side of my thigh with his other hand as he teases the tight ring of muscle I've never dared to toy with myself. "I like that I will be your only man. I'm all you'll ever need," he murmurs as I bob my head on his cock.

Looks like he's sure about the murders we're about to commit, but I don't think that far ahead, focused on the cock filling my mouth as he thrusts his hips up, pushing it farther down my tongue.

My head spins when his lips close around my own dick, but as delicious as that is, my focus remains on the entrance to my body. He's playing with it, and while that's an unfamiliar sensation, jolts of electricity travel up the inner side of my thighs as his fingers reach deeper, conquering my defenses.

I suck him harder, drinking up Saint's pre-cum as he gives an appreciative moan, but then he's pulling on my arm, and his fingers leave my body. "Face me."

That, I was not ready for, but I belong to him now, as per our agreement, so I do what he asks and meet his gaze. He must have sold his soul to the devil for that handsome face, and now I'm selling mine too. I'm letting him use me however he likes to get my revenge. And yet, there's already so much more tied up in this odd exchange.

My own lust for him is dark and sweet. I want this. I want him touching me. I want to be with this dangerous man. His presence makes my whole body throb, and I can only hope I don't get addicted to him, because I might still need to back out of this madness in the future.

"Like this?" I whisper, straddling his hips, painfully aware of his rock-hard cock under me. His eyes focus on me as if he's a hawk zeroing in on his prey, and then, the hard shaft rubs against my buttock, still damp from my own saliva.

"Look at you. You are so ready for this," Saint whispers as his fingers return to my hole, slickened with yet more lube.

But it's his dick I can't stop thinking about now. He's going to fuck me, and he's in charge of how that's going to happen. When he slips another finger into me more abruptly, I moan and fall forward, landing with my palms to the sides of his head.

I can't stop panting, and his smile becomes wolfish as his gaze slides from my flushed face, down my stomach, and all the way to my stiff cock. I breathe in sharply as he sits up, facing me up close, his scent intense in the air around me.

"You and I, we're going to have so much fun together. I promise you that by Christmas, you'll be taking my cock like a pro," he rasps, turning his fingers in my ass, gently stretching the muscles I no longer control. Working against me, they keep tightening up, but Saint has endless patience and massages them, as if he were trying to coax a frightened animal to work with him.

I often fantasize about sex in this way or another, but now that it's so tangible, now that he does what he wants with me, reality burns with so much more intensity than my imagination ever could. My legs are wide open to him, and when he sears my lips with a kiss, both his fingers drive into me up to the knuckle.

He chuckles when I whimper against his tongue, and only fucks me faster with his fingers. My nipples stiffen, hypersensitive to the touch as I move in tune with his digits and rub my chest against his.

"I'll be making you moan like this every day," he promises, watching me from under lowered eyelids. "You're going to get addicted to this. You're going to beg for my cock morning and evening, and I'm going to give it to you," he rasps as the tension in my backside subsides, letting his fingers move with more ease.

I shiver, breathless at the darkness in his eyes, but before I can utter a word, his mouth is on my neck, sucking, kissing, nipping my skin as if he's ravenous and I happen to be the only piece of meat capable of satisfying him.

He's holding me so very close as I move my hips, riding his fingers when my insides finally relax and every movement seeks that odd sensation that's been causing me to crave more since he first touched my hole.

Every time his fingers rub a spot inside me, I'm torn whether the sensation it sparks is uncomfortable or delightful, but I find it hard to stop myself as dirty, delicious words stream from his mouth, straight into my ear.

"That's it. So damn needy. So hungry for a dicking. I can't wait to come inside you, mark my territory."

I let out a whimper when he pulls his fingers out, leaving me stunned at the emptiness. He's right. I want to be filled. And that's what I am now. His territory. He can do whatever he wants to me. I agreed to it.

"Please..." I whisper, not really sure what I'm asking for. All I know is that I want him in my own voracious way. And when he takes my lips, I wrap my arms around him, too horny to think straight. The world spins as he rolls us over so I'm on my back, under him, and he stabs me with his slick fingers over and over, until I whimper in helpless need.

How is his cock going to feel? Bigger, yes, but will it be painful or pleasurable? Both? I can hardly imagine it, but when I somehow find myself on my elbows and knees, as if I lost consciousness for a few seconds, he's on top, and his hard, slick dick is nudging at my hole. I moan, and Saint tightens one hand on my throat, holding it rather than squeezing. He buries his face in my shoulder and bites me there too.

"Come on, open up to me," he rasps against my skin. "I own you now."

Those words are enough to make me moan. Because he does own me, he so fucking does, and he proves it by pushing half his cock inside me.

Can he feel my pulse quicken against his palm? Does he like how tight my ass feels? All I can think of is his pleasure even though my own dick is painfully hard and dripping pre-cum.

Saint moans. "Oh, you feel so good. Can't wait to be all the way inside you, pretty thing."

I spread my knees wider, inhaling his scent and drowning in it. It makes the sudden discomfort at the entrance to my body easier to bear.

He waits, kissing my shoulder and neck while perspiration makes his chest stick to my back. I'm trembling, but while the intrusion hurts, I don't want him out. In fact, I want him inside me. I want him to show me how much someone like me can be desired, and for him to take me in any way he feels like.

I breathe in relief when my body stops resisting, but the exhale turns into a low moan when I feel him move forward, filling my insides. He's gripping my hip hard as his other hand tightens around my neck, as if to remind me I'm fucking a murderer.

I'm playing with fire, but I don't fear getting burned.

The harder he squeezes, the more fearless I feel. It makes me want to laugh as if I'm crazy myself, but I only let out another moan when his hips press to my ass. Here I am, the boy afraid of having guests, fucking a dangerous man in a house in the woods. I can't remember ever feeling this alive. Maybe the fog of arousal will disperse by tomorrow morning, but right now, with Saint inside me, I feel invincible.

Not against him. *He* could snap me in half. But he's *my* monster. And since he desires me, I know without a doubt he will protect me with everything he has. With a man like him at my side, I will never have to be afraid again.

"Yes... I'm yours," I whine when he pulls back just to slam back into me. The sensation is still strange and unfamiliar, but there's something so addictive and fulfilling in surrendering my body like this, in being Saint's plaything. My limbs shake as I feel his rigid length push and pull through my tight channel.

"That's it, legs wide for me," he rasps.

As he braces himself on top of me, holding me in place with both arms, ecstasy streams through me as if the lube was an aphrodisiac. It's only started, and I'm already high on him.

"Fuck. Your hole's perfect."

I let out little moans with every thrust of his hips, and let him ride me like I'm his bitch, submissively pressing my face into the bedding as he fucks me. I can barely catch enough oxygen, torn between pleasure and discomfort. The sensation of his cock stretching my ass is so intense it borders on pain, but then every time I whimper, he pushes in deep and hits that spot that makes me want him to do it over and over. Arousal pools in my balls, but my orgasm will wait. I want to sate my beast first.

"Oh God... just like that," I utter to encourage him. I want it fast, I want it hard, and I drink up his delicious grunts.

His breath trembles as he uses both his hands to keep me still. He's no longer holding back, thrusting into me hard each time, and I can't fucking get enough of it. Each time he plunges in, forcing my muscles to accept him, it makes something in my brain switch off and numb my thoughts. I'm a sweaty mess, but as he licks my skin, humming in pleasure, I stop being self-conscious. This is how he wants me—dirty, loud, and obedient.

I've never been more aroused.

He stiffens, his balls pulsing against my flesh as he fills me with cum.

"Do you feel that? All for you..." Saint mutters in a voice so soaked in sex I could get off just on him talking to me like that.

And now that he's done, happy, I'm reminded of my own need. His cock is still hard and throbbing inside me as I reach between my legs and start jerking off. I want to come with his dick inside me.

I think of him not pulling out yet, of the heat of his cum, of his teeth on my shoulder.

"I want you to sleep with your hole full of my cum..." Saint rasps and licks me from shoulder blade to neck.

When his fingers trace a prominent scar on my thigh, I come so hard something seems to break inside me. I cry out as I clench my ass on his dick. Tears slide down my cheeks at the intensity of my orgasm and I gasp for air, crossing a threshold I didn't even know existed. Whatever's on the other side, I'm ready for it.

I whimper when he bites my neck, then leaves a series of wet kisses in the same area, hugging me. "That was... perfect," he says as his cock slips out of my body. It's almost strange that minutes before it was an intruder, yet now it feels odd not to have it inside.

I don't want to think about the sex being something that sealed an illicit deal. I just want to kiss him and feel his sweaty body against mine.

I turn around, still breathless and a little dizzy. "So good."

Saint's smile melts away, and he touches my lips. It's only then that I realize there's a coppery scent in the air, and when I see his fingers coming up stained with blood, my head spins.

"Did I do that?" Saint utters, his eyes wide as he reaches to the nightstand.

"Wha—? Oh." I pat the skin above my lip, only to realize I must have gotten a nosebleed.

He's right back with me and gently dabs my face with a tissue as if he's not a man with a head in his fridge.

Saint smirks. "That's a new achievement for me. Making a man come so hard he gets a nosebleed."

As the haze of afterglow disperses, I'm relaxed and sated, but a little voice at the back of my head forces me to see reality as it is.

Saint will go through with my revenge killings. He won't hesitate. He wants me to be his and will do whatever it takes to achieve that. I'm both flattered and terrified, because what if I... like him too much?

I could always try sabotaging the last kill so we're not done before Christmas, but then I'd miss out on revenge.

I watch him with my mind buzzing like a hornet nest. His elegant nose has a small bump that only makes it look more regal, and the symmetry of his face could land him a cover in a fashion magazine. His dark hair is in a bit of disarray after the vigorous fuck, but that, and the flush on his skin is so tangible I let my fingers draw shapes over his pecs.

But no matter how beautiful he is, I'm painfully aware that he's fucking deranged.

Which is either terrible or exactly what I need in a man.

Once he's done cleaning my face, he gives me the gentlest kiss. "When you're rested, how about I cook us something delicious?"

Oh, right. He's also a great cook.

CHAPTER 14

SAINT

I'm invigorated.

Elated.

Sated.

And as I cut the tofu, chicken, and all the other ingredients for our meal, I know I'm gonna enjoy the food far more than any other time in recent memory. The worry that Rowan might try to flee is still there, but his clothes are in the washing machine, the only key to the car is locked in a safe, and on top of that... well, I don't think the urge to run would be anything more than a reflex at this point.

He enjoyed himself as much as I did, and since I am the only one who can satisfy his thirst for revenge, he won't give up on our agreement so easily. I have him hooked. Collared. Addicted to my touch. And by the time

Christmas rolls around, he won't want to be anywhere but in my lap, eating gingerbread cookies from my hand.

I understand why he would be cautious, or unsure about his feelings, but we are a perfect match, and he'll soon realize I can be the answer to his deepest desires and the wall between him and his fears.

I can protect him. I can pleasure him. I can be the one who gives him a new, much happier life. He only needs to let me.

I'm mildly annoyed that I didn't prepare everything before our arrival, but I couldn't have known that we'd be visiting this place so soon. I don't yet have all the gifts, and only a narrow selection of food is available, but I am yet to meet a person who doesn't enjoy a nice pad thai. And if he hates it, I can always make pancakes.

Aromatic scents fill the kitchen as I fry the garlic and shallots, but the remaining ingredients soon join them in the pan, turning into the perfect fifteen-minute dinner.

I hear his soft footsteps before he speaks, and I glance back just to see his face. His cheeks are flushed after his shower, and his wet black hair glistens against pale skin. I even love his ears. They're a bit big, but they make him look so cute with their slightly pointed tips.

"There's no clothes in the wardrobe..."

I wave it off. "Yes, it's an Airbnb."

He pauses, hiding his nakedness behind the door frame. "So..."

"Let's just be naked. It's warm, and I even started a fire," I say, gesturing toward the fireplace.

"Naked..." Rowan huffs with a thoughtful frown, as if I didn't already see *all* of him half an hour ago. But in the end he steps into the room.

Good boy.

"You're not allergic to anything, are you?" I ask, draining the rice noodles before tossing them into the wok I always use when traveling. No matter what people say, you cannot substitute it with a regular pan.

"No, no allergies. I do hate beetroot though."

What a cute random fact to learn about my new boyfriend.

I love an open plan kitchen, so I can both cook and chat while enjoying my new favorite view, Rowan's naked body.

He stands in front of the fireplace and extends his hands toward it, in turn giving me a perfect opportunity to ogle his ass. He's on the skinny side, but there's a roundness to his buttocks, and his legs, while marred with scars, are long and lean. I almost burn the food when I realize I've been watching droplets of water slide down his nape and then spine.

"How are you feeling?" I ask, eager for feedback as I finish the dish, ready to wow his senses once again.

When he looks back at me, with the fire burning behind him, his eyes seem black. "A bit achy. In a good way." He gives me a shy smile, and my mouth stretches in response.

"As it should be," I say and plate our food. It's a no-frills kind of dinner, but that's the beauty of staying in a remote cabin, so I take the cutlery, the plates and lead the way to the plush sofa. As much as I enjoy eating at a table, right now I want to feel his body against mine.

He seems to understand what I want and comes to my side without prompting. He grabs a plate and smells it before digging in. "I probably shouldn't have an appetite after what happened tonight, but I'm actually starving."

I blink. "Really? I'm always hungry after good sex," I say, putting a pillow in my lap to support the bowl. I then put my free arm around him and bury my face in his hair. It smells of the complimentary shampoo, fresh eucalyptus, and while I like the scent of his own cosmetics more, this is a decent stand-in.

He frowns at me, stuffing his face. Ah, it's so rare that I get to feed someone and see them enjoy it. "I mean Ted's *head*. And you know, the literal kidnapping?" And yet here he is, sitting so close his thigh cuddles against mine.

I sigh. "As I said, it wasn't meant to be like that, but you forced my hand. You think I *wanted* to scare you like that?"

"I mean... you can stop pretending to be nice now. We both know the truth. But this—whatever this is—is delicious."

I blink, staring at him. "I *am* nice."

He raises his eyebrows and smirks. "Ted would beg to differ."

Dark humor. I like it.

I shrug and stroke the back of his head. "Ted deserved what happened to him, but that doesn't mean I can't treat normal people with respect. I am the revenge guy. I am *your* guy."

"What does it mean? Do you do this kind of thing often? You seem to be... proficient." His eyes are full of curiosity, and while I want to sate it, I have to tread carefully. I need him to see I'm his perfect match, not some desperate, lonely husk of a human being who can't connect to anyone without entrapping them.

I clear my throat, and think through my answer, taking my time to chew the pad thai. But there's no point in bending the facts now if he is to stay at my side. "It's my job. I take out people who the law won't get its hands on."

"How does it work? I'm guessing you don't usually find letters with people's fucked-up fantasies?"

It's kind of nice of him to take interest. After all, it will be his future too. And I get to actually tell him the truth, a refreshing thing in my world. I can only be honest with my victims. And those conversations never last long.

"I have a guy. He handles people, vets them. Sometimes, I find customers on the dark web, but some come to him, since he... he has a reputation. You know, one of those old school Mafia guys who have a restaurant as a business front? That's Marty."

I sigh and meet Rowan's gaze. He's curious, I can see it in his glinting eyes, and that makes me so proud of him. With the right guidance, he can become his best self, unafraid of the past or future. "It feels good when they're bad people. Someone might say a cheating husband, or a woman who sets fire to a bunch of paintings don't deserve to *die*, but I find out the story behind the request, and if I think that it's a hurt that needs retribution, if the payment is there, I provide the revenge my clients crave."

Rowan watches me with so much interest he forgets to eat. I nudge his fork. "So *you* decide?" he asks.

I shrug. "Someone has to. Why not me? Would you rather I didn't find your letter? Who'd have dealt with Ted? The police?"

Rowan shakes his head. "No, I'm glad you found it. My therapist keeps telling me I can't be the judge and juror for those men, that I have to let the system do its job, and you know what I think? I think it's a bunch of bullshit. They slipped through the cracks because of lack of physical evidence and alibis, but I know what they did. I was there."

I nod, pulling my leg up to the sofa so I can face him without moving much. There's so much passion in his eyes now, so much anger, and I can be the one to give him closure. "Do you want to tell me what happened? I did my research, but news articles and police information never tells the whole story."

He takes a deep breath but then turns his head to kiss my fingers. I'm so shocked I freeze at the tender gesture, ready to give him anything he might desire. It's been so long... too long since I've connected with anyone in a way that hasn't been strictly about sex. But here he is, giving me his attention, ready to see what I really am.

"I was sixteen when it happened. My dad ran a bicycle refurbishment company, and one of his employees was a junkie who just wouldn't stop stealing, so eventually Dad had to let him go. The guy got so riled up he talked his buddies into coming to our house. He told them we were rich, had lots of jewelry and stuff like that.

"We lived... not exactly in the countryside, but our house was secluded, so no one was able to hear the screaming and commotion. They dragged me and my grandma into the living room. They broke her arm in the process. She was crying so much, but still begged them not to hurt me. Patrick, the junkie, he tried to interrogate my dad, beat him up really bad, despite my dad telling them they could take whatever they want. But there were no riches, no safe, no secret stashes of cash.

"They wouldn't believe him, and the threats escalated. They thought he didn't want to give up his money, but there really was nothing to give up. Still, they broke my mom's hand with a hammer, and when they decided it wasn't enough, Grass, this absolute fucking psycho..." Rowan closes his eyes and takes a deep breath. "He cut my mom's throat. If the situation wasn't bad enough by then, all hell broke loose. They started arguing between each other. Not all of them wanted to kill us, but when they realized they wouldn't be able to get away with us as the witnesses, our fate was sealed. My grandma tried to get to the phone, my dad begged for my life, but they spared no one. My dad managed to free me, told me to run. I wanted to grab a gun from the kitchen, but I only got so far, and in the struggle, one of them, this guy Miles Brown, pushed me down the stairs to the basement.

"I was lying there at the bottom of the stairs, dizzy, with broken legs, and I couldn't go back and help anyone else. I only heard them screaming, until... they stopped, and the fucking bastards were just yelling at each other. All I could do was crawl away, hoping to hide. I heard them decide that they'd burn the house down to get rid of evidence. One of them asked about me, another said I'd just die in the fire if I wasn't dead yet. But as they doused the house in gasoline and set it aflame, I managed to crawl out through the basement window. I barely remember anything after that, until I woke up in the hospital."

My body cooks with fury. Every tendon, every muscle itches with the need to mete out violence, and as I swallow down the roar pushing at my throat, I focus on the dim gaze of my future partner. I know his pain, but my revenge was swift and brutal. He's been living with this burden, with this injustice, and the fear of those bastards targeting him eventually, for way too long. He deserves not only a fresh start but the bloodiest revenge imaginable. And I will be the one to give that to him.

"I'm so damn sorry. Nobody deserves such horror. I give you my word that I will dispatch them all for you. With or without your participation. That's your call."

He reaches out to stroke my cheek with his gentle fingers. "I want to be there. I want them to know who brings them death." His eyes contain so much cold rage it gives me a thrill. I found him beautiful when I secretly watched him work at the hunting goods store, but he's magnificent now, with raw emotion shining through like a beacon calling to me.

I want to tell him that, but it's not the right moment, not just after he's told me about the most traumatic event of his life. So instead, I pull his hand to my lips and kiss it, locking my eyes with his.

"We'll do it however you want. And... do you have any wishes for Ted's head?" I ask, nodding toward the fridge.

He stalls, glancing in that direction. "Can I... hurt it? I mean, I know he's dead, but can I... stab it in the eye? I want to see more. I wasn't ready when you first presented him." He licks his lips as if he's hungry for violence as dessert.

I growl and put my hand on his chest without thinking. He blinks, unsure of my reaction, but isn't pulling away.

Oh, we truly are meant to be. "Yes. He's yours. You can stab him, we can turn his skin into a lampshade, or anything you want."

He smiles at me and leans in for a kiss. "You're really something else. Cooks well, kills people, amazing dick, what else could I want in a boyfriend?"

Delight warms my heart even though I know he's trying to manipulate me a bit, play my own game, because he still doesn't trust me. It's understandable. In fact, I might have done the same, if our circumstances had been reversed, but I still like hearing him call me his.

It's the perfect beginning. The kind of story we would have told our grandchildren in the future, if we could have children in the first place.

But I digress.

"We should do it outside. Less mess to clean up," I say and finish my meal.

He's the first to get up, with the eagerness of a kid on Christmas morning. His bare feet flop against the wood in quick steps, but then he puts on my coat without asking, and dons a pair of slippers with reindeer antlers that the owners left for their guests.

In this ridiculous get up, he heads to the fridge and pulls the trash bag with the head out of the meat drawer.

Rowan turns to me. "Can you grab the knife?"

He looks so damn hot holding that head and weighing it in his hands. I can already see he'll make an excellent, fearless apprentice for me. Full of hope, I nod and hurry to the kitchen, eager to select an array of tools for him to enjoy. And if he stains my coat with old blood? Well, even if I end up having to burn it, it's a sacrifice I'm willing to make for my boy.

CHAPTER 15

ROWAN

I'M STILL DAYDREAMING ABOUT the moment I stabbed a kitchen knife into Ted Ashafi's eye. The head made a strange squelchy sound, and something slimy came out of his ear. How would a fresh body feel in comparison?

Saint was with me every step of the way, wrapped in a blanket, and didn't even demand his coat back. I'm starting to believe that even if his interest in me is misguided, since I'm definitely not the kind of person he takes me for, his weakness for me is real. He might be a dangerous man, but my presence is fulfilling his needs.

And he must need to have them met fast, since he's pushing for me to move in with him today. It reminds me of the insistent way he wooed me on the day I met him as my neighbor, and while I know his interest in me is shallow, it's flattering to hear that he can't get enough of me.

Anyone with half a brain would call it a massive fucking red flag, but considering there's a human head in the fridge, love-bombing is the least of my worries.

We've already fucked twice since the first time, and while both those times were thrilling, my ass is a bit sore, and I'm tired. Also, overwhelmed with the sudden glut of sex in my life.

I sip a coffee he got me on the way back into town. He must trust me more than is reasonable, because he gave me back my phone and everything. I groan when I check my work schedule.

"Fuck. You might as well take me straight to work. I can't call in sick again this month."

Saint frowns as he drives along the street, pulling down the visor as the sun reflects off the fresh snow, making both of us narrow our eyes. "What? No, you need to quit."

Wow. Yet another red flag. At this point, I'm just a bull, running at them with glee.

"That's not how the world works. I still need to pay rent while I work out what to do with my stuff. And the cabin is an Airbnb, it's not permanent." I'm still walking on tiptoes around him. He's a killer, and a professional one at that, but I'm finding my feet in this new reality in which he's not a threat to me.

I'm not afraid of him.

In fact, knowing he has my back makes my fears and anxieties so much less pervasive. And maybe it's my fucked-up brain acting out, but I also enjoy seeing that I have influence on him.

Saint shrugs, parking in one of the free bays close to the store where I work. "You'll move in with me, and I want you to focus on learning new skills, not waste your time on that place."

I want to fight him, just for the principle of not being told what to do, but it's not as though I love my job. The only good thing about it is discounts on bullets and survival gear.

"And how am I supposed to do that without an income?"

He switches off the engine and offers me a bright smile, as if he has all the answers. "You belong to me. I'll take care of you. But if you work with me in some capacity, then you'll have your own money. Trust me, it's going to be so much better for you."

I watch him, biting my lip. His hazel eyes eat me up. I'm tempted, so tempted. After all, I left all reason behind when I stabbed Ted's head in the eye. I'm also flattered he thinks weak, limping me can be his work partner. It makes me believe in myself too.

I've struggled on my own for so many years. Wouldn't it be nice to be *taken care of* for once?

All you have to do, Rowan, is sign on the dotted line. That's it, your soul is now his.

"I mean… hunting them down will be kind of a full-time job," I say even though it's not him who needs convincing.

"Exactly," he states, as if that's what he wanted to hear. He points at Chuck's shop and opens his door. "Just tell him you're quitting to be with the hottest guy in town, and then we can pick up the first batch of your things, get groceries, and call it a day."

My heart beats faster at the prospect and I lean over for a quick kiss.

I leave the coffee, grab my cane, and walk out. Every step reminds me about last night, but it's no high price to pay for the insanely good sex.

But when I walk into the store, and Chuck looks up with a grimace, the earlier confidence leaves me.

"There you are," Chuck says with a sigh, dropping something into a box. "One of your fucking rats snuck into the freeze-dried provisions. I'm so fucking done with this. You need to go to the back, and check every packet for bites."

I stand there, unsure how to proceed.

My boss cocks his head. "Why are you still standing there? Get on with it."

I clear my throat. "I... I was actually thinking that I might need to quit," I say flatly.

Chuck stares at me as his face grows redder by the second. "You're not quitting before Christmas, Rowan! What the fuck?"

"I mean... I could stay *today*. I just... need to tell my friend, 'cause he's waiting for me." I point to the door, out of my depth.

"Can't you text him? You need to stay the month, but we can talk about that tomorrow. I've got too much on my plate today."

"No, I... I'll just go tell him, and I'll be back in a sec."

Chuck points to the clock above his head. "Make it quick."

Embarrassment is like a lead collar around my neck, but I'm also angry at Saint for forcing me to do this in the first place. Of course Chuck wouldn't agree to let me go. Especially at this time of year. It isn't fair of me to even propose it, since it's such a busy time, and could mean Chuck would have to work late—

"Done?" Saint asks as I walk up to him. He's sipping his coffee by the car with a smile so handsome I can't initially bring myself to express my anger, but some things need to be said.

"No, it's not 'done'! He says I have to stay for my shift. And the rest of the month, really." I huff in frustration. "I told you it's not so easy."

Saint cuts me off with a snort. "You told me yourself he can let you go at any time, as per your contract. Why wouldn't it work the other way around?"

"This isn't funny! What am I supposed to do? Just not show up?"

Saint gives my hand a squeeze and pushes his cup into my hand. "You're too precious. Wait here."

I'm frozen and only look after him when the door of the store closes behind him. For a moment, I itch to follow, to tell him that I better stick to my schedule, since we don't even know if he can fulfill his obligation to me until Christmas Day, but that would have spoiled his fantasies about us being meant for each other. He didn't outright say it using those words, but it's definitely in the subtext of his deluded actions, and while I intend to wriggle out of our agreement once the time is right, until then it's in my best interest to play along.

As minutes pass, I'm beginning to feel nervous. He's not gonna... *kill* Chuck, is he?

I take a few steps toward the shop, but then Saint comes out and gives me one of the handsome smiles that grabbed my attention when I first met him. Which was only two days ago but feels like a much longer time.

He grabs his coffee out of my hand and passes me an envelope. "That's last month's pay and a bit extra for the few days you already worked in December. And you're done with this place, of course."

I stare at the envelope in silence, then glance at the glass door through which I spot Chuck kicking a box.

I follow Saint to the car. "Wh-what? How?"

He winks at me. "Don't worry about it. I know how to deal with people like him. You don't owe him anything."

I can't help but smile to myself as I close my seatbelt. My life is spiraling out of control, and I don't hate it.

As soon as we drive off toward my place, his hand is firmly on my thigh.

"Who taught you how to be like this?" I ask, watching his elegant profile as we drive past a group of teens in Santa hats.

"Like what? Suave? Good-looking? Effective at negotiation?" Saint asks and squeezes my knee with pride. After all, I am his trophy.

I snort in disbelief. So full of himself, and yet, doesn't he deserve to be? "So... uncompromising."

"Oh, I can compromise for the right reasons. But I always care first about my interests, and that of those I care about," he says, offering me a meaningful glance, as if he really believes we're in a relationship, not tied by a sex-for-revenge kind of agreement. Which, I won't lie, has its perks. I've gotten the good bits so far, but that did not mean the catches won't eventually fly my way.

"I mean, you weren't born an assassin." I prod, but I'm not sure if he's evading the question on purpose or really not understanding what I'm trying to find out.

"Oh. That's all on my uncle. I think, for a while he regretted taking in a very curious teenager, but once he brought me with him to be a lookout, and things went awry, I saw too much, and... well, he decided to make me his apprentice."

So the uncle wasn't a private investigator either. Got it.

We arrive at my building in no time, and I still can't believe I'm about to move in with this man. I've not even let anyone into my apartment since I moved in, so this is a massive step for me. And yet... I feel fine about it.

"You were just... okay with that? How many people have you killed since then?"

We leave our coffees in the car and step out of the vehicle. He's taking his time with the answer so intensely I can almost hear him chewing through my words.

"I don't count them anymore. Do you remember how many hunting jackets you sold last year?" he asks, as if those two were even remotely comparable. Maybe for someone like him—they are.

"So you find taking a life that easy? Did you grow up around violence?"

Saint shrugs, but I can see the sudden stiffness in his hands. He's ready to take a hike from this conversation. "Everyone does what they have to. And as you can see, I'm still here. Haven't been arrested once."

I might be socially awkward, but I'm not blind to cues, so I turn his attention to something he might find more bearable. "And how long since that streak started?"

"Twelve years since my uncle died," Saint tells me as we make our way to the entrance. As soon as we start walking, his hand is on my back.

He told me he's thirty-two, which means he was basically on his own since he was my age. But he's become a bit distant, and I don't want to ask if he misses his uncle. I'm not great at small talk, so we're left with uncomfortable silence as I wonder about his life.

He's a killer for hire, moves around a lot, there's that Marty guy he mentioned, but other than that, it's hard to squeeze much out of him. And yet he claims he wants to get close to me.

"But now I have you," he says and kisses my ear as the elevator opens on my floor.

I'm not sure how our relationship is meant to work out if he keeps withholding so much, but maybe it's just the topic of his work that is so touchy. I can try a different angle to get more out of him.

"And do you always find boyfriends by moving in next to them?" I laugh a bit nervously when I think back to how fast I fell for him.

"Not really. You're special like that," Saint tells me with a charming smile and pulls me that bit closer. "You know who I am. That makes it so much easier."

And the worst thing is, his words make butterflies flutter in my stomach, and I do feel special. "How so?" I can't help myself, and when we stand in front of my door, I stroke his chest. He's so firm, so handsome, and wants me. So why do I have to make it so complicated for myself?

'*Maybe because he's a fucking killer for hire?*' my inner voice screams.

Saint's mouth stretches in the handsomest grin in existence. If I didn't know him, I'd want a poster of him naked above my bed, so I could shamelessly fantasize that I do.

I stiffen when he leans in to brush his lips against mine, worried a neighbor might spy on us through a peephole, but I can't resist his touch. When his hand slides down my back and squeezes my ass, I raise to my toes as a wave of molten-hot pleasure flows through my body.

"You see the world for what it really is. You see that some people are rotten and need to be weeded out permanently."

No one has ever appreciated that fucked up side of me. To be fair, I stopped sharing it since expressing my rage and despair made people uncomfortable. Not him. He's more than happy to hear what I want to do to the bastards I have a grudge against.

I start opening the four locks, not yet sure how I will feel about letting him inside. "So it wasn't my charming smile, electric personality, and long eyelashes?"

Saint chuckles, and I shiver when his hand slides into my back pocket, massaging my ass. At least now he's standing behind me, and even if someone were to step into the corridor, they wouldn't see what he's doing.

"I barely saw your face when we first met, but the fire burning in every word of your letter made me itch for you even before I could see those pretty eyes," he says and leans in, kissing both my eyelids in a gesture so tender I can barely breathe.

He will be the death of me. Literally. I might not survive this relationship.

All the locks are open, but I can't make myself invite him yet, so I stall by wrapping my arms around his neck. When I kiss him, the world around us dissolves into a blur. His tongue is eager to reciprocate and he pushes me against the door, leaving me breathless. Saint's smell, the aura of danger that surrounds him, the touch of his hands... Every bit of him is so intoxicating it's hard to be rational and play mind games with him.

We're still kissing as the door clicks behind me and opens. Maybe if I walk in with my eyes closed, it will be easier. I have spent a day in his murder cabin, after all, and got used to his presence pretty fast.

He doesn't give me a choice, backing me inside with hands already tightening on my flesh, with his tongue teasing mine. It's exhilarating. And while I've been so cautious about letting anyone in, I let him not only step inside but also do so with his hand tightening on my neck.

I should be scared. I should stay outside and let him grab my things, but I don't feel in danger. In fact, I know that if one of the men who haunt my nightmares is somewhere in my apartment, he'll protect me. Maybe for his benefit rather than my own, but still.

It reminds me of that moment when we hugged for the first time, when I didn't yet know how *capable* he is. I felt so safe with him then.

And I feel safe with him now.

We're all the way inside when I open my eyes and look up at him.

"It feels natural to be here with you. I'm not scared when you're around." Even though I probably should be. I'm like a kitten cuddling up to a wolf. As long as I'm entertaining enough, he will take care of me.

He shuts the door with his foot and pushes me against it, smelling my hair, dragging his hands down my body. The jolt of lust for him, so new to me yet already becoming second nature, trails to my balls, making them throb in response to his fresh scent.

"No, I'll protect you. Always."

I don't even want to pull away to do the responsible thing and start packing. "How did it even work for you with your other boyfriends? Did they just get the censored version of you?"

Saint grins and grabs my thighs, pulling me up in a way that forces me to close my ankles behind him and embrace his neck. God, he's strong, and fit, and so handsome. Can the letter really be this much of a turn-on that he's desiring little old me?

"That's not a *version* of me. That *is* me."

The way he squeezes my ass is distracting, because it reminds me of the way he fucked me this morning, but I press on. "A sweet and caring guy who makes a picnic in the corridor? That's still you?"

Saint shrugs, carrying me down the hallway and into my living room. I used to be proud of the way I decorated it, but now that he's here, I wish I'd gone for something classier than a bright green wall behind the TV. And definitely tidied up more. Can't change any of that now though.

"I don't work every day, so I spend most of my time as the man you met. Reading, cooking, going on walks—"

That's... weirdly reassuring. "Not a writer though?"

"I dabble."

I shake my head. "Can I... I mean, I want to show you something I never showed anyone."

The haze of arousal lifts from his eyes, and he puts me down, watching my face as if he wants to remember every detail of my expression. "Of course. What is it?"

I take a deep breath and gently herd him to the sofa. "It's going to be useful in our hunt."

I go to the bedroom and retrieve my scrapbook from a box in the wardrobe. I hand it to him with trepidation, but I can't bear looking at him as he opens it, so I busy myself by going over to the wall.

I bought the large painting of a deer in a forest at a thrift store, and it's not very good, but it's what hides behind it that matters. I carefully turn it so that it hangs front to back, and step away so he can see my other project.

Saint's features are somber as he leans back on the sofa and takes in the product of years of research. I shudder, suddenly worried he might judge me, but if *he* can't understand my helpless rage, then who will?

"You have a murder board," Saint says, putting away the scrapbook and coming closer so he can see the collage of pictures and text hidden behind the deer painting from up close.

I stall, staring at the little arrows and sticky notes around the four mugshots. "What? It's not a... 'murder board'," I mutter, but he's kinda right. "It's just... a collection of facts and photos organized into visual form for ease."

Saint chuckles, eyeing me with a happy grin. "You tell yourself that. But those pins, those red lines around low-quality photos probably printed out from social media? I've seen this many times. You want those people dead. I would have been able to tell without even reading the letter," he says and taps Ted's face in one of the pictures.

I take a deep breath and put my hands on my hips. "I know it's fucked up—"

Saint shushes me, pressing his index finger to my lips and watching me with such glee, I'm instantly heating up under my clothes. "No, it's human. The society we live in tells us we shouldn't want retribution, but that's not natural, is it?"

He understands me, and that's a drug even more powerful than his kisses.

I shake my head and take Ted's photo off my *murder board*. Because he's dead. Eliminated. I rip it for good measure, and the act of tearing through the middle of his face gives me more satisfaction than I could ever imagine.

"So these are the men I want dead," I say with new confidence, meeting his gaze head-on. "Miles Brown. He's the one who pushed me down the stairs. Works night shifts at a mall. Lives with his mother." I then point to the photo of a man with a big nose and long, greasy hair. "Otto Grass. He cut my mother's throat. Spent two months in jail for domestic violence, but he's back out. Has a wife and three kids." Finally, I move on to the picture of a man whose eyes I'd like to carve out for the violence he inflicted on my family. "And last, but definitely not least, this fucking bastard, Patrick Galanis. He's the one who started it all. Broke my grandma's arm, wanted money. He's now a pastor in Fisher Lake."

Saint's inquisitive gaze slides to the photo of a clean-cut man with dark hair and pale blue eyes.

I'm breathing hard, unable to calm down. "I hate them so much."

Saint studies the pictures, and I can practically hear his mind working. We barely know each other, yet I already have a feeling I know what to anticipate. Is that strange?

"The pastor, I take it he acts as if it's all behind him?"

I slide my hand into his, needing the closeness to soothe my nerves. "I never dared to actually visit his congregation, but I would assume so."

Saint's fingers are smooth, warm and gentle as they rub against mine, and he pulls me close. "If he started it, he should be the next mark. I will give him to you."

I choke on a laugh, pointing to my board. "It's like an advent calendar."

"If you want his head recreated in chocolate, I can do that. We can make a mold before we dispose of it."

I don't know if I love or hate the fact that I'm not sure whether it's a joke, but when he winks, I find myself grinning at him and rubbing his chest yet again. Because he might be a monster who killed more people than he can remember, but he cares for my revenge in ways no one's ever done.

"That's disgusting, but I appreciate it. All I want is to stab him in the heart. So he knows how I feel every single day."

Is it wrong to be horny for Saint right now? Probably. But I push him back on the sofa and straddle his lap anyway.

He chuckles as his hands close on my ass. Hazel eyes, wide and joyful, watch me as he swallows. "Oh, you really are like me. Nothing's hotter than righteous anger. And you have so much of it," he whispers, rolling his hips so his cock brushes against my balls.

I rock against him like I'm in heat, and I can't get enough of his lips. "I don't think my ass can take another round just yet, but you can start teaching me how to deep throat," I whisper, watching his pupils dilate.

Oh, he is definitely as much into that as he is into my revenge quest.

Chapter 16

Saint

Sundays are my least favorite days. I might not be religious, but my family used to be, and I always get melancholic when walking past a church filled with people singing hymns. It takes me back to when my mother and father insisted I need to accompany them to mass each week for as long as I lived under their roof. I used to be so angry about it, but now I sometimes feel bad about expressing it when they were still alive.

If the past could be changed, I'd have likely never become a professional killer. Who knows, maybe I'd be cooking for a living instead, counting people's taxes, or doing something equally mundane? Maybe I would have liked mundane.

The life I lead so far has been a lonely one, but Rowan is the light at the end of that dark, cold tunnel, and if he needs me to sit on a bench and watch a white church in the middle of a small town, I'm going to do it. After all, not that much time remains until the deadline for delivering three more bodies to my new lover's feet.

He watches the church, and I watch *him*. His lips look a bit plumper from the side, and while this makes him even cuter, his dark gaze is so intense, he could probably kill with his stare alone if Father Patrick stepped out of the church. I can't get enough of him.

Since we've moved in together, I've been learning all about his little quirks. He won't go to bed before checking every door and window twice, he loves the big fireplace, and sitting outside under several blankets on a crisp, cold morning. He's still a bit skittish, so I make sure to walk around loudly because I don't want to scare him. His scars are ticklish, and on days when his knee hurts, a hot bath helps.

We butt heads about how to do things around the house as I'm a bit more particular, but he's very pliant in bed, a bit shy even, despite clearly enjoying both the dirty talk and getting fucked hard. He struggles to fall asleep, but not after he comes.

He doesn't abuse my generosity, even though I would get him anything he wants. At the store, he chose the same kind of shampoo he used before, and forced me to shop in the discount aisle for generic products. I still treated him to the best steak with fries I made myself out of russet potatoes, and he appreciated my effort.

Last night, he fell asleep against me while we were watching a movie, and I just sat there, admiring him and stroking his face. I didn't have the heart to wake him up, so I stayed put with my arm slowly dying until he woke up to empty his bladder.

We work so well together it feels as if we've known each other for ages, and in an ideal world, I'd be spending a lazy afternoon with him, walking through the woods around the rented cabin, cuddling, then fucking on the floor in front of the fire.

Instead, we're watching a church.

This whole revenge thing could be dealt with so much quicker if I did it myself, as usual, but I need to be patient if I'm to honor his wishes and teach him my trade. But that doesn't make me any less bored.

"We could easily snipe him from there," I say, pointing to the roof of the 1930s-style building with a pharmacy on the first floor and balconies on the two floors above it.

"No. He wouldn't know what happened. I need to look into his eyes. He deserves pain and fear."

I sigh and glance back at the church. Its walls are white and the tall turret at the front has a sharp, conical rooftop making it resemble a rocket about to launch into space on this crisp, cloudless afternoon. Being here makes me feel like I'm some old-timey gent with a revolver, trying to hunt down the man who murdered my own family, but the smell of gas is killing the illusion.

Rowan's right though. If I had the opportunity to take revenge on my parents' killers? I'd want them to suffer for hours and endure double the pain and fear they inflicted. I'm sure my uncle gave them hell, but I wish I had been there.

I take a chunk of the apple cake I made yesterday and bite into it. "It will take a while until the service is over. We don't need to stay so quiet."

"Does it get any easier? You're so chill about all this, and I feel the cops are already onto me."

Rowan takes a piece of cake for himself, and I love to watch him eat my food. It's yet another way in which he accepts me. I take pleasure watching him wear my scarf for the same reason. He didn't even ask if he could keep it, a cute kind of entitlement. The scarf is there around his neck when my hands can't be.

I sigh when the sugary taste spreads on my tongue like a promise of sweet love later. I'm romantic like that.

"Yes. The first time I saw my uncle kill, I nearly pissed myself, but if I can skin a rabbit, why not do the same with a bad man, you know?" I shrug, watching him. "There's an art to avoiding the cops' attention though. I'll teach you."

"I… don't know if it's even possible for me to be as proficient as you when it comes to the physical side. Because of the knee." He takes a big bite of cake, but his expression gets gloomy. "But I'm a really good shot. And I'm good at seeming all innocent if I need to."

I nod and put my hand on his, squeezing it gently. There aren't many people about, no one who can see us touching like this, so I don't worry about attracting attention.

Damn, he's so perfect.

"Being a team doesn't mean we both need to have the same job. I need a lookout, a sniper, someone who'll patch me up on the rare occasion I get hurt. Or watch me sleep when I'm forced to track a target for days on end, so I don't need to wake up every hour to make sure I'm safe."

I want him to be that for me.

He lights up and sits straighter, not even paying attention to the church anymore. "I could be that. Of course, hoping you'll never need medical help, but I took several first aid courses at survivalist classes. And you might think I'm messy, but if you teach me what to watch out for, I could take on cleaning up any messes so you can rest after a job."

He's so earnest about it, I have to believe he means it.

It warms my heart, and I itch to kiss him right here, in the middle of town, right in front of a church. That's how perfect he is to me. And as unlikely as our first meeting was, something brought us together. Some grand design or fate? I don't care what, but I am intent on making things work.

"How is it that you're single?"

He nudges me with his elbow. "I'm not."

"You know what I mean."

Rowan sighs, sending a cloud of vapor into the cold air. "After the... whole *thing*, dating anyone was the last thing on my mind. It's a small town, so it's not filled with gay men, but realistically, I know I'm strange. I was too anxious to let you into my home, or go to yours. Who would have the patience for that? And I come with all this baggage. On which date do you even tell a guy that your whole family was murdered, and you're *not* okay?"

I entwine our fingers and swallow the rest of the cake as the sun briefly comes out from behind clouds and makes the church appear even brighter. If God does exist, maybe this is him telling me he wants that liar out of his home?

Not that I need permission or reasons other than Patrick Galanis's crime against my lover.

"Oh, I do know. Dating apps made everyone so impatient. They all want to fuck you on the first date and see where it goes. Not that I mind *that*, of course," I say with a little smirk as I remember my very first date with Rowan. "But it takes time to build trust, and people drop you like a hot potato if you're not exactly what they want."

He bites his lip. "When you hit on me, I kinda thought you might be a sex addict looking to have someone to fuck while you're in Rosehill Pines. I couldn't really comprehend you wanted *me* in particular."

I roll my eyes with a smile. "Ew, false modesty! Come on, you're beautiful, funny and passionate, and you know your way around hunting gear. What's not to like?"

Rowan laughs and shoves my arm. "Stop it or I'm gonna have to believe you! I'm still learning my way around parts of you." His gaze shamelessly slides to my crotch, and the winter sun hits his eye from the side, making it twinkle with mischief.

But the church bell rings, and that's our cue to infiltrate it.

"Ready?" I ask, but he's already getting up after shoving the rest of his cake into his mouth.

Rowan nods, rubbing his palms together, eager as if he were about to get his hands on my dick.

"I've got something for you," I say and reach into my coat before handing him a knife in a nice leather sheath. "Since you lost yours in the forest."

He takes it from me with reverence. "It's even got the extra strap, so you can attach it inside the jacket..."

I give him a quick kiss. "Just don't use it until I tell you to."

CHAPTER 17

SAINT

CHILDREN SING ABOUT THE birth of Jesus, no doubt rehearsing for the upcoming nativity play, and their shrill voices echo off the white walls of the church while adults gather in a large side room, sharing coffee and cake.

With so many people present it should be easy enough to blend in, and while we're on the lookout for Patrick, I take stock of where the exits are, how many windows the church has, or if there are significant obstacles if we need to flee. It's just a precaution, but it's always better to be prepared.

The smell of sugar and vanilla soothes any worries I might have, but I'm really only worried about Rowan. He might do something brash, being so new to this job, and while this outing is part of his training, the matter with Patrick is personal. He can't get arrested or hurt on my watch.

Several groups and clubs have their tables arranged into a horseshoe so people can walk around and get to know what's on offer or ask questions. Someone gives guitar lessons for donations to a homelessness charity. There's the *Chess in the park* club, which I doubt can be popular in this weather, and a Bible study group for teens.

Rowan sticks very close to me, which is sweet of him. I know by now that he can speak his mind and is very opinionated but gets anxious in crowds. It doesn't matter though, because I can be his shield, the support he needs when life gets a bit too hard to handle, even though I can't touch him the way I want to among these people.

"You seen him yet?" I whisper in his ear, and he nods, taking a sip from a paper cup as we walk alongside the different tables, wondering who would be the best person to approach. I don't want to chat with too many people, as I'd rather not be remembered when I'm planning a murder, but intel from a naive congregation member could prove essential.

"He briefly talked to the kids."

I scowl. "How did it feel?"

Rowan hums. "Like not seeing *him*, but some fake person. It's strange."

"Did he look different then?" I ask, pulling him into a corner, so we can speak more freely while my gaze scans the crowd for the pastor I've seen on the murder board, which now graces the wall of our rented cabin.

The churchgoers occasionally peek our way, likely not that used to seeing new faces, which makes me glad that I brought glasses for both of us. It's a disguise that doesn't work nearly as well as it does in the *Superman* franchise, but a small change in appearance can be the difference between a bystander being able to correctly describe my features or not.

"Yes, he had longer hair, in a bit of a mess, and crazy bulging eyes, one of them pink from a burst blood vessel. I wish I didn't remember it that clearly, but I do."

"Sorry to bother you," someone speaks behind us in a soft voice, and when I don't initially spot the stranger over my shoulder, I turn to see that a young, blond wheelchair-user is holding on to Rowan's forearm.

"Y-yes?" Rowan asks, a bit too nervous. We'll have to work on that. Whenever we go out into the field, he is to appear confident, as if he's exactly where he's meant to be. Though if we're playing the role of two men looking for a new church, maybe his uncertainty might work in our favor this time.

I don't need to assess the man consciously. I've been doing this for long enough that my attention focuses on threats and points of interest. And this guy? He has a rainbow badge featuring a cross. It's pinned to his baby blue top, which he'd clearly chosen to show off his chest and biceps.

"I've noticed you're new here. I don't want to seem pushy, but I looked at your cane, and I wanted to let you know we have a group for folks with limited mobility." He points to a stand at the end of the horseshoe.

Rowan clears his throat, glancing at me for a second, but then turns back to the stranger. "Oh, and... it's a gay-friendly church?" he asks, pointing out the pin.

The man's eyes light up, but all I can see is that his hand is still on *my* Rowan. What does he think he's playing at when I'm standing right here?

"Yes, the pastor's making it a very inviting place for us."

I sense Rowan stiffen next to me as the stranger introduces himself as Pete, and I take it as the perfect opportunity to disperse any doubts about mine and Rowan's relationship. Because we are not brothers, cousins, or best friends who share one house.

"Sebastian. And this is my husband, Rob."

Rowan's face flushes, but I'm glad to see the fucker's hand slide off him. I can see the light of disappointment in Pete's eyes and I'm glad to be the cause. Rowan might not yet understand what a catch he is, but I remember how easily he fell into my lap. I'll be keeping an eye out for guys who think they're smooth enough to steal him from under my nose.

"H-hey," Rowan utters with a smile. I wish I knew what's going on in his head.

"So nice to meet the two of you. I'm sure the pastor will love to meet you as well. He's been a blessing to our church."

"Really? Tell us more. He sounds like an angel," I say.

Pete sighs, leaning back in a way that shows off his pecs. He's hot, I have to give him that, but he is not going to flirt with Rowan.

"He runs a soup kitchen on Fridays, and he's been outspoken about his past drug issues, which has made many people comfortable enough to seek support. Addiction can be a lonely experience, shrouded in a lot of shame. Father Patrick is there for those who struggle."

Rowan looks a little pale, so I step in. "We can't wait to meet him. But I'm not sure if we should bother him today, when there's so many people around. Are there any days and times when he might be more available? You seem to be well-informed."

Translation: *when and where will it be most convenient to kill him?*

Pete smiles for the first time since I cut him off from my man. "Oh, I work with him quite closely, since I'm the president of our LGBT circle. He's usually around between ten and three in the afternoon on weekdays."

"That's great to know. My husband's a little shy, so he might prefer to come back when there's fewer people around."

Pete's grin widens. "Nothing to be afraid of, we're a friendly bunch!" He proceeds to pat Rowan's forearm, and I kind of want to rip his hand off, but seconds later, he's wheeling back to his table.

"Husband," Rowan says and laughs nervously, but I spot the threat heading our way before he does, so I can't entertain my sweetheart with jokes.

"Watch out," I whisper, but Patrick Galanis comes up to us with a somber expression that suits his all-black outfit. It will be what he's found dead in, if we choose not to get rid of the body.

"Rowan..." he says, and my man grabs my hand, no longer caring whether we're alone or not.

CHAPTER 18

ROWAN

THIS ISN'T HOW I imagined speaking to Patrick Galanis for the first time after all those years. In my mind, I always beat him down with something heavy, and then, once blood glistens on his tan skin and his speech slurs, I tell him about all the ways in which he ruined my life.

But he was polite, almost cautious, when he invited us to his office at the back of the church. He left us to wait, saying he would be back as soon as everyone left, because he needed to talk to me. By the time I sat down in the room with wooden panels for walls and a large picture of the Holy Mary holding Baby Jesus behind the desk, the bloodthirst that led me here feels... tainted.

Maybe Saint was right? Maybe we should have killed our mark quickly, because seeing all the proof that the beast I remember Galanis as no longer exists, spoils my desire for revenge.

There's a distinct, sour taste at the back of my mouth whenever I attempt to imagine the bastard dead, but now I can't do that without envisioning all those parishioners mourning their shepherd. And I can't help but wonder if years of hate didn't make *me* into a monster selfishly wanting to take him away over something this new reformed Galanis would have never done.

But as I contemplate my choices with a heart of lead, Saint walks around the office with a small device in hand and hovers it around all the walls.

"What are you doing?" I mutter.

"Checking for cameras," he says, bringing me back to the reality of what we came here to do. What I want to do.

"Do you think he wants to record us saying something incriminating?" Maybe that's why he told us to wait here? So he can go back to his secret lair and turn on the cameras hidden in the eyes of statues.

"No, but better safe than sorry," Saint tells me as he approaches the desk and casually opens all the drawers, as if they contain his own belongings. "I also need to know if we're not at risk of being filmed as we take care of him, but there's no cameras here."

"Wait... what?" I utter, startled. "Here? Now?" My heart speeds up because it feels like too much too soon... Sure, I've seen Ted's head, the concept of killing these men is more than real, but after talking to the living, breathing Galanis, I'm no longer sure if I can mow him down without thinking it all through.

Saint shuts the drawer, hides the device in the pocket of his coat, and sits in the chair next to mine. It's only now that I realize why he insisted we both wear gloves. He came here intending to deal with my former tormentor right away, and he doesn't want us to leave any incriminating evidence.

Shit.

Fantasizing about murder and actually planning it are two different animals. Right now, I wish I could slide off this one's back.

Saint shrugs, looking elegant as he looks my way with his legs crossed. I'm suddenly reminded that the man who made me avocado toast with goat's cheese for breakfast is in fact a wolf with sharp teeth and an appetite for murder.

"It's the perfect opportunity. The sun is slowly going down, he is asking his congregation to leave. We will be alone with him. It would be a shame to not seize this kind of opportunity."

My breath speeds up, and I'm getting a little sick. I don't know if it's because I'm terrified or excited. "And wh-what would we even do with the body?" I settle on a practical question because that's easier than the moral dilemma I'm grappling with.

Saint reaches to my lap and squeezes one of my hands, which, I only now realize, I was clenching into a tight fist. "I have plastic sheets in the car. Are you having second thoughts about participating?" he asks with a gentleness I don't feel I've earned.

What the hell is wrong with me that I want to see a man who managed to turn his life around dead? What would be the point, other than empty satisfaction? Then again, do I not deserve retribution? Why should my needs be less important?

"No, it's not about that. If it's happening, then with my participation, but the question is if it's happening at all. I'm... confused. What if he really changed? What if it was drugs that affected him to the point that he did... what he did?" I swallow with my stomach aching at the memory of Galanis's bloodshot eyes, and him yelling at my father about money that wasn't there.

Just reaching back to those memories makes my heart beat faster, and I hug myself, trembling in the face of a decision I might not be fit to make. Do I really have the right to sentence a man to death? Galanis might be single, but his congregation clearly loves him, and he would be orphaning them all.

Saint leans in, staring into my face with a deep frown. "We agreed that I'd kill them all before the twenty-fifth."

I try to swallow, but it feels impossible when my throat's so tight. "And what? I can't take it back? Like it's some deal with the devil?" It's not him I should be angry at, but I hate feeling trapped between my dark desires and the scraps of morality still left in me.

Saint exhales in exasperation, letting go of my hand. He crosses his arms over his chest. "We technically don't have a contract, but I treat it as a gentlemanly agreement. I *can* dispatch him, so if you don't want me to, it will not affect the end result come Christmas."

Because now that he put his claws in me, he won't let go. And I won't lie, I've been enjoying his love bites more than I should.

"I don't know, okay? Am I a bad person to still want him dead? After everything we've seen out there? This man changed."

"Did he though?" Saint asks, resting his elbow on the side of my chair and piercing me with his gaze as if he wants to drill straight to my soul. "He might no longer be a criminal, but did you hear from him at all since he and his buddies invaded your family home? Did he try to get in touch? Did he go to the police, confess, or atone for his actions? Did he help you when you were struggling?

Whatever change he's made, he made it for himself and his own comfort."

Saint's words are like a punch, and I clench my teeth so hard they ache.

I have to take a deep breath before I speak. "No, you're right. He's out here just living his life as if nothing happened. Maybe even treating the crime against me as his stepping stone to salvation."

The warmth of Saint's hand soothes the tension in my back, and while I know his actions are entirely self-serving, I can't deny that I needed this pep talk.

"Most people will excuse their actions, because we all need to feel like we're the good guys. That's why, for a moment, you hesitated. That's why I only kill for people who want revenge, even if petty, and that is why our friend Patrick found God."

"How do you excuse pulling me into this? Or does it need no excuse because I want revenge?" I watch him with goosebumps on my forearms, even though my decision about Galanis's fate feels sealed.

"*Pulling you in?*" Saint mutters, facing me. "You were the one who wrote down that you wanted those men dead. I didn't push it on you."

Only we both know I would have never taken the step of attempting to kill anyone if he hadn't appeared in my life. Maybe I would have led an existence full of self-loathing and fear, but my conscience would have remained clear. And even if I stopped all this now, one of the men I mentioned in the letter is dead because of me.

I feel no remorse about *that*, which says something about me, I suppose.

"You didn't ask for money though. You gave me a devil's deal." I don't even know why I'm prodding him like this.

Maybe I'm nervous. Maybe I'm frightened of a future that's coming at me all too fast.

Whenever I'm with him, there's a strange mixture of danger and safety in the air. But deep down, I know he chose me, stalked me, seduced me, and sealed the deal by playing on my vulnerabilities. He will make me his by taking my soul and turning me into a killer.

Which I shouldn't find hot. But I do. Because he wants me like no one else.

"I don't need your money," Saint says as his gaze scorches me, leaving no doubts about his intentions. If he could have his way, he'd have me blow him right here, while we wait for Galanis.

And the worst thing is that thinking about him exercising such power over me is making me throb with heat. He didn't even put that idea in my head. I'm the one who came up with it because I'm horny and fucked up. He's the answer to my secret prayers.

A man who makes me dinner and fucks me so hard I forget the emotional torment in my life. When he bites me, when his dick is inside me, I only live in the moment, and that's always so cathartic, deep down I know I'm the one who doesn't want to let go of this new drug.

"Let's just see what he wants from me," I decide, and the fact that it *is* my choice makes me feel powerful, even if I still need Saint to end Galanis.

He shrugs, but his lips remain pressed together, since he doesn't attempt to hide his feelings about my waffling. Maybe to him my hesitation seems weak? After all, *he* admitted himself that some of the vengeful kills he carries out are petty and he still has no issue going through with them. My indecision must be a nuisance.

The silence becomes uncomfortable, but I simmer in it, trying to distract myself by looking around. A metal box with a little padlock sits on a shelf behind the desk with the word *donations* scribbled on it in the hand of a child. Yet another reminder of Galanis's charity endeavors, since he's *such* a good guy now.

Or is he? Can he really be called that if he didn't take responsibility for his past? His confession would have added to my witness statement, and the bastards could have been convicted. Instead, he got himself an alibi.

I stiffen when the door behind us opens. Saint glances over his shoulder, but I can't bring myself to follow his example, so I only see the somberly-clad pastor when he sits down across from us.

It's shocking that if I haven't looked him up over the years, I might not have even recognized him in the street. Gone is the messy hair, the dry skin patches, the dark circles under the eyes and shaky hands. The man before me is a picture of good health, with neatly cut hair and a depth to his gaze, which might have converted many a lost soul.

But the longer I study him, the more familiar he seems, and I sink into the padded chair as the reek of smoke and blood reaches my nose. I'm crawling through the basement, legs broken while Galanis and his buddies scream at each other. He might have claimed death and pain wasn't what he wanted for my family, but he was still ready to sacrifice us so he didn't have to take responsibility for his actions.

He doesn't deserve mercy when my family paid such a big price for his return to health.

But I sit in silence, waiting for his move. What kind of pathetic apology will he come up with to excuse what he did?

'Oh, I was on drugs, I didn't know what I was doing'?

Galanis takes a deep breath. "We need to speak alone, Rowan."

Saint straightens, and despite our little spat, I couldn't feel safer. His presence is the only cure for the anxiety I've been living with since the attack. He'd sooner rip Galanis's throat out than let the fucker anywhere near me. A comforting thought.

"Anything you want to say, you can say in front of him." My voice is dull, but I manage to speak, which is no small feat.

"Oh, so he's your muscle," Galanis says, resting his elbows on the desktop and entwining his fingers as if he were about to pray.

I'm thrown off by his words but don't say a thing until he meets my gaze, pinching his lips so sharply they turn pale.

"It's been years. How dare you accost me like this?"

Saint squints at Galanis but says nothing, giving me the space to confront my demon.

"E-excuse me?" I utter. "'Accost' you?"

Galanis's face darkens with a flush, and in this moment he's no longer a benevolent pastor, or a pillar of his community but a rabid dog who claimed a juicy bone and would rather bite than give it back. "You heard me! I'm a changed man, doing great work for my congregation. What's done is done, and you're here to what? Shove the past in my face? Ruin what I managed to build? You've got some nerve."

'What's done is done'? *That's it*? I stare at him in disbelief. It's as if he's grown horns right in front of me. My tragedy, my broken life, my nightmares, my anxiety and fear are just "*the past*" to him.

I suppose they are. He's not the one who had to live with them all these years.

The knife Saint gave me burns the inside of my jacket.

"You fucking bastard..." I whisper, filled with right-eous fury.

Galanis glances at Saint, but then his attention settles back on me. "What could you coming here possibly change? You've gone to the police before, and the matter was closed. You should take that as a sign. I did! A sign from a higher power, that there is redemption for each and every one of us." He gets up as if he were about to give us a sermon on how God gave him an alibi and the murder of innocents was actually a good thing, because it inspired him to become a pastor. "I understand. Everything has a price," he scoffs at me with an ugly twist to his lips. "I'll give you money, but I never want to see your face again."

My eyes go wide when I realize he's turning around to the donations box with a key in hand.

What the actual fuck?

The multiple homicide this bastard committed was only a step on his road to self-improvement, and my arrival is an inconvenience he believes he can buy his way out of, just like he had when he paid someone for an alibi. This time, he wouldn't even be using his own money.

I can't believe this.

"Told you," Saint says in a cold voice and gets up from the chair. He's calm as ever, and his sudden move throws Galanis off guard. The key falls to the floor as the man from my nightmares backs away toward the religious picture behind him.

"I will call the cops if you put one finger on me."

I blink, struck that he has no idea death might come for him too, as unexpectedly as it did for my family, but Saint doesn't hesitate. I see a tiny bottle in his hand, and a piece of cloth, and then he's shoving Galanis against the wall, with the cloth pressed to his face.

The chair swallows me as I watch my knight wrestle with the beast from my past, but by the time the sharp scent of whatever Saint used reaches me, the struggle is over.

I jump to my feet, pulled out of my stupor. "No! Wait. He... Is he dead?" I utter as Galanis slides to the floor.

Saint frowns, glaring at me as if I just told him aliens have attacked. "No. But it'll be easier to deal with him if he's not screaming. I've had enough of his yapping anyway. Figured his words were enough proof that he doesn't deserve to live."

I rush over with my head ringing. "Yes, but not like this! You heard him. Everything I went through is meaningless to him. He doesn't deserve to die unconscious! I need him to know why he's dying." I'm breathing hard as Galanis's words play back in my head, filling me with rage again and again. It's as if he changed something in me. I was at a crossroads, but now I won't stray from my path until all those who wronged me are dead.

Saint takes out a small Ziploc bag and puts the bottle and the cloth inside. His eyes settle on me as he contemplates the body at his feet. "So you've made your decision? We're killing him?" he asks, staring at me. I swear the '*don't you dare change your mind again*' is waiting to be spoken out loud.

"Y-yes," I say, breathing heavily as I pull the knife out, but he puts his hand on mine.

"Rowan. You just said you don't want to kill him while he's unconscious."

I lower the knife, grateful that he's looking out for my needs even when he's annoyed with me. "Right. How long until he wakes up?"

Saint rubs his chin. "It will be a while. We can't just wait around here. I guess we need to take him."

I put the knife back into the sheath and give him a kiss on the lips, still shaken by what just happened. "Thank you."

Saint exhales and puts his chin on the top of my head as we both stare at the limp form on the floor.

"I live to please."

CHAPTER 19

SAINT

We barely managed to reach the cabin before the snowfall became a white wall. It would have been inconvenient to get stuck somewhere with an unconscious pastor in the trunk, especially in this weather, but now that we're safe, I can calm down. The hot chocolate in my cup has the faintest aftertaste of chili, and I lean against the doorframe, watching Galanis struggle in the chair I've fastened him to.

He can't get away, of course—I made certain of that—but I can imagine waking up in a strange place, in a room covered with sheets of plastic and dolls watching you from behind the translucent film would make anyone frantic.

I didn't put the toys in the room to freak him out. The small nursery just happens to be the farthest away from the living room and least in use.

Rowan hovers around Galanis, giving him more attention than the bastard deserves. He's squeezing the knife I gave him, his eyes are wide and attentive, but for once, I'm not sure if he's frightened or excited.

Maybe he's psyching himself up. After all, this is going to be his first kill. Mine was tough too. My uncle expected it of me, and when it happened, I wasn't ready. He later apologized for pushing me, but not wanting to do harm and not causing harm are two different things. It's been years since. I've gotten used to death and all the inconveniences it came with, but I still remember the taste of blood on my lips as it squirted straight in my face that first time.

My uncle had me do an STD test and everything.

But as annoyed as I am that I could have dealt with Galanis long ago and freed up our evening, I don't want to make the same mistake my uncle did and stay back, giving Rowan space.

He's in his own head and doesn't speak or even look my way as he circles his prey. His black T-shirt sticks to the front of his body, damp with perspiration, and each turn around the small interior makes the plastic sheets whisper in reassurance. I know he can do it, but this first kill would be infinitely easier if he chose not to wait until his mark's eyes sharpen with awareness.

Outside, the wind howls so loudly it's like another presence in the room, and every now and then, a strong gust rattles the window as if it too wants to get to the pastor and choke him before Rowan can.

The eerie silence that settled over the cabin is broken when Rowan speaks, taking a deep breath as he faces Galanis.

"You thought you could get away with what you did. That I'm some weakling who would never approach you.

That you're invincible thanks to what? God's benevolence?" He shakes his head with a sneer.

Rowan's not a big guy, but right now, with the knife in his hand, he looks powerful. I find it so hot that all his wrath, all his darkness is packed into such a compact body. Every day, he seems to get tougher where it matters, yet as soon as he's under me, he gets so sweet and pliant I melt into him. It's as if the softness is only for me while the world gets all of Rowan's sharp edges.

Galanis mumbles into the gag, eyes wide, but Rowan doesn't take it out for a conversation. He just wants to say his piece without being interrupted. I understand that, even though it's giving final speeches that always gets TV villains in trouble.

That's okay. He's not a villain, and I'm here to back him up.

"You will die tonight. And guess what? Your buddy Ted is already dead. That's right. I'm not here to make empty threats or take your money. In fact, we added a few bucks to the donations box you were so eager to dip into. Your congregation will be better off without a wolf in sheep's clothing."

Rowan speaks in a raised voice, and my mouth waters a little when he steps even closer to Galanis, the sharp point of the knife aimed at the man.

The wolf's eyes widen, and he whimpers, trying to twist away from the blade, but it's too late. He's had years to atone and save his miserable life, and yet he didn't. Why would anyone take pity on him now? I don't.

Rowan's breath is loud when he presses the tip of the knife into Galanis's chest. It's sharp, I made sure of that before gifting it to him.

"I hate you so fucking much, and I will sleep so soundly knowing you're dead. Just two more of you to go, and the world will be a better place."

Galanis writhes in the chair, jerking away as Rowan pushes the knife into skin, but the motion makes our prisoner swing right back, and the very tip stabs into flesh, making him shriek.

'Do it', I think as if I can encourage Rowan with my mind alone. 'Do it, *he deserves it*'.

But Rowan stills with the knife barely digging into Galanis, who is only making things worse for himself by wiggling as if he believed he can come out of this murder room alive.

I put the mug of chocolate down on a side table and take a step closer. "You need momentum, baby. It's hard to stab without a good swing."

Rowan huffs and pulls his arm back, but seconds pass and he's not making his move. In fact, he's not making any moves, as if the cold outside has frozen him stiff. When Rowan once more pushes the knife against his victim's chest, Galanis screams into the gag and stares at him with pleading eyes.

His next twitch makes the chair stagger. The blade slashes through his shirt, releasing a steady stream of blood, but by the time our mark collapses on his side, he's not only still breathing but on his way to perfect health once the new wound closes.

I want Rowan to finish the job, but as much as the need to be done with this irks me, I stay back. It's his kill. I promised that to him.

Rowan kneels on the plastic sheet, but as I still, convinced he's going to use his weight to plunge the knife into that bastard's heart, his shoulders drop, and he glances my way. His eyes are clouded, as if he were lost in the fog and in need of my guidance. "I know, I know. I'm just..." He takes another trembling breath. "I want him dead, but it's just hard to..."

The wind rattles the window again, as if to encourage my boy. I know he has it in him. He doesn't seem worried about the blood dripping from his knife, or about Galanis squirming like a maggot that just won't die. Maybe it's stage fright. Or that instinct most people have that makes it so exponentially hard to stab something into another person's body.

I can't help a smirk when Galanis starts sobbing. With hands and legs both cuffed to the sturdy chair, he has no means of escape, and I know that one look at me tells him I'm not going to back away. I've been told I have this aura about me, of someone who carries out every job to the very end, and I'm proud of it. I can only hope Rowan will be proud of me too.

"How do you want me to do it?" I ask, kneeling next to him. He's trembling, but no matter how much I want to, I cannot make this any easier on him.

Relief washes over his face, and his shoulders sag as he passes me the knife. He doesn't back away though or run out of the room. No, he wants to be here, wants to see it, just isn't ready to take that final step.

When his bloodied hand rubs my arm, I don't have the heart to tell him he's leaving stains on my shirt. I can get a new one, and we will only have this moment together once.

"Stab in the heart," he says, and I focus on his soft lips releasing those words.

It's as if he releases *me* from my cage with this not-quite-command. I stayed back because I wanted to accommodate his needs, but the beast within me was clawing at the bars, ready to bite.

Now I get to kill the man who hurt my Rowan so much he couldn't bring himself to live a normal life, and the smile that fact brings to my face reflects at me from those pretty eyes. "Of course, baby."

The knife feels perfectly balanced in my hand. It's light but sturdy, and its blade could cut through a sheet of paper if the fancy struck me. What point is there in waiting when the night isn't getting any younger and I have so many activities planned for us?

My blood feels hot when I trap the wriggling beast with my knee and then push the blade in, avoiding bone. Pallor sets in as Galanis fights a battle he can no longer win.

Seconds later, it's all over.

Rowan puts his hand on Galanis's chest, not blinking once. "I could feel it stopping," he whispers, flushed. He's so beautiful with the storm raging behind him it takes my breath away.

I'm elated at his reaction. Maybe he wasn't ready to take a life, but he stayed with me every step of the way and didn't flinch when the blade sank into flesh.

I was right. He's the one.

"Exciting, isn't it?" I ask, letting go of the knife before blood can stain my hands. Turning toward him, I scoop him into my arms and press our lips together. The kill itself was like many others before it, but sharing it with my lover means everything, and as warmth spreads through my chest, I realize just how much I've missed this kind of companionship.

It's such a primal need to want to share your kill.

He glances at Galanis as he wraps his arms around my neck with a shaky exhale. "Yes. It's done. Irreversibly. He's gone because I chose to erase him from society." His eyes meet mine with the intensity of a wolf cub hungering for blood. "Thank you for finishing the job when I couldn't. Maybe the next one will be easier."

I'm melting.

He is the epitome of perfection, and I want him at my side. Forever.

"I can be your blade for as long as you need," I promise, pushing my forehead to his and then cocking my head so our noses touch.

He's eager to kiss me, and I love toying with his tongue. I don't care that Galanis is right next to us, dead as a rock. My other plans can wait, because it looks like Rowan isn't ready to go and clutches at me, starting to shake.

"Baby?" I ask, eager to give him whatever he needs.

In the dim light, Rowan's eyes are so dark I could drown in them. "You're not only my blade. You're *my* monster. One everyone else should be afraid of."

His words pump the air out of my lungs, because he sees me for who I am and not only doesn't run but provokes me. The rusty scent of blood looms in the background, but the peppermint I've learned to associate with him becomes ever more intense as his body heats up against mine.

"They should. I'm good at hiding what I am, but that part of me is always there, ravenous," I whisper, closing my hand on his throat as I lean above him, ready to strike.

His bloodied fingers wrap around the wrist of my other hand, and in a gesture that makes my breath hitch, he pulls it between his legs. "*Show* me what you are. No holding back," he rasps. His lips are so ripe for the taking, and when I squeeze his crotch, I can feel he's getting hard already.

The kill might have been nothing new to me, but this? *This* gets my adrenaline pumping.

"You want the monster? The beast?" I rasp, pushing at his chest. He holds his breath, falling to the plastic-covered floor, but his eyes become somehow even more intense. It's as if the blood staining his fingers soaked into him through the skin, and I want to taste this new version of him even though I know it'll be even more addictive.

"Raw you." Rowan pushes some hair off his face, leaving another blood stain on his pale skin.

He might not know what he's asking for, but I'll give it to him anyway.

A smile pulls at my lips as I stretch over him. I toss my shirt at Galanis's face, but don't miss the way Rowan's eyes slide down my chest. His pupils dilate with a familiar hunger, and he doesn't even flinch when I drop my hands next to his head, caging him against the floor.

I can't wait to be inside my pretty little killer in the making. The blood on his hands predicts his future, *our* future, but he needs to know where he belongs before he can commit. By appearing in his life, I threw him into dark rapids filled with boiling blood, but I'm also the one who'll be his anchor.

I grab his wrists, and when I pin them above his head, he whimpers and rocks his body against mine without a hint of protest. Lips parted, cheeks flushed, he's an offering to me, a reward for doing his bidding.

I killed for him, and now it's time for my feast.

I dive in, snapping my teeth close to his cheek, and while he shivers, his hips go up, as if he wants to be mine as much as I want to make it so.

My sweet companion. My pet. The only one who'll ever know me inside and out.

How I longed for him all this time.

"Two gone, two to go. I'm closer to making you mine for good," I rasp, tasting his cheek while he writhes, tightening his thighs on my hips.

"I never knew this was what I needed."

He arches his chest to me, and I rock against his hard dick to give him a taste of how I will fuck him. I love coming inside him, and while I admire the strength of his character, it's when he's vulnerable with me that I want to claw into him most. I want to overwhelm him, give him more than he thinks is possible, leave him shaking and dripping with my cum as he moans my name.

I nip on his cheek, then his chin, before biting those juicy lips just hard enough to make him moan and stiffen. But there's no fear in his eyes. No, they're like burning coals, hot with the need to be overpowered. Taken. Only I can give him what he wants. I'm the only one he trusts enough to let in. Inside his house, into his life, and into his body.

"You are mine. And I'll spill even more blood for you, until you're satisfied," I whisper, rocking between his thighs, high on lust. "But now, you'll open your legs for me like a good boy."

He gasps and nods as I grin, my balls heavy with need. I reluctantly let go of his wrists to flip him over, face down. As much as I love watching his face twist in pleasure, tonight I want to see his pink hole taking my dick.

I don't even have to ask. Rowan is already opening his own jeans and pushing them all the way down to his knees. There's something so arousing in seeing him offer himself like that. He knows I could overpower him. Hell, I could kill him if I chose to, but he plays with fire anyway, as if he understands that he can't free himself from the chains of his past without it.

I am the fire. The beast he can ally himself with. His protector. I am important to him already, but I will make myself indispensable.

"All yours," he whimpers, spreading his thighs under me, and I love the sense of power it gives me.

As he buries his face against the plastic sheet I spread in the whole room to protect it from blood splatter, all I can think of is me on top of him, buried deep and furiously staking my claim. I don't even want him naked tonight. I want him fast, and hard, and more than once.

"I'll keep you safe, but you know nothing's free, hm?" I rasp, shoving my pants down and plucking a tube of lube out of my pocket, already seeing stars whenever I blink. His ass still bears marks from the last time I fucked him—small bruises where my fingers dug into flesh in a moment of passion. "You're going to take my cock and moan my name when I come inside you."

"Yes, make me feel," he whispers, and arches his back so deliciously I could eat him up. Maybe another time.

I love how eager he is to satisfy me in bed. Or on the floor for that matter. I may dote on him, but between the sheets I want to feel he's mine to do with as I please, so I rock my cock between his ass cheeks as I slide my hand under his T-shirt, all the way to his stiff nipples.

He's so responsive, so wanton, even though I'm the first man to ever have him, but maybe this was simply meant to be? I'm not a big believer in anything—not in gods, and not in fate—but how else could I explain how perfect he is for me?

"Feel what?" I tease and lick up his nape.

"Like you decide if I live or die."

"What if I do?" I ask, grabbing his nape with my teeth hard enough to make him arch with a little hiss. But if the way he cozies his ass up to me is anything to go by, this taste of danger is making him hotter than a furnace, so I push two lubed fingers down his hole, twisting them to make sure I won't hurt him as my other hand grows ever tighter around his neck. I can feel him swallowing beneath it, and there's condensation on the plastic sheet, right next to his mouth.

Rowan answers with a moan, writhing under me as if he wants to fuck himself on my fingers already. He knows what I am yet can't get enough, which is so naughty, so delightful. Because yes, I do decide if he lives or dies, and we both know it. I could crush his throat if I chose to, but he's made himself far too precious to me to even entertain such thoughts. If anything, the way he gives me his body and how he anticipates my needs makes him irreplaceable. He makes me feel seen for who I am and accepted, claws, sharp teeth and all.

"What was that?" I whisper into his ear, pushing him down with my hips so that his dick is trapped against plastic. "You need your hole filled with something thicker?"

"Yes. Please," he moans as I slide my thumb between his plump lips.

His words are like honey, so I lick his skin, from the base of his neck to the hairline and push in as soon as my fingers are out.

Pleasure blinds me for a second, and we both stiffen, not yet locked together, but then his body lets me in, and I moan, resting on top of him so he can feel how easily I could overpower him. But I wouldn't. I want him pliant, willing, drinking every sweet word from my lips.

"Fuck... Your tight little hole feels so good." I squeeze his jaw in pleasure, sensing every wiggle of his hips as he adjusts to my presence inside him. "I might just have to be inside you more often, make you sit on my dick and keep it hard as we watch TV. I bet you'd like that."

He sucks on my thumb when I push it into his mouth. It gives me the idea that maybe he could spend some time on the floor and suck on my cock as I read. My pretty plaything, naked by the fire. Maybe with a plug up his ass so he's all needy by the time I'm ready to fuck him.

I shove all the way in, covering his body with mine. Our legs are tangled in fabric, but I have just enough freedom of movement to rock back before driving into him again. It's almost as if he's restrained, a gift to my innermost needs, and as I paw at him, holding him in place, he doesn't resist, sweet and pliant.

The plastic sheet rustles as I get into a rhythm, taking him the way I like most. There's something visceral about rough quickies without much foreplay, and I love that he's so responsive, so very easy to arouse and get in the mood.

"It's only been just over a week, and your hole is already so well-trained. Just imagine how good this is going to feel in a year," I tease him and bite his ear.

"Oh fuck... oh fuck..." Is all he manages between one thrust and another.

His back arches, meeting my chest, and the muscles inside him are so tight around me, so hot. They squeeze and throb, ready to milk my dick. There's a slight plumpness to his ass that makes slamming against such a pleasure. When I'm inside him, rutting like a madman, my mind blurs, and all I can think of is holding him against me, making sure his legs are spread for me. I live in the moment, focusing only on how his hair feels against my face, how he smells, and on every little moan he makes when I drive into his hole.

Rowan claws at the plastic, clenching it in his hands, but he's not going anywhere.

"Saint!" he cries out. "God. Just like that!"

His ass tightens around me, and I feel his pulse quicken as his body goes rigid. Rubbing his dick against plastic must have been enough to finish him off, because he's coming.

When I still, just to tease him, he rocks back onto my cock, fucking himself on it needily, like a cat in heat. The little shivers going through his body are a thrill, and I lean forward, kissing his cheekbone as I slam into him faster, driven by the insistent urge to plant my seed inside him.

He whimpers, reaches back to grab at me but doesn't protest, his insides hot as lava when my brain switches off.

It feels so good to finish inside him, right here, on the floor, next to a man who hurt him so badly but whom we dispatched as partners. It's a beautiful moment, and as I slide out of him and collapse, the desire to still hold him doesn't let up.

"Come here."

He can't catch his breath long enough to answer, but crawls into my arms with his eyes closed. The way he looks now, with a post-orgasmic flush blooming on his cheeks is for me only. Everyone else gets the polite version of Rowan, but with me, he can be himself.

We found each other after years of being lost, and I nuzzle his face, longing for gentleness, even though I enjoyed the delicious roughness of our sex. I need to know that he wants to be around me, not just lose himself in me. And I want him to know I feel the same about him.

"You're so intense," I whisper.

When he opens his eyes, they overflow with fondness. He seems almost shy, even though I know what a horny boy he really is. I slide my hand to his ass and tease the slippery hole, which so easily responds to my touch now that it's been thoroughly stretched.

Rowan is still catching his breath as he hugs me. "I... I... what a fucking day..." He chokes out a laugh, looking at his bloodstained fingers.

Air is trapped in my throat as I kiss each one, cuddling up to his copper-scented hands. The storm of lust tends to be over fast, but I don't think I've ever enjoyed the aftermath as much as this.

He might be afraid of what we decided to do together but sees the wolf in me and still chooses to embrace it.

"Tired?" I ask.

"Yeah. I was so tense. You fucked it out of me," he says and leans in for a kiss.

Pride bubbles up in me. I gave him what he needs. But as he lies so sweetly in my arms, it's obvious that I don't want to stop at this, so I kiss him. Slowly. Gently. Until he sighs, submitting to me again.

"You might need a warm bath after this."

Rowan glances back at the dead man. "I don't want to leave you with everything."

But I've been doing this on my own for years. I'm just happy he's mine. "My treat. You can help with the next one. I just want you to relax."

He smiles and gives me one more kiss that I end up deepening because I just can't get enough of him.

CHAPTER 20

ROWAN

There's something wrong with me.

I don't know if I was born this way, if it was caused by the attack on my family, or if Saint triggered it in me, but I know what we're doing isn't right. I should be terrified of the killer I'm living with, worried about the murder I took part in, and definitely not aroused enough to have sex next to a dead body.

But when I entered the bathroom, my head was full of pragmatic thoughts rather than regret. I decided to wash my hands before entering the tub, so I don't bathe in Galanis blood soup. And once that was done, I opted for a lovely cherry bath bomb. In hindsight, that might not have been such a great idea, because it tinted the water a reddish pink, which makes me feel like I *am* in fact bathing in Patrick Galanis's blood.

And yet it wasn't enough to put me off. I'm not freaked out after not only witnessing but also actively participating in someone's death, and I think it's sweet Saint offered to deal with the body.

Sweet.

Like he's not a stone-cold killer who held me down so hard I have bruises. But the truth is that before stepping into the bathtub, I studied my body in the large mirror on the wall, and got a thrill from seeing all the marks and love bites.

Is it because he's my first, and he's shaping my experience of sex, or do I like it 'cause I'm messed up?

I'm not innocent enough to not know that there are people who get off on pain and humiliation, but he and I didn't discuss any boundaries, made no contracts, didn't agree on safewords and... well, we didn't even discuss safe sex. He's just taking whatever he wants, and I can't get enough of it.

I shouldn't like it, yet even now, the afterburn of our rough tumble on the plastic sheets, and the memory of him coming inside me makes my balls heat up. I should be angry that he never asked if I wanted to use protection and resent him for the way he spoke to me during the sex, but my own body keeps betraying me.

Can you be a pervert and not know it until someone brings it out in you? I guess my fantasies have always skewed toward dominant men stronger than me, maybe because a part of me believes they could protect me from another attack. But at the end of the day, in my dreams, I'm in charge. Here? I'm in way over my head.

Me, the guy afraid to let someone into his apartment, now living a life of crime.

For a while, I entertain the idea of staying with Saint as his apprentice. Could I possibly be smart enough to evade the police? To cover our tracks? Will I one day no longer flinch when I press a knife to someone's flesh?

I consider myself quite smart, despite never finishing high school. I read a lot, I'm interested in understanding the world around me, so I do have to confront the fact that Saint circled me like a predator and caught me by telling me exactly what I wanted to hear.

I'm pretty sure love-bombing is the term for that. He escalated closeness so fast, and I fell for it, because I'm so desperately lonely I eat up any scraps of attention. The way he spoke to me, all the interest he showed in me, the date, the scarf he gave me, the picnic in the corridor, the cooking, the hugs and kisses... it was all planned. And I fell for it.

I don't know how to deny him anything, or if I even want to, but I need to acknowledge that he hunted me down as if I was one of his victims. He maneuvered me into giving him sex whenever and however he wants, and for all I know, he might just discard me first thing after Christmas, like old wrapping paper, because why keep a liability like me when he can find a fresh replacement?

But as much as this fucks with my head, I know I won't run. For years I've been trapped by the expectation that I'll eventually get better in therapy and move on, trusting in the system that failed me. The price I'm going to pay for the real solution to the trauma I've suffered might be high, but I'm willing to take my chances.

I don't know how long I've been in the tub, but the water's now making me shiver, so I climb out, thankful for the existence of towel heaters. I'm not ready to face Saint and his unnatural seduction, but I'm going to do that anyway, because he is my only chance to take back the control I've been longing for. If that means sacrificing my body and sanity, then so be it.

Saint left me a green and white pajama set with red details around the collar and sleeves. If that's what he wants to see me in, I might as well oblige. It features one of those classic horizontal patterns with Christmas trees and reindeer, and is made of warm flannel. It feels cozy against my skin, even though I'm uneasy about wearing it while Galanis's body cools. Because what is this even? Are we on a murder spree or in a holiday romcom?

Then again, whatever gets the job done, I guess. The job being—killing Otto Grass and Miles Brown.

I feel self-conscious when I walk out. My knee stopped aching in the hot water, but I'm still limping a bit today, and I don't feel particularly attractive in this Christmas outfit. It's on the tight side, and I've no doubt that's on purpose, because he's obsessed with my legs and ass.

I wouldn't call myself ugly, but my looks don't warrant the kind of attention Saint's giving me, and while it's easy to get drunk on all this attention, I know I shouldn't be complacent. He's a murderer, a master manipulator, and probably only gets off on having wrapped me around his little finger to use as a sexual outlet.

I keep all that in mind as I step out of the bathroom, and while I wasn't sure what to expect, it's certainly not the dense scent of vanilla and spices.

A pop Christmas classic flows through the cabin from the playlist he made on YouTube, and as I approach the main room, I hear Saint singing alongside Mariah Carey. My heart beats faster, and it passes through my head that I might just walk in on him cutting Galanis's body into smaller, more convenient pieces. But when I enter, he's by the stove, whipping something on low heat, and the large kitchen island is crowded with several trays of gingerbread men.

How long have I been in the bathtub exactly?

Saint's eyes light up, and he lifts the whisk, showing me he's working with melted chocolate. When is he going to show me his true face? Because this man seems so utterly harmless I have to remind myself of the ease with which he killed a perfect stranger earlier.

We're even wearing matching pajamas, though his aren't nearly as form-fitting.

"I was worried for a moment that you fell asleep in the tub," he tells me as he takes the pot to where all the cookies are. "You did say you were very tired. Not too tired for cookies, I hope?" He could star in a Christmas ad for Macy's with that smile.

I glance at the reindeer head-shaped clock. Two in the morning. Weirdly enough, despite all I've been through today, I'm wide awake.

"No, it's... I mean, I could eat." I'm getting a sense that I'm not just his *sex* toy, but also the boy he can dress up and play house with. "When did you bake all this? Did you deal with Galanis so fast?" I'm wary but doubt the cookies are poisoned, since he takes too much pride in baking to waste them.

Also, why do I have it in my head that he wants me dead, when he's been so good to me? Or am I as deluded as he is to think I can date a killer?

Saint approaches and closes me in his arms, bringing me to his chest. The faint aroma of his favorite cologne is still there, but I rather like the warmth of his natural scent too.

"Oh, the weather sucks right now, so I just packed him up and stashed him in the shed for the time being. I'll dispose of him tomorrow, and now we still have time to decorate some cookies."

I raise my eyebrows but can't help myself and stroke his side. "Shouldn't we be planning the next kill? I feel ready."

Saint huffs and cups my face. "We just killed one of your marks, didn't we? Don't be too greedy."

I roll my eyes and point to the cookies. "I don't get it. This just doesn't feel very important right now. We're killers. Even if I'm just one in the making. Pretending we're having a lovely time decorating cookies is just... weird."

Saint's brows drop low over his eyes, darkening them. "I like baking. Killing is what pays for the flour and eggs."

"Can we at least talk about who we're targeting next as we do this?" I back away, unsure what to make of it all.

Saint lets go of me and glances at the counter filled with several dozen cookies. "We planned this. You know I took out the butter early so it softens. And it's two in the morning. Why do you want to make plans *now*?"

I shrug, approaching the cookies. "I don't know. Why do you want to *bake* at two in the morning? It's as good a time as any. We're already having sex, you don't need to woo me." Okay, maybe I'm *a little* bitter.

"It wasn't two in the morning when I started," Saint says behind me as I glance at the little men, each with a head and four limbs. It suddenly hits me that maybe he sees real people like these cookies—just there for him to play with. And maybe him trying to be so nice is yet another part of the game, the icing to cover the chipped trust. "It's you who disappeared for hours and let me start on my own. We did what *you* wanted, and now it's my turn!"

I shake my head, because it looks like we won't be getting anywhere near planning the next step of my revenge quest tonight. Not when he's throwing a tantrum. And I have no idea why he's so set on this, but I rather not prod the beast when he's already raising his voice.

The cheerful music is in such contrast to the dark waves in my head that I have to ignore it, but when all I get instead is Saint's silence, my stomach drops. I've angered him, and while he isn't lashing out yet, maybe I shouldn't completely ignore the need for self-preservation. Would pretending I enjoy this charade really be such a big price to pay?

"Fine. What do I do?" I ask, standing by the stone counter, the snowstorm outside mirroring how I feel.

"I don't know, decorate the fucking cookies? I prepared everything," he eventually states, gesturing at a collection of colorful icings, sprinkles, buttons, and chocolate.

I huff, because this feels like a strange thing to do at two a.m. after killing a man, but whatever, I can do this if he wants me to. Maybe I'm also annoyed, because as I grab the pen with liquid icing, I have a flashback to doing something like this with my grandma. Who died in horrific circumstances. The music, the smells, the cheery decor rub my face in what I don't have anymore, and never will.

In a bout of frustration, I give the gingerbread man an upside-down horseshoe for a mouth and Xs for eyes. That's how I feel. I grab the small ladle from the pot of chocolate icing and pour it all over his body. This cookie is in mourning for Christmas, not celebrating it.

I can sense Saint's gaze on me from the other side of the counter. His gingerbread man is smiling and wears a sweater with Santa's face, which Saint carefully drew on with a toothpick, as if any of this matters. He can pretend we're a real couple if he wants, but I *know* what this really is, and I can only play along for so long.

So I rip off the next cookie's hands and splash him with red icing, because that feels way more appropriate than acting as if any of this is normal.

Saint's voice penetrates the dense soup of my thoughts. "What are you doing?"

I look up and show him the gingerbread man, then snap off his head before pushing it his way. "This is Ted. Get it?"

Saint's lips thin, and the muscles in his jaw twitch as he stares me down with eyes like two knives. "This isn't funny."

"I mean, I guess we're not cannibals." I say but eat the head anyway. I have to admit it's fucking delicious.

Saint's eyes widen. "Those are for next week!"

I groan and swallow, because what am I supposed to do? Spit it out now? "Why? Who is gonna police when we eat cookies?"

"Fuck you." Saint stares at me, gripping the edge of the counter, and I can almost physically sense the sparks inside him.

I should be afraid. I know he's dangerous, but the anger in me leaves no space for fear, and for once, I'm glad of it, because I'm sick of living in its shadow.

"What did I do now? I'm decorating the damn cookies, in the outfit *you* chose, listening to *your* playlist!" But the mood soured like week-old milk left on the radiator and we both know it.

"That's what we agreed on. I am fulfilling my part of the bargain, so suck it up!" Saint yells, and I freeze, realizing this is the first time he's ever raised his voice in my presence. The song ends, leaving us with a moment of dense silence that's already choking me.

"No! If I can't decorate them how I want to, I don't want to do this at all!" I blow up and throw the decapitated cookie at him in a fit of helpless fury.

He ducks, then takes one of the bowls with sprinkles and tosses it my way. I expect it to break my nose, but it flies above my head, scattering bits of sugary chocolate over me before breaking as it collides with the wall.

"Why are you doing this?" Saint roars, heading my way like a grizzly bear that's had enough teasing.

"What did I do?" I back around the counter, watching his every move. "I was decorating, like you told me to, but no, I have to be as bland about it as you! I wanted to inject my personality into them, but *that's* not good enough. Stay away!" I warn him, grabbing the pot of warm chocolate.

A food fight. This could be funny. Quaint. Adorable.

But I'm not laughing, and he eyes me as though I've ruined Christmas.

"Don't," he mutters, tense like a bow about to release an arrow.

When I swing my arm to get the pot out of his reach, he grabs my wrist, and I splash the chocolate on his face, the stupid pajamas, and the floor.

He either moves unnaturally fast, or I've lost a second, because the next thing I know is the wall against my back and his hand squeezing my throat. He's done this so many times before, but his grip is actually tight this time, as if for once he means it.

My heart starts beating all too fast, but then he sneers and squeezes my neck with more force. This is the real him. He's not my pet wolf. He's feral, maybe even rabid, and he will bite when prodded. I try to gasp in panic, but it's no use, so I grab his wrist and forearm, desperate to wrestle it away. His chocolate-stained face should amuse me, but it kind of looks like blood, and laughter is the last thing on my mind.

He's going to kill me.

He's going to kill me over cookies.

I catch his gaze with a pleading expression as my vision gets blurry. He blinks, scowls, and then tears his hand away, recoiling as I slide down the wall, struggling for breath.

Shock sets in as I freeze, focused on the plush gray slippers on his feet. I can't force myself to look up when he takes a step back, then another, as if needing to create some distance between us.

I shouldn't have teased a professional killer who *owns* me, no matter how upset I was, but my heart somehow hurts more than my neck.

"I'm sorry about the chocolate," I mutter when I'm able to speak.

He's very quiet, and George Michael singing about giving away his heart on Christmas feels like mockery, but I wait, knowing painfully well I might have sealed my fate. Would he still kill the two remaining men on my list after putting me in the ground, or would he leave, wanting to forget me as soon as possible?

"Just... go to sleep," he says in a voice so dull it sounds almost like one of those century-old recordings.

"So... do you want me to sleep naked?" He usually does, and I also enjoy the sensation of our bare skin touching, but I'm not sure what's expected of me now.

"No. I'll clean up and sleep on the sofa tonight."

I swallow, backing into the living room on my hands and knees. I should be glad that I don't need to sleep with him tonight, yet I worry what this means. Will he lose interest in me now that I've spoiled his fun? "Are we still going to look for Miles Brown tomorrow?" I ask in a tiny voice.

He mutters something, and I flinch when another dish breaks, colliding with the floor. "Yes. Sure. Why the hell not?" Saint tells me in a voice sharp as a collection of razors.

"Okay," I mutter and dash down the corridor.

My heart pounds as if it wants to leap out of my chest and find safety elsewhere. I should have just gone with his plan and enjoyed the cookies. But on the other hand, he shouldn't have choked me, regardless of my mood. I shouldn't have yelled at him. But he raised his voice too. I splashed him with the chocolate. But he threw the sprinkles at me. Then again, I started it all by tossing the gingerbread his way.

I'm so mad, so upset, and still a little frightened. But what did I expect getting in bed with a killer?

I crawl under the comforter and put a pillow over my face so he doesn't hear me sob.

Chapter 21

Saint

I DIDN'T GET MUCH sleep, tossing and turning on the sofa until daybreak. I can't say I wasn't tempted to knock on the bedroom door and apologize for losing control, but I was too afraid he might have locked the door to protect himself from me.

I wouldn't blame him.

He knows what I'm capable of, but it scares me that I didn't. For years, I lived on my own, never truly engaging with anyone, never seeking closeness beyond the occasional fuck and conversation. But I thought he and I shared more, and having it thrown in my face hurt so much I lost my mind.

Now, our relationship feels as brittle as the damn gingerbread men. I wanted a perfect evening, and I made a mess of it instead. Usually when a guy pisses me off, I leave, but with Rowan, the stakes feel so high, and I want it to work so badly that I didn't back off.

Maybe he was more stressed after the first kill he witnessed than he let on. I should have taken that into account instead of flying off the handle.

I don't want him to shut down and keep himself from expressing anger just because he's afraid of how I might react. As much as I want my life with him to be this perfect snowball diorama the truth is that we both have darkness in us, and I need to come to terms with that.

I spend the morning lighting the fire, removing piles of fresh snow from the porch, and reading up on how to apologize to one's partner. After all, I've never had one, but every website mentioning a situation like the one last night advises me to call a helpline for perpetrators of domestic violence, or contact my church.

Well, that last one isn't going to work, since the only pastor I know is currently frozen in the shed.

I sizzle in the fire of my own guilt as I trash all the cookies, because now they're tainted, and I don't want to see them anymore. I never thought of myself as a violent person. I kill people, yes, but it doesn't give me pleasure other than satisfaction of a job well-done, and I've always prided myself on being gentlemanly in my everyday life. And yet, I snapped, and it feels as though I don't know myself anymore.

I'm on pins and needles and close my laptop as I hear the door to the bedroom open. When Rowan comes into the living room, he's already dressed in a large knit sweater, his hair brushed so it doesn't point in every direction, like it usually does after he gets out of bed. Did he change his morning ritual so he could avoid me for a few moments longer?

Just thinking about it makes my chest ache, but I've made my bed, and now I'll need to lie in it.

"Morning," he says even though it's almost noon. To be fair, we did stay up late.

I want to touch him so badly, but now I don't know how to do that through the invisible wall that's grown between us overnight. There are so many things I want to tell him, but while I might not have much relationship experience, I'm not naive enough to think apologizing would make it all fine.

He hurt my feelings and fucked with a family tradition that I intended to bring back, but I'm the one who really crossed the line when I started choking him.

Maybe I'm more fucked up than I thought?

Maybe *that* is the true reason why I never connected with any guy, not my profession?

Excuses gather at the back of my throat, but deep down I know he'd see them as empty, and it leaves me so lost that I just make a broad gesture toward the windows and mumble, "We're snowed in."

Life comes back into his eyes as he looks out at the pristine pillows of snow reflecting sunshine. "What? No... We can't go?" The disappointment on his face is so visceral it cuts me.

I'd give him anything, but I physically can't move tons of snow from the forest road. Not without a snow plow.

"I called a service, but we're not a priority," I tell him, bracing myself against the kitchen island. The hot coffee, my second today, steams up my chin. It's hot, and bitter, and right now I hate its very existence.

His shoulders sag, and he presses his ass against the back of the sofa. "I just..." He takes a deep breath and rubs his eyes. "I just wanted it so much, you know?"

I do. Just like I wanted a nice evening in. But maybe I don't deserve nice things.

"Coffee? Food?" I ask, not yet ready to talk about the elephant in the room, and it seems neither is he. Great. If only we could forget what happened and move on.

For the first time this morning he meets my eyes, and I can't miss the fact that his lips are trembling. "I don't know. It feels like this revenge is my only purpose now, and I don't know how I'm supposed to do anything else in the meanwhile. I quit my job, I moved, I don't plan beyond tomorrow, and you're the only stable thing in my life."

I know this wasn't meant to sting, but it does, because he deserves so much better, yet I still want to keep him. "I'm sorry," I mumble, hanging my head. "We should have just stayed in town. It would have been easier."

That would have kept us from enjoying this cozy cabin, but I'm sure that's the last thing *he* would call it after last night.

He shakes his head. "This makes more sense, it's completely secluded. I'm sorry for yesterday too. Everything feels so meaningless when those two fuckers are still out there, alive and unaware of what's coming for them. I don't want you to feel neglected, but I'm not used to living my life this way."

Oh, he's trying. Of course he is. He needs me to go through with his plans. It's tempting to just go with this narrative, but I can't, because I want this to be real, not just a tit for tat. Sighing, I leave the coffee cup and walk around the kitchen island. It pains me to see that he stiffens as I approach.

It's my own damn fault.

"I fucked up. Not with the cookies, that was nice. But I—you know," I finish lamely as I stop next to him. I'm usually so confident and find it easy to be charming. But what's between us isn't superficial, and that makes me more nervous than lying ever did.

Rowan swallows, and it seems that his dark eyes can see parts of me even I don't realize I have. He grabs my hand and my heart speeds up when he leads it to his neck.

He makes me close it around his throat, so soft, gentle, and so easy to break. His eyes are filled with new determination, even if they're bloodshot.

"If you *own* me, take care of me. Don't ruin what's yours."

The world disappears, and all I can see are his beautiful, deep eyes, begging for me to love him. I start nodding, and then he's in my arms, and I cradle him against my chest. "I'm sorry. I just... I'm not used to this. I won't hurt you."

He melts into me, filling me with such relief I can hardly breathe. Rowan's arms snake around me, and he squeezes the back of my sweater in his fists. He's so much stronger than I ever imagined. I might be the killer he needs, but he's the one who has me by the balls, because I'll do anything not to lose him.

"I feel so safe when we're like this," he whispers against my shoulder. "I felt that way from the first time you hugged me. I don't want to lose that."

I kiss the top of his head, overcome with relief that this thing developing between us isn't lost after all. I lead the way to the sofa, because I need him in my lap, tickling my face with his warm breath as we watch the snow outside.

"Me neither. I just want us both to have a good time. To for once not spend Christmas watching TV on my own."

Rowan wraps his arm around my neck, his warm thighs such a comfort on mine already. "I don't see you as someone who struggles to find company."

I swallow, pulling him close until his head rests on my shoulder. He's warm, and smells so nice I find myself rubbing my nose over his temple, reassuring myself that he really is here, longing for my touch. It means so much.

"I don't struggle to find hookups and chat to random people, but I don't want to lie to those closest to me. I don't know how those secret service agents do it, having families."

The warm orange light from the fireplace dances in Rowan's eyes and hair. It's as if he has a halo around his head and *he's* the saint for putting up with my bullshit.

"You never told me what happened to your family. Saint, we... can't get close through cookies alone."

I open my lips. "Meaning?"

"I had a long night thinking about everything, and I think I'm missing something. What happened last night wasn't about the cookies, was it?"

The weight of his warm body is so soothing, but the question could lead us both down a dangerous path. He already knows a big secret of mine, sure, but it's one that still keeps me in control. If I allow him a glimpse of the things I've kept to myself, he'd have the tools to play me. Can I afford that risk?

I take a deep breath, looking at the snow weighing down the trees surrounding the cabin. When a whole pillow of wet snow slides off a spruce, a branch springs right back up, showing off its green needles. Will that be how I'll be when I shed my secrets? Renewed?

Rowan isn't rushing me. He plays with my hair, cuddling up to me even though a bruise peeks out from under his collar. He's not shying away from me despite the danger I clearly pose to him. He's giving me a chance, but I have to pay for my transgression.

Truth will be my penance.

"My mom would always make me bake with her," I say, sinking deeper into the sofa as cookie-scented memories flood my brain, making me high on sugar. "I refused to do it the year she died. I felt it was something good for kids, and as a teenager, I was way too grown up to paint smiling faces on gingerbread men."

Was that part of the reason why I lost my cool so badly? Because his rejection reminded me of the way I'd acted toward her when all she wanted was to have a nice afternoon with the son who was growing up all too fast?

Rowan kisses my temple, and it feels so soothing. I don't deserve it. I'm not a good person.

"And when did you decide to do it again?"

I laugh, but not a single fiber in me feels any joy when I think back to it. "The year after my uncle died. It was dark and cold outside, and I was in a quiet apartment by myself on Christmas Eve. My uncle was the kind of guy who didn't say much, but he was *there*. Without him, there was this giant hole that I needed to fill. And, somehow, when I decided to bake those stupid cookies, it made me feel like my mom might enter the room at any moment, as if she wasn't dead in the ground."

"I'm sorry. You're always cooking, so I didn't know how much that meant to you."

I've never told any guy this much about myself, always preferring to keep up the facade of suave charm, yet being this real with him doesn't make me feel pathetic. He's letting me uncover my pain. I never knew *this* would be the way we connect when I chose him. I thought he'd understand my violence, that he'd accept my job and participate if I played my cards right, but maybe *this* is what I've been missing all along? It scares me that the stakes are this high, but he's right. If he's to understand me, he needs to know more, so I clear my throat and take the plunge.

"My parents were killed early in January, and Christmas was such a big thing in my house. Dad would always put up the most extravagant, embarrassing decorations, and Mom would go all out inside the house. So... this season is bittersweet for me, I guess."

Rowan freezes, watching me with a blank expression. "They were killed?"

Until now, I spoke about my past in vague terms. I told him they weren't there anymore, that they passed away, but it's time to be real. After all, he's confided in me already, and while I'm happy to be his well of sorrows, sometimes the void should speak back.

I shrug. "My uncle had enemies, and they went after his brother and his wife, to scare him, I suppose. I was the one to find them later. It was... I don't remember much of that night, to be honest. But he came for me, and I moved in with him the very next day.

"I told you I was a lookout for him. Well, the first time I did that was when he went to avenge my parents. I was shaken, followed him where I shouldn't, and saw too much. But while I panicked when I saw the bodies he mutilated, I didn't feel sorry for them when my uncle told me it was their fault my parents were dead. And then, a few years later, when someone got *him*, I was the one to chase down the killer. It didn't bring him back, but yeah, it fucking felt good." I clench my teeth, looking into the fire as Rowan's gentle fingers stroke my neck.

"Is that why you decided to take on these revenge jobs?

I nod and kiss his forehead, gradually relaxing, because those questions are an attempt to understand me better. "And I'm careful. I don't get involved with gangs. At the end of the day, I just want to live my life with someone who gets me," I add, meeting Rowan's gaze.

He licks his lips. "I... I used to bake with my grandma. Just for Christmas. I mean, she did the baking, but we decorated as a family. I think I got so upset last night because it felt like scratching at an open wound. But, maybe instead of denying myself all the nice things that remind me of family, I should embrace their memory. Who will carry on the tradition, if not me? And... if you feel the same, could we try again tonight? But you'd have to accept my family's tradition of eating them as soon as we want to." The way he smiles, all shy, makes me squeeze him, and I rub my face into his hair as the peace of the cabin settles on us.

So maybe we'd both have liked to go after our next mark today, but I still have ten days until the deadline, so I might as well enjoy his company and let him know me better. "We can always make another batch."

"Do you want to take advantage of the sunshine first? Do target practice, or even some tracking in the woods? I want to learn, so I'm not useless when you need me."

His excitement brings a smile to my face, and yes, my heart does feel lighter now that I've shared my pain with him. But I want to lift him up too, so I lean in for a chaste kiss and stroke his back.

"You will learn. If you think I was the perfect killing machine from the start, I need to stop you right there. One time, I slipped on blood and got a concussion. My uncle wouldn't speak to me for two days," I say with a chuckle and get up, sliding him off my lap.

He's right. We might as well make the best of this day while it's so nice and sunny.

In the morning, I feared our whole relationship was irrevocably broken, but now he smiles at me, and I vow to myself I will do what he's asked me to. Take care of him. Always.

He laughs, rushing to put on all the layers needed for going outside in this weather.

"Nooo! I don't believe it. You? Failing at something?"

"I think you already know how imperfect I am," I tell him as I wrap a warm scarf around my neck and follow him outside. The sunlight is blinding, but when I take a deep breath of cold air, my heart feels light.

"In being a boyfriend, sure. I just didn't expect to hear about your blunder at work. You seem so... *proficient*." There's a pinch of admiration in that word that makes me feel taller.

"Here's another one, though I do admit that was years ago. I baked a batch of muffins, injected poison in one, then ate it by accident. I wasn't even hungry, it was just mindless eating. I spent an hour making sure I threw up every last bit and then ate a whole blister of activated charcoal."

"Should I worry about what you feed me?" Rowan snort-laughs, staring at me, and I'm realizing that it's nice for him to know the *imperfect* me too.

I shake my head. "You? Never."

He leans down, and just as I think he's about to tie his shoe, Rowan scoops some snow with his gloved hands and sends a snowball my way.

I duck, narrowly avoiding the projectile.

"Not fair!" Rowan complains, but I grin, already forming my own snowball.

"How is it not fair? *All* is fair in love and war."

"You're a professional. Of course you'll always duck on time," he complains, rushing behind a tree.

"It's a good skill to learn. We'll work on your reflexes." I throw a snowball in his direction when he peeks out from behind a branch.

"You missed!" Rowan laughs, but his voice turns into a squeak when the snow cap from a branch above him, which I aimed at and hit, drops on his head and shoulders.

My smile dies when he falls over. Snow crunches under my feet as I run toward him in panic. "Rowan!" I yell and kneel in the snow to check if he's okay.

He turns to me, pulls on my scarf and shoves a handful of snow under my collar.

"Noo!" I cry, trying to get it out.

"All is fair in love and war." He smirks, but this isn't over.

I grab some snow, hold him by the arm, and slide it under the back of his sweater. He squeals, laughing, and this doesn't even feel like a fight anymore. I kiss his wet cheek, then his lips, and as he hugs me, I barely even feel the chill of the melting snow on my back.

CHAPTER 22

ROWAN

"THIS IS... SO WRONG," I utter, choking on my breath as Saint's wet, deliciously hot lips polish the length of my cock.

He's on his knees, with the wolf skull balaclava pulled up to reveal the lower part of his face, and while my instincts warn me the curtain concealing the changing cubicle might be pulled aside at any moment, I can't bring myself to stop him. The slow, deliberate strokes of his tongue make me tremble and whimper, but when I look down, every single thought comes straight from the gutter.

His hands are the perfect size to cup my ass and pull me close, and as he buries his nose in my pubes and utters a grunt of utter delight, I kind of want to rip the mask off him and tighten my hands in his hair. But I won't, because seeing him dressed to, literally, *kill* yet taking a moment to suck cum out of my balls has my brain stewing in its own juices.

Our eyes meet, and I bite my lip to avoid moaning too loudly. He pulls me into these situations with such ease... Then again, maybe it's not just his charm, but me wanting to fall into his traps every time. On the other hand, can his lips be considered a trap when they envelop my dick with such skill?

"Oh, God... Almost there," I whimper, clenching my fingers on his shoulders and grasping his black sweater. He's wearing cashmere even for work.

So smooth. So elegant. And yet, he can be so damn dirty. I love it.

He utters a hum that travels up my prick and resonates in my balls as I cover my mouth, about to blow. And then he's pulling back, cheeks hollowed around my shaft, gloved fingers moving up my thigh all the way to my ass. I come as he teases the tightened cleft between my buttocks, imagining him somehow fucking me while he sucks me.

I try to muffle my moan with my arm, but if someone's outside the cubicle, they would hear us anyway.

I can barely keep my eyes open, but I still look down to watch him swallow my load. It feels so wrong to do so when he has the mask on. It's as if he broke into this changing room while I was dressing just to steal my cum. I might have to ask him to fuck me wearing the mask one day.

My biggest fear is somehow becoming my biggest turn-on when he's the star in it, and maybe that won't cure my trauma, but it's definitely taming it. Some days, I can't believe he only entered my life two weeks ago, because he's already turned it upside down. Maybe I'm just fucked up, but I trust him to keep me safe despite witnessing one of his kills. When he's around, the need to check every lock thrice isn't as pressing, and when I fall asleep, he's the guard dog to ward off any and all nightmares.

And while I sometimes don't feel that I bring enough to the table in exchange, there's no doubt he needs me as much as I need him.

"You want—" I try, catching my breath.

Saint shakes his head, his hand already on his dick as he kisses the inside of my thigh.

We were snowed in for a week, and while it was far from optimal for our revenge hunt, it helped us get to know each other's tics and quirks so much better. I worried I'd get cabin fever after day three of not being able to leave, but with Saint, in the beautifully decorated house, I felt as if someone pressed the fast-forward button on my life.

We painted faces on the target practice boards, he showed me some moves a smaller guy like me could utilize for self-defense, and taught me where to punch or cut for maximum damage. At the same time, he showed me where to cut for minimum damage but maximum pain, which I appreciated. We burned Patrick's body and Ted's head, then discarded the ashes and remaining bone fragments in the nearby river. It took us a whole day, but Saint treated it as an opportunity to teach me about covering one's tracks.

That's not all there is to him though, and at times, I struggle to understand the extreme dichotomy of him being so casual about death and then initiating the most mundane activities, like inventing dishes out of the ingredients we have on hand or looking up Christmas crafts on Pinterest for us to do together. We decorated more cookies than two people could possibly eat, watched movies every evening, and once I even made a sleigh out of a laundry basket and talked Saint into pulling me around the house in reindeer antlers. I wish I took a photo, but I was too busy laughing my ass off and jingling bells.

By the time the snowplow arrived to get us out, I wished our solitude would have lasted a bit longer, but Saint was set on leaving as soon as possible.

It's so strange that I've so far lived with the conviction I would never be able to land a boyfriend, or even have sex, but his confidence, and the odd mixture of danger and gentleness brought me out of my shell. Everything is so easy with him, and while I see myself falling ever deeper into his arms, I don't have the strength to deny myself. It's only been less than a month, and now I'm scared of him losing interest. My plans to use our agreement and then somehow trick him out of the reward have sunk to the depths of the dark ocean, and it's me who desperately longs for our relationship to continue.

I'm falling for him. Not just crushing on a hot neighbor or hooking up with no strings. Everything about Saint feels *right*.

But caring about someone awakens feelings I've long buried, along with my family. Because if you love someone, they become a part of you, and the possibility of losing them is a threat to your very being.

I rub my leather-clad thumb over Saint's soft, wet lips just as he comes, gorgeous even in the mask. The skin around his eyes and mouth is flushed so deliciously I want to get a taste of it, but then he rests his face against my thigh and cleans up with tissues.

"Oh... this is hot. We need to watch out so fucking on jobs doesn't become too much of a tradition," he says with a grin and gets up, closing his pants.

I pull up my jeans without haste. "Sounds like a good tradition to me…" I'm teasing him, but I know what he means. Work won't always offer us so much dead time.

We entered the mall Miles Brown works at before closing time, hid, and now we're stuck in a locked department store, waiting for one of Saint's contacts to let us know that the cameras have been disabled. I wish I was an IT specialist so I could be more useful to Saint, but unfortunately hacking is outside my realm of expertise.

But I'm very eager to become even better at shooting, either as backup or for jobs where sniping someone is enough. Despite my bad knee, I feel confident I can also be a good lookout. I'm not big, not very memorable, and my experience in customer service means I find it easy to pretend I'm nice and normal. I can also become a getaway driver if I polish my skills, and we're already working on learning a system of codes built on one Saint used with his uncle, including special whistles.

Because yes, if he chooses to stay with me, I'm ready to become his apprentice. His partner. His fuckbuddy, and lover, and everything in between. I don't know what kind of person that makes me, but this path doesn't feel… wrong. Sure, it's not hard to want revenge on people who brutally murdered my own family, but as I adjust to all this and learn Saint's every lesson, the thought of giving others the relief he offers me feels good.

Simple murder for hire? That I couldn't do, but if Saint and I only target people who hurt others severely enough to warrant revenge? I can get behind that. I want to be the justice the law never gave me.

It makes me feel powerful after years of lacking control over my own life.

When I follow him out of the changing rooms, watching his toned form from the back, I feel so enamored, a dumb smile emerges on my face. For ease of movement, the sweater he's wearing is form-fitting, and that emphasizes the difference between his wide shoulders and narrow hips. And yet this dangerous, beautiful man, this beast in a balaclava, chose *me* because he saw qualities I didn't know I possessed.

I reach out to stroke his back as he turns to me, and when he realizes I want to touch him, he pulls me into an easy hug. It's dark, and for a moment I think he's smiling at me, but he's just pulled the mask down, and the teeth I'm seeing belong to the skeletal wolf printed at the front of the balaclava.

"Ready for Brown?" Saint asks, and it's not the first time he checks in with me, which is quite sweet.

I nod. "I'm a bit worried. Seeing him will be stressful, but I'm also... looking forward to it? Does that make sense?"

Saint kisses me on the forehead through the fabric. "That's how it should be. The moment you get overly confident and stop worrying, that's when you lose your edge. Trust me, I've seen it," he says. There's a tinge of sadness in his tone, and I know he's referring to his uncle's passing, but while I can't do anything to give him his family back, I can be there for him now, so I wrap my arms around him and rub my face against his chest.

I'm so peaceful that the sudden tremor at his hip startles me, but then he reaches into his pocket and plucks out the phone. The cool glow of the screen reveals his eyes, and I swallow in sudden excitement. He doesn't need to tell me that's our signal to start the hunt. I already know.

"The stage is set," he says and strokes my nape as we walk along the shelves and rails.

There's something magical about elaborate Christmas decorations, especially in winter, when the day comes to an end so early. The bright, colorful lights make long nights more bearable, but now that all the Santa figures, piles of presents, and trees are dark, the department store looks creepy rather than cheerful. Being here without Saint, watched by so many dead eyes, would have been a nightmare, but he's here, and he'd protect me even if the LED Rudolph turns out rabid and charges at me.

As we pass clothes, discounted gift baskets and whole shelves filled with fragrant candles, it strikes me how much my life has changed. I was quite the law-abiding citizen before I met Saint, and now here I am, breaking into a store in the middle of the night, sneaking around with the intention to kill. I don't know what that says about me, but it feels natural. As if I shed my sheep skin to reveal the wolf that was always there. The wolf born in blood, the night I lost everything.

"Ah! Almost forgot, since I've been doing this alone for so long," Saint says, and reaches to one of the shelves.

He presents me with a... ski mask. It's red, with a Santa hat, openings for eyes and mouth, and a white woolen beard.

I take it, squinting at him. "Seriously? You get to look so cool, and I get *this*?"

His eyes narrow, and in the soft glow of the flashlight, I can see the little wrinkles that form around his eyes when he smiles. "You want us to match, since it's the season?" he asks and picks up another one.

I slap it out of his hand, laughing. "No! Don't you dare. Fine. I'll wear the stupid one. But I warn you, you'll be getting a blowjob from Santa on Christmas Day."

Saint chuckles, and the sound of his voice makes me feel things I never felt before. I want to pull up the sexy, dangerous-looking wolf balaclava and push my tongue into his mouth, but this is not the time. We still need to get rid of Brown's body once this is over, and we can always make out while celebrating our success later.

Shaking my head, I secure the Santa balaclava on my head, ignoring the price tag digging into the back of my head, and grab his hand as we make our way through the store, toward the exit. Saint's IT person was also to disable the alarms, but as we get to the glass doors and he scoots down with two small tools, about to open the lock, I strain my eyes, searching for movement.

"If he's not alone, we back out," Saint reminds me. "No random casualties unless your life is at risk."

I nod, even though he's repeating rules we've already agreed on. It's always best to know we're on the same page, and I like that he doesn't want to involve innocent bystanders. It speaks to his character. Makes me trust him more.

"But he *should* be alone, right?" I ask to confirm, as Saint deals with the lock with expertise I should have expected. Apparently, picking locks, starting cars without keys, and escaping out of binds and cuffs were skills his uncle drilled into him early on. Saint has already promised to teach me. Since he's the better fighter, and probably always will be, I'm eager to not only become just as good as him in everything else but hopefully even outmatch him one day.

Up till now, he showed me several ways of getting out of handcuffs, including instructions on dislocating my thumb if I deem it necessary, but I didn't have the stomach to actually go through with it.

He opens the door for me, like a gallant man from yesteryear, and I give him a little bow as I step into the corridor with shops lining walkways with a view of the floor below. There's a railing, of course, but I've hated heights since the night Miles Brown shoved me down the stairs. I survived, somehow, but parts of my mind refuse to heal.

I shiver as the dead silence of the massive building dawns on me. I've been here many times, yet in the dark, with the blueish light coming from the skylights, there's something spooky about this place. The massive sled hanging above like a gray demon about to come alive in reds and greens amps up the creepy atmosphere, even though I know it brings smiles to children's faces during the day.

The soft click of the lock behind me makes me flinch, but that's just Saint making sure we leave as little trace of our presence as possible.

Having his hand in mine is instant reassurance, and as we face the quiet mall, knowing I have this amazing guy at my side while Brown is hiding somewhere, on his own, makes my blood fizz with anticipation. Tonight, the man who's plagued my nightmares for years will be gone, and I won't ever have to fear him again. Tonight, he's the rabbit, and I'm the wolf.

I might not have taken matters into my own hands if it wasn't for Saint's push, but as grateful as I am for his presence, I feel strong enough to stand on my own two feet. This time, I won't flinch and give away my kill.

Unable to resist the urge to move, I let go of him and lead the way to the escalators. They're the only kind of stairs I can handle, so nothing will stand in the way between me and Brown's death. I've spent so much extra time whetting my knife that I can't wait to make Brown feel the sharpness of my rage.

My mouth waters as I approach the stairs and tap the button meant to turn them on, but... nothing happens. I swallow and push the button several times more, getting frantic, because Saint is right behind me, and I can't stand him seeing me fail. How can I possibly be a partner for him if I'm anxious about something as mundane as *stairs*?

But the escalator won't budge. Of course. I've never been here at night, and it just makes sense for the electricity to be cut when there are no customers around. I should have seen this coming.

My heart drops as I stare into the pit of darkness below.

CHAPTER 23

ROWAN

I CAN SEE THE first half of the steps, but they descend into a dark chasm, and as I squeeze the handrail, my head spins so rapidly I lean back, worried I'm going to fall. I might not be as lucky as I was last time.

Saint's hand lands on the small of my back in a reassuring gesture, but I still flinch as if he were about to push me.

I curl my fingers into fists in anger so intense that my eyes sting. "I don't want you to see me like this," I choke out through clenched teeth.

A sigh, and then, in the dark quiet of the mall, Saint places his hands on my shoulders. They're so warm, comforting like the fire in our cabin, and yet all I can feel is shame. He might be here for me, but I feel like a disappointment. What use will he have of me in the long run if I can't overcome my fears?

Am I shivering?

Goddamn it. Yes, I am.

"I'm sorry," he says in a voice so soft I shudder, because I don't want to be coddled. Not anymore.

I rub my eyes, feeling so ridiculous in my Santa ski mask. "I just... It's because of him that I have this irrational fear, and now I can't even get to him!" My breathing quickens as I stare down the stupid fucking stairs, but they're not like the two or three porch steps in our Airbnb. They're steep, made of grooved metal, and go on forever. My imagination shows me all the ways in which they can break me, and I turn away from them, unable to face the void below any longer.

The glow of the moon and the stars coming in through the glass ceiling reveals Saint's eyes. They focus on me, soft and beautiful, and all I want is to lean into his embrace, ask him to do this for me after all, but how can I live on like this, never quite having the guts to reach for the things I want?

"Maybe... Maybe I could carry you downstairs, like before? The security office is in the basement," Saint tells me, squeezing my arm, as if he were worried I might faint and roll all the way down.

I bite my lips not to scream and take a deep breath through my nose. "I appreciate it, but it would only make me feel like even more of a failure." I force my foot forward and put it down on the first step but nausea rises in my throat and I'm right back up. "Fuck."

He's still, watching me as the mall turns into the darkest of caves. This is a test, and I've already failed it. I will *always* fail it.

In my nightmares, Miles Brown always wins, and that's never going to change.

"It's not your fault," Saint finally whispers, stroking my shoulder. I don't know if he's too disgusted to touch me or afraid that I'll break, but both of those options are *horrible*.

"Maybe I could—" go down on all fours? Backwards? Slowly? How humiliating would that be? I'm getting frantic, because he will see how impractical it is to take me anywhere, especially to a job where my issues can be a liability. I sigh, and my shoulders sag. "Falling down was so quick, I barely remember the moment itself, yet whenever my brain forces me to think back to it, it feels like... like I never even landed. Does that make sense? Like I've been falling for years now."

The same warm hands that baked bread for us earlier and which held me back at the store, now cup my face and lift it, so I look at him. I shiver, prepared to see annoyance, but his eyes watch me softly, as if I haven't lost any of his respect.

"I'll catch you."

I swallow the lump in my throat, because I have to harden. I can't cry over every little thing. But his eyes are so intense I know he means it.

To anyone else, he's just Saint, but to me, he is my patron saint. If I were Catholic, I would have chosen him at confirmation, and carried a photo of him in my wallet.

I get to my toes and kiss the fabric covering his lips. "I trust you with my life."

He shivers, then his arms cradle me against him, and we kiss again. There might be a barrier between our lips, but every touch feels so intense I swear this moment is going to be forever ingrained into my memories.

He presses his cheek to mine and sighs, stroking my back so very gently, as if he's not afraid of all the ways in which I could fail him. "Then maybe I could bring him to you?"

I glance down the stairs, calculating. I need to face Brown so badly, and Saint's giving me the chance. "You'd go there alone?" I ask even though he has over a decade of experience doing such things on his own. It's me who's out of his depth.

When he shrugs, spreading his arms, it's the most adorable gesture I've seen him make. "It's just one guy. If that's what you want, just wait for me."

"But if you're in trouble, do the special whistle, okay? I'll come, I don't know how, but I will."

I roll my eyes when he pets my white woolen beard.

"You can count on me, Santa," he says and dashes down the stairs before I can smack him. I can't see his grin, but I somehow know it's there, that his eyes glint even in this darkness. Because of me.

As I watch him descend, then disappear, a predator in the night, I lean against the railing and wait. To think that what led me here, to this moment, was the letter I wrote out of spite. A letter even my therapist didn't want to finish reading, but Saint did. He read it over and over, excited by my uncompromising need for revenge. If I'd known whose hands it would fall in, I would have signed it with three kisses.

I might be struggling with the steep stairs, but my blade is sharp and ready. Miles Brown will feel my wrath, and I will meet his eyes before I kill him. I will show Saint that I'm capable, even if there's still a learning curve ahead of me.

As I wait, I'm struck by the strangest realization.

There might be danger hiding in every shadow, but I'm no longer afraid of hands reaching for my neck or shoving me to my death. Not anymore. And while Saint isn't here to watch my back, I can still sense his presence in every passing second. His pulse is normally so slow when I lie with my ear to his chest, but when it speeds up my man becomes a powerhouse everyone should be wary of. Everyone but me, of course.

Whenever a twinkle of fear appears inside of me, I take slow breaths, tuning into the solid heartbeat I remember so well, and my own pulse matches that of my imaginary Saint. It allows me to think straight, and I look around the dark mall without seeing demons in the Christmas decorations. No one is hiding behind the massive tree in the middle of the corridor, and no knives are about to fall on me from the glittering Styrofoam snowflakes hanging from the ceiling.

I shiver when I remember the way he said "*I'll catch you*". With him at my side anything feels possible.

The sound of footsteps tears me out of my mushy thoughts, and I scoot down, in case the intel wasn't accurate and there's another person here for whatever reason. Still, instead of falling onto the floor and hurting my knee, I duck out of sight, already thinking of excuses that might encourage whoever this is to set me free. After all, we don't hurt innocent bystanders.

The stranger's foot squeaks on the tiles making up the floor, and there's a raspy noise, followed by a thump, but just as I get ready to lie flat, to make myself near-invisible, a familiar whistle reaches my ears, soothing as hot cocoa.

"Saint?" I ask, dragging myself up right in time to see him emerge out of the shadows.

Brown is a skinny guy, so Saint is able to carry him over his shoulder like a sack of potatoes. With a narrow face and a stupid mustache, Brown reminds me of a rat. He mumbles something through a gag, but with arms and legs expertly bound, he's more reminiscent of a sausage than a person.

Saint drops him at my feet without care, and Brown's head hits the floor with a dull thud, since he can't protect himself with his hands.

"Ho, ho, ho, I brought gifts," Saint says and his eyes glow with pride. "Maybe I should be the one with the Santa mask after all."

I look down at Brown with a growing smile. He's trying to crawl away like the maggot he is, but I push him over to his back with a kick. Power buzzes in my bones as I stand over him, knowing that for once I'm the one with an advantage.

"Might just be one of the best presents I ever got. Can I... Is it safe to take the gag out?" It's not just that I want to hear him scream. I hope he begs for his life, like my family did. And I won't give him mercy.

Saint switches on a flashlight and puts it on the floor. It doesn't give us much light, but it's enough for me to see the blood already smeared under Brown's nose. His eyes are bloodshot, and as he squirms, watching me as if I were the terror from his secret nightmares, my stomach twists in a mixture of delight and guilt. A part of me still believes vigilante justice might not be the way to go, but at the end of the day, that is the only justice some people can get.

"Knock yourself out. Just don't let him bite your finger," Saint warns me.

I nod, careful as I pull the gag out of Brown's mouth.

"Who are you? What do you want? I've got no keys to any safes!" he says, his face twisting in pain.

Maybe Saint broke his tooth? I hope he did.

I gesture at my mask, and when Saint nods, I pull it off. The cameras are dead, as Brown will be soon, so there's no one to hide from.

Brown goes silent, and I swear I see blood drain from his face. I can only hope it's because he recognizes me. I'm shocked that I'm not afraid to be in his presence, but then again, I'm the one holding a knife, and he's on the floor. And while I'm still torn about whether I should end him, this is *just*. And I love it.

"You thought you got away with what you did to my family?" I rasp.

"You're a fucking psycho, and you won't get away with this! I did nothing!" Brown yells.

I don't know why he'd say that, but maybe he thinks I brought a hidden camera, and all this is meant to make him incriminate himself. His loss, if he doesn't understand I'm long past trying to get any of them arrested.

"You can tell that to whoever's on the other side." I chuckle, cocking my head. "That actually might be your buddies, Ted and Patrick. Have you kept in touch? I mean, *before* we killed them?"

The raw terror in his eyes is so delicious it feels sweet on my tongue. He didn't have pity for me or my family. Why should I feel sorry for *him*? He doesn't deserve my forgiveness. In fact, he didn't even deserve the years of freedom he's enjoyed while I've suffered in silence. Today, I'll get to balance the scales.

"Otto was right," he rasps in a weak voice. "Something *did* happen to them!"

Behind me, Saint shifts, and before I can say anything more, he joins me above the pitiful bastard on the floor. "You and him still friends?"

Brown grasps on to this like a lifeline, staring at Saint as if he was the good cop here. He has *no* idea...

"Kinda. Not really. We just... keep in touch, just in case. But he said he was 'going underground'. I never wanted to join his gang. I want none of that shit. I kept on the straight and narrow since... *then*."

Saint's voice is soft when he speaks, kneeling next to our mark and nodding. "He's the one we want. After all, you didn't actually kill anyone. You might get away with broken legs if you tell us where Otto is hiding."

Everything inside me balks at that, but I keep my anger in check. I know he's bluffing, since it's the smart thing to do if Otto Grass really disappeared.

"I don't know, man! He wouldn't tell me. Please, I promise I'm not protecting him, he's a fucking nutjob," Brown says quickly.

Saint cocks his head while I burn with helpless anger. If I don't get rid of them all, Otto will try to come after me, because he *will* know what this is all about. I shiver at the thought that he might have found my apartment in town and rummaged through it, but there's no trace of my current location there. The cabin's still safe.

"Okay then, what's his number?" Saint asks.

Brown takes a shivery breath. "He's under GrassMan. Phone's in my pocket, PIN is four-four-eight-nine. Please... I don't want any part in this."

Shouldn't have tagged along to my family home then. Or pushed me down the stairs. Or threatened my father with a broken bottle. Or helped set my house on fire. Memories of that night flood my brain with screams and cries for help, but Saint remains calm, looking out for me, as always.

"Four-four-eight-nine. Thanks, man," he says, pulling the phone out from the bastard's pocket. He types in the four digits, and then swipes the screen several times while I try to swallow the fact that Brown is not dead yet. Each of his breaths is an insult to the world.

"Good, he's here all right," Saint says before pocketing the phone and grabbing the prone body.

I meet Saint's gaze. He knows what I want. Brown might be lanky, but it still takes a bit of effort to pull him back to his feet while he's bound, but eventually Saint helps him up and offers me the tiniest of smiles. Brown's facing us from the very top of those treacherous metal stairs.

Once more, my man and I understand each other without words. It's so thoughtful of him that he would offer me this poetic justice.

He lets go.

I push.

Brown's eyes go wide as he falls, but there's nothing that can save him. His scream fills the silent interior of the mall when he drops, head-first, tumbling down the escalator like a useless piece of meat and bones. Several cracks make me hold my breath as I remember my own broken legs and hip, but I'm filled with a sense of satisfaction.

When Brown hits the floor at the bottom of the stairs, I exhale, and it feels as though I'm fully exhaling for the first time in years. The relief of seeing him tumble into the darkness below is so overwhelming I need to hold onto the handrail, but moments later, Saint puts his arms around me as we face the descent together.

And somehow, it no longer paralyzes me, as if dealing with my personal nightmare weakened my greatest fear.

As I lean into my lover, we both stiffen at the sound of a wheeze coming from below. Saint pulls away, grabs his flashlight, and sets it to a high beam, illuminating the grooved steps and the twisted shape just beyond them. I freeze at the sight of twitching limbs, and the food I ate earlier threatens to come up my throat.

There's something so visceral about seeing a mangled body, yet I know who this man is, and push down my compassion, because Miles Brown has earned every single bruise and broken bone. Still, he's alive, like I was after he tossed me to my death, so this is not the end. Pushing him felt so *right* moments ago, but now he's down there, out of my reach.

Saint will have to do the deed for me. Again.

His hand slides to my hip in silent support, and while I feel utterly pathetic, I know he won't judge me. He wants to help, and I lean into his warmth as he clears his throat.

"Should I bring him back up?"

I take a deep breath. I've just thrown a man down the stairs. If I could do that, then I'm also capable of killing the monster from my nightmares.

I slide my fingers into Saint's, because I don't think I can do this alone, but there's nothing wrong in asking for help. "Walk down with me?" I whisper, unable to find my voice, but the moment he squeezes my hand, I know I can overcome my fear. Anything's possible with him by my side.

People say relying on others is a mistake, but nothing has ever made me feel better than needing him. As he moves down first, pointing the flashlight at the step below my current position, I grab his free hand and descend by those few inches.

The darkness around us might be spinning, but I'm at no risk of falling off this carousel, not as long as he watches over me. With every step, I'm closer to the wheezing at the bottom of the stairs, and it gives me some satisfaction that Brown will suffer a little longer before I get to him. He didn't offer me pity or help. In fact, I still recall him telling his buddies that I was *as good as dead*. That the fire would finish me off anyway. I owe him nothing.

Saint is such comfort to me, and as we move together, I realize that needing his support doesn't mean I'm a failure. This is me going against my fears, and by the time we reach the first floor, I can hardly believe I've done it.

My heart flutters as I look at Saint, squeezing his fingers in my sweaty hand. He's given me so much confidence, and I am no longer afraid of the teeth on his mask.

I'm also no longer afraid of Miles fucking Brown.

"Sorry it took so long," I say, approaching my past tormentor as I pull out the knife. "I've been struggling with stairs since *someone* pushed me down□"

"Fuck you," Brown chokes out, spitting blood. "I wish I'd made sure you were dead. Fucking psycho! Otto's gonna get you."

I smile at those empty threats and pull on Brown's hair to expose his throat.

Saint sucks in air but stands back, supporting me in silence, watching rather than offering his guidance. The glow of the flashlight reveals the extent of Brown's injuries. It's possible he might die from them soon anyway, but my fall had been horrific too, and I'm still here, so I won't be taking any chances.

"And how would he know who to look for?" Saint asks, making Brown smile despite the blood on his lips and glassy eyes.

"We... you're the only one... we did together. Otto's one smart fuck, he will—"

His voice dies when I press my knife to his throat. It's so sharp even that touch cuts through skin, but I look back at Saint, a bit lost. My heart is beating so fast, I want this so much, but it's my first kill, and I don't want to fuck it up.

"Do I... just press, or... pull the blade across?"

Saint kneels next to me, his smile just as encouraging as his touch. "Cutting will do the job more efficiently. It works the same as slicing into a chicken breast."

Brown mumbles in panic, and his weak writhing gives me an immense power trip. Finally, I get to avenge my family and this piece of trash will no longer haunt me.

I reposition the knife, pushing it under Brown's jaw, and Saint puts his hand over mine to gently guide it. It's romantic of him to show me how to do this, in our own fucked up way. But it's me who presses and pulls the blade across, cutting through skin, arteries and tendons.

Hot blood splashes my gloved hand, and I hear a gurgle as my vision blurs. A part of me doesn't want to see life dimming in another person's eyes, but as Saint embraces me from behind, I blink away the haze and stare at my tormentor while his blood soaks into our pants and creates a growing puddle on the floor.

That's it.

I've killed Miles Brown. Right in front of Santa's Grotto.

I should probably question my sanity, but all I feel is relief. There isn't even a shred of guilt in me as I sit back against Saint, inhaling the scent of blood with a growing smile.

"Just the way I dreamed. With him knowing it's me."

Saint's lips stretch into a smile under the mask, and he leans in, kissing my lips. "You did so well. I wasn't sure you were ready, but you've exceeded expectations again."

I pull away only to sit on the first step of the stairs, since it offers a great view of Brown's broken body and his throat wide open in a silent scream.

"I feel so thoroughly... cleansed. Like another weight has just dropped off my shoulders. Even the hate I felt died with him. Nothing will bring back my family, but knowing those three are already dead, that they suffered a fraction of what I have, gives me so much satisfaction."

Saint chuckles. "Unlike the floor. We'll have to be quick with the cleanup," he says, pulling off the backpack with all the supplies we need.

I shake my head, not looking forward to it, so I stall. "I kind of like that Otto's afraid. That he's hiding somewhere. Even if it means finding him will be more difficult."

Saint rubs my back. "You can just sit back for now. I think you need a moment after your first kill. And as for Otto... we will get to him sooner or later," he says, pulling out a plastic sheet.

I smirk, weighing the bloodied knife in my hand. "Aren't you worried? Only three days until Christmas, and we don't know where he is. *Tick-tock.*"

He catches my gaze for the longest moment. "Then it's a good thing Brown's off Santa's list," he says grimly.

CHAPTER 24

SAINT

Tick-tock.
Tick-tock.
Tick-tock.

It echoes in my head over and over, always in the same cheerful tone, and while I'm trying to focus on the task at hand, I'm at a loss where to start, which is ridiculous, since I've been cleaning up after myself for over a decade now. And now I'm struggling with indecision while the sticky red pool spreads farther over the tiles. Do I start with the body? The stairs, which surely bear traces of this fucker's DNA? Should I soak up some of the blood first, to avoid getting it on my clothes?

Tick-tock.
Tick-tock.
Tick-tock.

But none of my worries are about the work.

My cortisol level rises because of the reality behind Rowan's words.

He did an amazing job with Brown. Watching him felt like a pivotal moment. He even walked down the stairs with me despite being so nervous. But then he made the comment about the time remaining until my deadline, and now all I can think of is that he might not be joking.

Just because we've been having a good time for the past week doesn't mean things between us are set in stone. The three days remaining until Christmas seemed like more than enough when I thought I knew where to find Otto Grass. But him hiding somewhere changes everything. Without time pressure, I always get my mark, it's just a question of patience. But now I feel like I'm dealing with a time bomb.

The possibility of Rowan slipping out of my grasp makes me feel so frantic it's cutting my brain into ribbons. Because what if he *is* only focused on taking his revenge and silently hopes that I can't deliver it on time?

This thing between us feels so genuine, and right, and sweet, and it's blurring the hard boundaries I usually uphold. I can't imagine needing to give him up, and if I don't keep my side of our bargain, it will give him a convenient excuse to leave me behind.

A part of me refuses to believe that he doesn't care for me at all, but this wouldn't be the first time I've convinced myself a relationship was something more than it actually was.

Three years ago, I fell for a guy I was hooking up with, took his friendliness as a sign of something more, and abducted him because he claimed to never have the time for his dream vacation. I'm lucky he didn't press charges, because I didn't have the heart to intimidate him once he started freaking out. And I would have needed to.

It's not as though I can ask Rowan if he's pretending to have feelings for me. If he is, he'll just continue lying. What I need to do is make sure we finish his revenge quest, so I can lock him in.

Which doesn't sound great, but if he really does enjoy my company, he won't mind, and if he doesn't… he will in time.

Or I'm just paranoid and losing my mind.

Should I even try to pull him into a cold arrangement if he doesn't actually want me? Only for him to resent me for years to come?

Those are questions for future me.

Rowan stares at Brown's body with a small frown. "What does it even mean that Otto 'went underground'? If you were a guy like him, worried about being hunted, where would you hide? Then again, you're smart and he's not."

Genuine compliment or flattery? I don't know anymore because all I hear is him saying "*tick-tock*" and it's bending my mind into a pretzel.

"We'll just have to get to it right away, because once he finds out this fucker's gone too, he'll be certain there's someone after him," I say and once again stare at the fresh corpse.

Ugh. At least it's not even two in the morning yet. We have time, though I'd rather not deal with dried blood. That stuff can be so hard to remove.

"He won't find out for quite a while. Oh!" Rowan raises his hands. "What if 'underground' means he's living underground *here*?"

I scowl, because I don't have the time to play detective. "That's ridiculous. I'll start with tracking his phone."

"You really mean… now? It's two in the morning. It's not like we can get to him tonight."

"Why not?" I ask, plucking out my phone already. "I have a guy. I could call Grass, pretend I'm someone else for long enough that we get an approximate location for him."

Rowan gets up with a growing frown. "That sounds like a great plan… for tomorrow. Why would we rush like that?"

Maybe because time is *ticking*? Maybe because I need to be sure he's mine, no questions asked? But I can't *say* that without sounding like a nutjob. I have in fact learned my lesson.

"Why do you want to stall?" I ask him, meeting his gaze, and the cartoon reindeer sticker wrapped around the pillar behind his back mocks me with a wide grin, as if it knows something I don't.

"I can think of better things we could do tonight once we're done here." Rowan wiggles his eyebrows, and while his words frustrate me, I can't ignore how pretty he looks right now, dressed all in black, with a smudge of blood on his forehead where he must have pushed his hair out of his eyes.

He's fucking perfect, and I need to have him. If Otto slips through our hands, our relationship will sour even if he stays, and I can't have that.

"Oh really? What kinds of things?" I ask, already browsing through my list of contacts, because I am not sabotaging the thing I *need* with the thing I happen to *want* in the moment.

He comes closer and scoots down to kiss me through the mask. "You know what kind of things…"

Thank fuck my guy is online and happy to take my request (and my money).

Rowan's dark eyes suck me in like twin voids, but I need to focus.

"No, we'll go as soon as we get an address."

I hate the look of disappointment on Rowan's face, but it's for his own good. He gets back up with a groan and spreads his arms. "Fine. I guess I'll just drink five Red Bulls or something. Speaking of drinking, I need to go pee." He points to Brown. "Okay if I leave for a sec?"

It's not an extreme reaction, but now that he planted the seed of doubt in my head, I can't let things rest. I'll only be at peace once Otto Grass is six feet under. Or burnt to cinders. Or dissolved in acid. Whatever's most convenient. "Sure. There's bathrooms down the hall, by the food court."

He doesn't seem pleased when he turns around and starts walking, but we can't always get what we want, and he'll get over it.

I'm about to spread the plastic sheet—again—when my phone buzzes. It's the IT guy calling me back, so I immediately pick up, pacing around Brown's cooling remains while we talk details. My contact wants more money if I want him to work at night, which is new, but we eventually settle on a price, and I end up finishing the call, mildly annoyed that Rowan isn't yet back. Then again, what if the reality of what he's done only hit him now, and he's struggling with guilt, all alone?

My feet move, carrying me to the food court, and his name is on my lips as I jog into the men's restroom, but the stalls are eerily silent.

I open each one for good measure, and I'm pretty sure there's a blood mark on one of the doors, so I grab some toilet paper to wipe it off. Rowan still has a lot to learn—

I freeze, certain I heard *something* outside.

Maybe I just missed him, and instead of coming right back to me, he went to one of the food stands to pick up snacks. After all, we do have a long night ahead of us.

But as I walk out, wary of my surroundings, a darker thought settles in my gut.

What if he... ran away?

Tonight is the first time we've been out of the cabin after getting snowed in, and the first time he's been able to roam freely since I abducted him. I paid much closer attention to his movements when we were tracking Galanis. Did I get too confident about him?

What if he was biding his time, happy to get whatever revenge he could, but not wanting to stick around a professional killer?

Unless, of course, I'm going crazy, and he's just sulking because I was pushy about Otto Grass.

I grab my phone, because in my frantic search, I've forgotten it's in silent mode, so I wouldn't hear a text from Rowan even if he sent one to let me know that he needs a bit more time. I did get a message from my IT guy, which makes me roll my eyes, but I suppose I might as well make the call to Otto now and be done with it.

Soothing myself with an exhale, I type the number into my burner and click *call* as I make my way down the long corridor, but I almost stumble on my own feet when I hear the faint echo of an old-timey telephone ringing somewhere ahead.

"Ro... wan?" I utter, but the ringtone comes to an abrupt end as the noise ahead dies down.

I leap forward with my heart on fire. "Rowan!"

I shouldn't have left him alone.

I shouldn't have fucking left him alone!

CHAPTER 25

ROWAN

IT'S MY NIGHTMARE ALL over again. I'm sixteen and my hands are tied behind my back as I kneel and watch Otto Grass slit my mother's throat.

Only this time, the restraints are steel, not rope, and, and if I don't manage to do anything about my situation, Saint might join my family in the afterlife. Because he'll come looking for me, and this is a trap.

When Otto and his buddy snatched me from the mall, I was as easy to overpower as a baby. I got one punch in, and a kick, but that was that. Moments later, I was tied, gagged, and being dragged toward a dirty van.

Did they watch us kill Brown at a distance, yet did nothing, as if he were expendable? How else could they have accosted me so easily?

A shudder goes through my overheating body as Otto paces around the room, casting a shadow on a wallpaper with a geometric pattern. It's eerily clean here, and I even spot some of those wooden words that were popular decor a few years back. One says *Love*, the other—*Family*, and as my initial panic is replaced by a numb sense of anticipation, I wonder where the person who takes care of this house is, because it's certainly neither of the thugs who imprisoned me here.

Otto is flanked by two dangerous-looking guys. One is bald and has a moth tattooed over the left side of his face, while the other is a brute with a massive orange-red beard. They must be accustomed to kidnappings, because they don't seem fazed by the fact that I'm cuffed to a chair.

Mothman is sitting on a salmon pink sofa, focused solely on his phone. He's already commented to Otto that women who reject him on Tinder because of his face tattoo are "*shallow.*" I imagine the ink is the least of his problems when it comes to dating. Beardy just took off his leather jacket and is now spraying something on his elbow.

Otto frowns at him. "What is that shit?"

Beardy shrugs. "Heat spray. What? I've got joint pain."

Otto waves him off, annoyed. His face is flushed all the way to his ears. Or it's just rosacea. Hard to say. What's more important is that I know of at least two guns in this room. Otto has one, and before taking care of his elbow, Beardy cleaned the other weapon and stashed it into a holster under his top. Mine got taken off me and left with the two guys downstairs. If Saint's coming here alone, he'll be at a disadvantage and may get hurt—a truth that keeps rumbling in my head like pre-shocks before an earthquake.

And yet, I hope he does come for me. Maybe I'm a coward who simply wants to be saved, but if he steps in here, guns blazing, it will mean I'm worth something to him. I know he enjoys my company, and the sex we have, but none of that would be worth the risk of dying if there wasn't something more to our relationship. Something I don't dare name, worried I might like the truth too much.

I hope he comes for me.

My Saint.

I stiffen as heavy footsteps echo on the stairs, but when the door swings open, I see that it's one of Otto's buddies, a brunet with the plainest and most forgettable face I've ever seen.

I'll need to wait a bit longer.

"Tamara called and said there's goulash in the freezer. You guys hungry? Me and Pete want some anyway."

Otto dismisses the guy with a wave. "Last time I had her goulash, I spent the evening shitting myself to death. I'm good."

Once the man disappears, Otto's cool blue eyes settle on me, and I hate every second of it. Just being in his presence makes all the hair on my body bristle.

"So. Little asshole, all grown up, thinks he can take me on?" he asks, shaking his head. "I don't know how a weakling like you got to my old buddies, but what I'm sure of is that you're not working alone."

He looks different. Just as horrible as he used to but different, as if he's aged twenty years, not four. Patches of dry skin cover his face. He has premature wrinkles, and the stubble that's almost becoming a beard at this point makes him look unkempt.

He's wearing a denim jacket, and a purple T-shirt with puffy, balloon-like letters that read *Dream Big* printed at the front, but there's also a gun tucked into the back of his jeans, and his eyes keep wandering.

Is *this* his idea of a big dream? Me, cuffed to a chair in his friend's home?

"He wasn't alone," Mothman says, absent-mindedly swiping his screen. "I saw another guy."

Otto pulls out my gag, but I don't scream. I don't think there would be a point to it. "Some people, like you, are meant to be losers. Prey. And people like me, natural predators, will hunt you if we choose to. You stepped out of line, and you *will* regret that."

The smack to my face comes out of nowhere, and it's so harsh it makes my head ring. I let out a yelp that makes Beardy glance our way, but he's not going to intervene, too busy polishing his gun again.

I look up at Otto with a scowl. *He* thinks he's at the top of the food chain? How pathetic. He might be a vulture at best. Now Saint... that's the real deal, and Otto is right to be afraid. Just knowing that I have Saint on my side relieves some of my terror, because he *will* come. I know it.

Otto exhales and cracks his neck, never taking his eyes off me. "You were lucky to come out of that fire alive. You should be grateful we didn't finish the job. How fucking stupid are you, huh?" he asks but slaps me again before I can answer. This time, I taste blood, but it's far from the worst thing that's happened to me.

This time, I have an ally, and Otto won't kill me until he's certain no one else is coming after him.

"With that fucked-up leg of yours, you couldn't have been the one who killed the others. Who's the guy helping you?" he asks.

My brain still rattles a little, but I'm shocked that I'm not hyperventilating and about to faint. I've changed. It was so gradual I didn't notice it, but now I have the confidence to look into Otto Grass's eyes without seeing him kill my mother. The memory is still there, like a shard of glass stuck so deep I won't ever be able to remove it from my flesh, but being with Saint and becoming my own champion of justice changed me. I'm no longer the scared boy I was.

"I hired a hitman," I say plainly and give him a menacing grin despite the blood on my tongue. I don't want Otto to think my connection to Saint is personal, so he can't use it as leverage.

Mothman raises his head in attention. "You? Hired a hitman?"

"Yes, I did. So if you kill me, he will still come for you."

Otto lets out a raspy laugh. "Hired him with what? The peanuts Chuck was paying you?"

I freeze as my confidence dwindles at the memory of Otto coming to the shop and taunting me by staring from the other side of the interior, as if he reveled in my distress. But Saint is coming, and I need to make sure he's as safe as he can be.

"Lottery win. I told no one," I whisper and hang my head, staring at Otto's dirty boots.

"You should have kept it. Left the state, or even the country. But no, you had to be a dumb fuck. The thing with killers for hire, which you wouldn't know, since you're painfully unaware of how the world works, is that they are in it for the money only. They have no loyalty, and no remorse. At best, one more thing they care about is their reputation. All I need to do is call him and offer a better deal."

He doesn't know Saint, but I won't volunteer any information he could use. Saint might be able to track Otto's phone if he's stupid enough to make the call.

I look up with pleading eyes. "No... Please... Maybe I made a mistake." I don't believe for a second my begging could change Otto's plans for me. In fact, I hope he'll call Saint, just to hurt me. But that is the goal. I need him to believe that Saint doesn't care whether I live or die.

"Why are we even keeping this clown alive? He'll be wasting Shawn's water," Mothman says before chuckling to himself as he starts typing on his phone. I bet he's popular with the ladies. Not.

"Ever heard of keeping a hostage?" Otto snarls, but my heart leaps when he pulls out his battered cell. "You can even use them as human shields, if necessary."

Mothman rolls his eyes. "Yeah, like that ever happens in real life."

Otto growls. "Who's your fucking boss, huh?"

"You are," Mothman grumbles.

Otto holds the phone between his head and shoulder as he approaches a dirty coffee table in front of the sofa. The room is oppressive in its normalcy. I had a sack over my head on the way here, so I don't know where we are, but there are lights outside so it might as well be some suburb. To think that less than a month ago, I was afraid to even enter someone's house with them. I guess such fears become irrelevant when one's life is on the line.

"Let's cut to the chase," Otto says into the phone and carefully scatters white powder from a Ziploc bag he pulled out of his pocket. "I've got your client, and I don't appreciate being hunted."

The other two men both look up, listening to the un-intelligible whisper coming from the phone. I can't hear the words either, but I would have recognized Saint's speech pattern anywhere. I choke up and my eyes sting, suddenly on the verge of tears when I think back to the way he held me as we made our way down the stairs, to finish Brown. Maybe it's selfish of me that I want him to risk it all for me, but I don't want to die yet. I want to see where life can take us, if I can hone my skills and be his lookout, maybe even partner.

I want to *see* him come to my aid.

Otto snorts and uses his driving license to form two lines out of the powder. "I get it. I'm a bit of a businessman myself," he says, waving his hand at Beardy, who snickers, shaking his head. "But I'm sure we can come to an agreement."

I close my eyes and focus on Saint's voice, but I can barely work out anything more than *"alive"* and *"money"*.

"Yeah, yeah," Otto says. "I'll text you the address, and a hair won't fall off his head until the money is in your hands."

Soon after, the connection ends. I look up in time to see Otto snort a long line of coke... or whatever that is.

Beardy raises his brows. "You're really gonna—"

"Of course not!" Otto sucks in air and sneezes. "Fucker's as good as dead when he comes here. And you..." He faces me and pulls out his gun.

I stiffen, because maybe I've overestimated Otto. Maybe he's not reasonable enough to keep me alive as insurance for the time being. After all, he's getting drugged up to his eyeballs instead of staying sharp.

Or maybe he just thinks Saint is the kind of guy he is—a sociopath with no morals, who cares only about cash. That's why he murdered my mother for nothing. That's why he might kill me before Saint even arrives.

My breath quickens when he presses the barrel of the gun to my forehead. "*You* will learn what a bad idea it is for dumbass maggots like you to hire killers. You really thought you could get *me*? I'm Otto fucking Grass! I deal with people like you before breakfast."

"You don't have breakfasts," Beardy says, and Otto steps back with a roar. At least his gun no longer digs in my flesh so I can catch my breath.

"Why are you like this! It's a figure of fucking speech! You ever heard of them?" Otto asks and approaches the coffee table to inhale the second line.

"No one needs that many words when you have guns," Beardy replies, not at all offended.

Mothman shakes his head, but his eyes remain on the small screen in front of him. "I should say that to the girl I'm talking to. She just goes on and on and on…"

"So, is he coming?" Beardy asks.

"Oh yeah. And he's getting a bullet in the head, not a suitcase filled with money. Even your hitman is a halfwit," Otto tells me, knocking on the side of his skull.

I swallow, staring at him. "I mean… I just got him off the dark web," I say because the less those fuckers know about Saint the better. Let them think he's some random dude who finds killing easy, so they're not prepared for the storm coming their way.

I'm scared, but as I imagine Saint stepping in here and sending each of those fuckers into the embrace of death within the first three seconds, I have to keep my joy hidden, even though it's tugging at the corners of my mouth.

But I need to be ready to help him in any way possible, even if just by removing myself from the line of fire. I tug on the cuffs, but my hands, while slim, won't go through, unless␣ Nausea rises in my throat when I think back to Saint's lesson about dislocating one's thumb, but I can always just tip over my chair.

All I have to do is stay sharp, ready, and focused.

Otto laughs, and the other goons chuckle as well. "Heard that, boys? This dumbass thinks he's hard. Got a hitman on the 'dark web'. This is just so precious. I guess if you're just like us, I might as well share."

I frown, not sure if he means Tamara's goulash, but then I realize he's approaching me with the little Ziplock bag filled with drugs.

"No... no need," I utter, trying to stay cool, but my voice comes out as a squeak, prompting all three men to laugh again. Because of course it's the funniest fucking thing on the planet.

"Oh no no no, you're our guest. It's only fitting that you get some of the best stuff," Otto tells me with a wicked grin. He's enjoying this, and as he drops the baggie after sprinkling some of the powder on his fingers, I'm tempted to tell him I did not expect him to be so eager to touch my lips. But that might have gone down badly.

I don't even fight him when he grabs me by the jaw, because what chance do I have? If I bite him, he'll just hit me until I comply.

To my terror, he's not making me snort it. I hoped for that. Then I could have sneezed out some of it. No, he pushes two of his fat fingers under my lip and rubs the powder in without mercy, all over my gums.

I gag, but that won't help.

I'm fucked.

The bitter taste makes me drool, and I spit some of it out, but Otto doubles over with laughter, and the slap I've been expecting doesn't come. Neither does the instant high. Maybe it's not really a drug but some counterfeit powder? How am I supposed to know when I've never taken any drugs?

"Oh, my God, you looked like a dog that licked shit instead of peanut butter," Otto roars, sliding onto the sofa as fits of giggles shake his body.

Minutes pass, but as I wait, listening for signs of Saint's presence, my pulse quickens, triggering a euphoric sensation. Oh no... Maybe it *was* cocaine after all because it's hitting me, and I don't think I like it.

It feels as if the synapses in my brain are snapping, and the world around me becomes unnaturally sharp in some places, while remaining blurry in others. Otto's laughter is booming in my ears, but the sofa he's sitting on along with Mothman becomes a blur.

I have a vague idea that coke sharpens the mind and gives you energy, but while I feel like doing jumping jacks, I'm also woozy as if I am about to float up to the ceiling, like a balloon filled with helium.

The smell of Beardy's heat spray reaches my nose with new intensity, and the moth tattoo flutters its wings, about to fly off Mothman's face. And then there's Otto, whose eyes bulge out of their sockets. He's simultaneously far from me, and all too close, which makes me want to throw up again. I don't know what kind of unholy mix of drugs Otto's rubbed into my gums, but I fucking hate the sensations it's producing.

I'm stuck rolling my head from side to side, uselessly trying to get rid of it, but there's nothing I can do.

Time passes differently now, and while I struggle to stay still while my mind races, leaping between the pain of my past and the fear of my life possibly coming to an end tonight, I don't lose hope. Maybe that's what ultimately drove me to crawl out of that burning building and how I survived years on my own? I somehow always believed there was a light at the end of the tunnel. Tonight, that light has a name and a face, and I focus on them, imagining Saint's arms around me, his soft voice promising me this horror will be over soon.

I believe him.

I believe him so completely that I'm not even surprised by the shrill yet melodic whistle tearing through the air. He taught me the exact sound so I always know he's coming.

He's here.

He came for me.

"What was that?" Otto asks, putting down his beer, and Beardy dashes to the window. He leans against the wall next to it and peeps through the glass, as if he thinks he's a character in an action movie, but after a moment, he just spreads his arms. "I don't see anyone."

I don't mean to laugh, but the chuckle still comes out of my lips. It seems the drugs fucked up my impulse control.

Oh well.

Otto looks back at me. "The fuck are you so happy about?"

I don't even hold back my laughter anymore. "He's here. My boyfriend is *here*, and you gave him the address. And now you're all dead. You just don't know it yet."

"Shut the fuck up!" Otto steps up to me and smacks me in the face so hard blood fills my mouth, but I can't stop cackling even as it dribbles down my chin.

"You're so fucking dumb! He's gonna rip you into shreds and make ornaments out of your intestines."

I don't even know where those fantasies are coming from, but the moment I release them into the air, satisfaction blooms in my chest. Yes. That is exactly what I want. Their fucking bones and intestines decorating our mantelpiece at Christmas, gift stockings made out of their skin.

I'm sorry, Tamara, but your man chose the wrong crowd.

Even Mothman is alarmed enough to leave his phone and get up, heading for the entrance.

"What the fuck are you saying?" Otto roars and grabs me, shoving the muzzle of his gun at my cheek. I hear a click as he pulls off the safety, but for once I'm not afraid.

I slam the side of my hand against the chair, now glad that he made me high, and slip my hand out of the cuff. I'm sure it hurts, but I can barely feel anything as blood rushes to my head. All I know is that I can't be Otto's hostage. I need to clear the way for Saint.

When the door swings open with a thud, Otto's gun leaves my face, and that's the moment I've been waiting for. He's standing close enough for me to kick him in the balls.

Time slows as I twist my body along with the chair and knee the bastard's crotch. I spin and fall to the floor, but the bullet meant for my man hits the ceiling, making plaster rain down on us as Saint steps in, his handsome face sprayed red already.

I bet the two men downstairs are dead. He's not even covering his face, because those bastards aren't getting out of here alive. The shitty yellow lightbulb makes his eyes shine like liquid gold, and there's bloodlust in the way he curls his lip.

He might be a hitman, but he didn't come here for business. This is personal.

CHAPTER 26

SAINT

DON'T GET TOO SURE *of your skills. You might be a better shot and fighter than anyone else in the room, but you might still get unlucky. Minimize the risk.*

My uncle taught me many things. How to be a man. How to take care of myself. How not to die on the job. He did die at work, of course, but that's because he broke his own rules. And while this is personal for me, I'm being careful. Deliberate.

I didn't care if the thugs I killed downstairs knew who I was or why I wanted them dead. They signed their own death warrant when they took my Rowan. And using the recording of my whistle as a ringtone on a burner placed in front of the house is a tactic that's a personal favorite of mine.

I'm not a knight in shining armor. I don't play fair. I only aim to be efficient and go back to my own home once everything's over.

One of the bastards who took Rowan stands by the window, checking out the whistle, and I shoot the back of his head without hesitation. Brains and blood spray the glass around the web of cracks left by the bullet, and then his hulking body collapses to the floor, leaving me to face Otto one-on-one.

I step forward, taking in the scene in a split second. A coffee table, a sofa, Rowan on the floor. His face is sprayed with blood, but he's very much alive, and that's what matters.

I'm about to shoot Otto, no questions asked, when a massive arm swings at me from behind the door.

Fuck. A third guy, who I didn't see during my brief survey of the house.

He's trying to grab me by the neck, so instead of fighting it, I twist myself his way, and smack his elbow hard. He loosens his grip. But in the corner of my eye, I spot Otto aiming at me.

I dread what might happen to Rowan if he remains so close to the bastard who took him, but the smart boy is crawling behind the sofa.

The guy who lunged at me throws his head back, about to headbutt me, but I manage to twist us around in a deadly tango. Otto shoots, and I hug my enemy so he can become my shield.

His broad form trembles in pain, and I feel him weaken, but he can still be of use.

There's something so strange in moments like this one. I've heard a travel vlogger say that moving to strange places, or making big changes to one's life makes every day and night seem longer, richer. For me, it's danger that does it. No other second lasts as long as one spent with a pistol aimed at my head. It almost feels as though I have all the time in the world to improvise.

I toss Brown's cell phone at Otto, and as he ducks in an attempt to protect his head, I charge at him, pushing the injured goon in front of me, as if I were driving a bulldozer.

Otto tries to shoot at me again, but he's too slow, too surprised. When his dead buddy lands on him, he loses his balance and pulls the trigger a second too late. By that time, his arm is already in motion and the bullet goes through the ceiling instead of my head. Plaster falls on us like snow, forcing me to squint so it doesn't get in my eyes.

I open them in time to spot Otto aiming at my face again. I act on pure instinct. My head whips to the side, and I grab his hand even though he's already firing. My ears ring from the booming noise, but I can worry about my poor eardrums later.

We wrestle awkwardly, with the warm body between us.

"You're not getting me!" Otto yells, but he's lost his breath for nothing. As he tries to roll from under his buddy, I punch his hand, and the impact makes him let go of the gun, which flies out through the broken window.

Well, fuck.

I'll have to kill him with my bare hands then, but the now-dead goon comes in handy, since he and I weigh more than enough to keep Otto still. He's desperately pawing at the floor as I punch his ugly fucking face and close my hand on his throat before pulling myself up so I can use the other to—

A sharp, hot cloud kills my vision as he sprays something from a can, and my eyes burn as if he just poked them out. I twitch away from the fiery mist, wary of breathing it in.

I can't see, since every time I attempt to open my swollen eyes, the pain is unbearable, but I refuse to die and take a blind swing at Otto. He smacks the can into the side of my head and shoves me off. I fall over to my knees, disoriented and breathless from the burn in my throat, but as I attempt to get up, a brutal kick in the side rolls me over.

My heart stops when I hear the click of a gun's safety being taken off. So this is how I die. At least in my final moments, I attempted something good, and maybe Rowan will still be able to get away somehow. Desperate to give him that chance, I snarl at Otto, ready to lunge at him, but Rowan's voice comes loud and clear from behind the acid fog in my stinging eyes.

"Get the fuck off him!"

That click. Was it... Rowan's gun? One of the other goons might have dropped a weapon.

Otto snarls. "You don't have the balls—"

The deafening bang of a gunshot makes me drop low to the floor and cover my head. Otto lets out a choked cry, and then the wooden floor creaks under someone's weight before he stampedes down the stairs. In the distance, I can almost hear a siren, but for all I know it might be a hallucination caused by whatever's making my eyes burn and my windpipe swell.

"Rowan?" I utter, attempting to get up and open my eyes, but it's no use. They hurt way too much.

"Fuck! I barely grazed him," Rowan says. "He ran away—Saint. You came. Are you okay?"

When I squint, I can just about see a blurry shape in front of me. With my vision gone, sounds seem more prominent. There's a rattle of cuffs, and yes, definitely a police siren.

"The cops are coming. We need to go," I mutter, reaching out toward the voice. Now that Otto has fled, pain radiates all over my body, but the warm touch of Rowan's hand is so soothing I lean in until my face presses to his stomach.

"I'll guide you. Let's go," he says, and while I need to wash my eyes, his sweet kiss to my temple is the next best thing I could have hoped for. He's alive, whole. We can deal with Otto later.

"I'm sorry I left you in the mall," I say as he helps me up, because it feels important.

Rowan strokes my back. "I went off on my own. It's not your fault."

"Should have gone with you. I was stubborn," I whisper, holding on to him as tears roll down from my aching eyes. But we can't stay so I need to suck it up. There is no way. "I parked the car in that narrow alley to the right, close to a big tree. We need to disappear."

I almost stumble when the front of my foot presses to something soft—a body?—but Rowan steadies me and leads the way. My arm rubs against the doorframe as we step into the hallway, but the insistent wail of the siren prompts me to breathe faster, and I reach out with one hand, seeking the railing by the stairs.

And then it hits me that I should be the one leading the way down, just like I had at the mall. But I can barely see anything even when I manage to force my eyes open. I'm ready to come up with a plan, but he speaks first. When he wraps his arm around me, I can feel the empty cuff dangling from his wrist against my chest. Even now, when I have so much adrenaline running through my veins, I love the sound of his breath.

"Be careful."

"I'm sorry," I whisper but stall when I feel him taking the first step down before me and immediately follow his lead, holding onto the railing with my free hand. My head is spinning, and everything hurts, but he is so steady next to me that I speed up.

I'm so proud of him. Not only is he facing his fear for my sake, but kept his cool with Otto, and shot at him to save me.

His breathing becomes trembly, but the sound of sirens in the distance is a constant buzz, so we can't stop. I can only hope my presence helps him down these stairs as much as his is helping me.

"Nothing to be sorry for. You came through," Rowan whispers.

"Are you hurt?" I ask as I take another step only to discover that we've reached the bottom and are now free to go.

He speeds up, pulling me toward a cold draft, and then we're outside, stepping over the grit scattered in front of the house. The icy air makes my face burn less, but we're not out of the woods yet, and the siren is getting ever closer, like a hornet that needs to be kept out of the house by shutting the windows.

"I'm... good enough. Otto got a few punches in me." He gently pulls on my elbow. "Now we turn."

"Are there... people watching us?" I whisper, unsettled that I'm no longer in control, that if we got attacked now, I wouldn't be able to do anything to help Rowan. We need to get away, regroup, and then go after Otto, but for that, I'll need working eyes. I shiver when at least two vehicles rapidly brake not that far behind us. There's shouting, but I'm focused on getting away, on not being noticed.

"No, we're almost by the car..." Rowan says, but his voice drifts off.

Something's wrong.

"What is it?" I urge him, stiffening. Is one of the cops approaching us on foot? I can only hear some commotion down the street, but who the fuck knows?

"Otto is being arrested," Rowan mutters, guiding my hand to the car door.

A weight settles on my heart, heavier than the dead guy was when I tried to use him to my advantage. Rowan's voice tells me that he understands what this means too.

Otto will be out of my grasp. He could spend *days* in jail, and we don't have that long until Christmas. Unless he's released on bail, which is unlikely, I will have no way to reach him before the deadline.

I sit in the car, feeling like a trapped panther with its claws cut at the knuckle.

I have failed.

CHAPTER 27

ROWAN

IT'S A RELIEF TO be back home. Many bad memories are tied to the apartment I've lived in for the past two years, but it has running water for us to wash away all the blood, and for Saint to deal with his eyes.

We both needed a change of clothes, but that can't change the fact that neither of us got any shut-eye. My head throbs now that the cocaine has left me with its own kind of hangover, so I make us coffee and approach Saint, who sits on the sofa with bloodshot, puffy eyes.

I've got my own set of bruises, which he kissed ever so gently after I washed off all the blood, but he hasn't been very expressive since our lucky escape. I don't want to prod at him since we're both so tired, but soon enough, we will need to talk about our next steps.

"How are your eyes?" I ask, handing him the mug.

He shrugs and takes a generous sip. "Dry, but I'll be fine. I just... it's disappointing that I let him escape."

I shake my head. "It's *disappointing* that he dodged my bullet. And you dealt with the other guys. If I manage to learn a quarter of your skills, I'll be golden."

Saint downs his coffee so fast I worry about him scalding his throat, but he gets up with a determined look as soon as he's done. "We can't leave that thread hanging. Are you ready?"

"I... what? Ready for...?"

"We need to go watch the police station in case a Christmas miracle happens and he gets out."

I'm not even halfway through my coffee, but Saint is already putting on his coat, so I don't want to stall. "Is it really such a good idea?" I ask, even though I'm getting my boots.

"We don't really have a choice. He could leave, go underground, and remain a threat. We can't have that," Saint tells me, stepping into his boots.

But I notice that he even pulls on his shoelaces with the force of someone trying to use them as an impromptu garrote.

If this is the first job in a while that he considers a failure, I don't want to ask unnecessary questions to avoid stressing him out further. I might think going to sit in a car outside a police station at dawn is ridiculous, but he's the one with years of experience.

We get ready within minutes and my coffee is probably still warm by the time we're out.

I'm locking the door when something creaks behind me. But when I turn my head, ready for another fight, relief floods my body. It's just Mrs. Treville.

"My goodness, you're up so early?" she asks, stepping out of her apartment in a puffy coat.

Saint takes off his woolen hat. "Yes, we planned to walk in the woods first thing in the morning."

She chuckles. "See, I also like to move first thing even before the sun is up. Keeps the blood pumping. It's nice to see you two... get along so well." She gives me a meaningful smirk that transports me back to a more innocent time when I wasn't killing people.

I stroke Saint's arm. "It's been a crazy time."

Mrs. Treville glances at us as she locks her door. "I haven't seen much of you. Have you been away?"

Saint speaks before I can come up with a sensible excuse. His smile doesn't give away even a hint of how he really feels about tonight. "Oh, we've been around. Just so busy being cooped up with each other. Are you sure we didn't chat last week? About the cake Rowan got us? I could swear we did."

Mrs. Treville stalls. "We might have..."

We chat for a bit more, and even take the elevator together before wishing Mrs. Treville a Merry Christmas, in case we don't see her until the twenty-fifth.

As soon as we're in the car though, Saint's face falls.

"People can be very suggestible. It's good to have an alibi, in case we need it," he explains without me needing to ask.

I nod. "Right. An older person might think they just forgot when they last saw you."

"Works the same with young people. Memory can be funny like that. It's surprisingly easy to implant false memories in another person when they don't expect it. People like to be in the center of events," he says, driving onto the empty street. The town is quiet this early in the day, and while we have stumbled upon our neighbor and seen one delivery truck in front of a grocery store, we reach the police station without seeing another soul.

Built out of red brick, the single-storey building looks more like a doctor's office, but it's a small town, with few cops. The dead bodies at the house where I've been taken? Miles Brown's corpse at the mall? I doubt this department ever dealt with a night like this one.

I hope to doze off in the car, because I don't expect they'll be letting Otto go anywhere. I'm fatigued, and while my headache has gotten a bit better, in an ideal world, I'd be curled up against Saint under a warm comforter.

Saint, on the other hand, looks as awake as Otto was after snorting his two lines. His lips are in a tight line, and he grips the steering wheel so hard his knuckles turned white.

"Fuck. I left Brown's phone at that house. That'll tie Otto to the murder. They will not be letting him go," he says and slaps the wheel before leaning back in the seat, defeated.

As if that bastard finally getting busted for something was a bad thing.

Exhaustion pulls on my eyelids, so I rest my head against the window, about to get some shut-eye, when Saint taps my hand. "Have you ever been inside? Maybe there's a way to enter unseen? A station this small might not be fully secure, since they probably deal with DIUs and theft most of the time."

I glance at him, unsure why we would even consider taking such risks. "I've been in there, but... why are you asking? He won't escape, if that's what you're worried about."

Saint exhales and kneads the steering wheel, as if that motion could somehow get the vehicle moving. His lips are twisted, and a deep groove appears between his brows. "Because we won't reach him once he gets transferred. Now might be our only chance," he mutters and pulls out his phone.

I shrug, surprised I don't really care that much. Worst case scenario, we'll get him a few years down the line, or he rots in prison for the rest of his miserable life. If we're lucky, maybe someone shanks him, solving the problem for us.

But I entertain him with a sleepy smile. "Or we could start firing our guns so they arrest us too."

Saint grunts, browsing something on the screen. "Those cops are innocent. I bet they do their jobs well enough most of the time. But maybe if I can find plans for the building somehow—"

"Saint. That was a joke."

Something's off and I can't put my finger on it.

When Saint turns my way with his teeth bared, I recoil at the snap in his voice. "Why would you joke about it? I just told you this might be our only chance to get him. There's only two damn days left until Christmas!"

Oh. I was so overwhelmed by tonight's events that I didn't even take that into account. I kind of... forgot about the whole revenge agreement.

I grab his hand and squeeze it, surprised to find it trembling. "It's okay."

Hazel eyes darken, and he shakes his head. "No, it's not. We agreed I do it until the twenty-fifth, and if I fail, you can just walk away. I need to prove I can do this for you," he chokes out in a voice that gets raspier and lower with each word. His hand squeezes mine to the point of pain, but I can't make myself move as a sense of peace swells in my chest.

He's worried? Afraid I will leave him? Unfathomable.

"Saint? Look at me," I ask and shifting closer, annoyed that there's so much space between us and that I can't just push the stick aside. "Just because I can, doesn't mean I will. I don't want to. We can kill him whenever, or *never*. I'll still be yours." The words tighten my throat, because I mean them with every cell in my body.

It's not that revenge doesn't matter anymore, I still want to get Otto, but Saint's affection, his need for me, has created a buffer around my heart. It soaks up the blood from the many cuts my soul has suffered and softens the jagged edges that pushed people away. He embraces me as I am, and I'm ready to always be that for him too.

He swallows, stiff as if a part of him was already dead and my touch is the only thing capable of bringing him back. Air trembles as he exhales, blinking rapidly when he looks away from me. "I just... it's been so lonely without you. I can't let go."

I see all of him. Not just the powerful beast who plowed through four people to get to me, but also the man who's been alone for twelve years, unable to connect with anyone.

Fuck it.

I scramble over the stick and hit my head on the roof, but I manage to straddle his lap. "We'll get to Otto eventually, but you have a new job now," I lean down to kiss him. "Making sure I'm safe, so you don't lose me."

It's still quite dark, but in the glow of the lamps mounted at the front of the police station, I see the damp sheen in his eyes. He blinks it away, leans in to touch our foreheads. Then, after a moment of stillness, his arms are around me. "Really? You want me for good?" he rasps, teasing my neck with his breath.

"For good, for bad, forever." I give him another kiss, wishing I could melt into him. "No one has ever empowered me like you. You make me feel like I matter, like I deserve revenge, like what I've been through wasn't just a blip the world doesn't care about. And not just that. You came for me after Otto took me, despite all the risk."

Saint kisses my neck and pulls me against him even more tightly, so I can sense every tremor in his body. "I've never been so damn scared. Of course I came."

I chuckle, feeling reassured by this show of vulnerability. It's so difficult to discuss feelings without worrying about having them thrown in my face—even in therapy—but if he can tell me the truth then so can I.

"With you, I feel so cared for, so important, and I need you to know I feel the same about you. Not just because you're stupidly handsome," I kiss his soft lips again, "but because we're bound in ways I could never experience with anyone else. You *get* me."

Saint shivers, watching me with the softest gaze, as if he were about to get on his knees and worship me. "You get me too. You're the only one. The One."

The gear stick digging into my leg is nothing, because just being close to him soothes any and all discomfort. My heart is full, even though we've been through so much last night. Even though Otto Grass still breathes.

I'm not even a little bit sleepy anymore as I give Saint's lips a teasing lick. It feels so good to be chosen by this amazing man. "And you're my first and my only. My own, personal wolf." I stroke the back of his neck, and as we lock eyes, I can't help myself and... I grind against him.

His eyes widen, as does his smile when his hands slide down my body, to claim my butt with a firm squeeze. "I can be that and so much more. I'm offended you didn't mention that I'm also your personal chef," he muses as his hips move up, rubbing against my denim-clad ass.

The earlier stress and anguish are both gone from his gaze, replaced by a haze of lust.

I moan, cuddling up to him. "Oh, you're right. I'd fuck you for those cakes alone."

We both chuckle, but my laugh turns into a whimper when he squeezes my cock. He frees it from my jeans in a few movements he must have perfected over years of hooking up with guys way hotter than me. And yet, it's me he wants at his side. I'm the one he's willing to take risks for, and who almost made him cry.

"This is for good," he whispers, and I grin because it's neither a question nor a request. He's just informing me what my future is going to be like.

"Or what? You will hunt me down?" I tease, pressing my dick against him.

Saint's teeth sink into his lips as he gives my cock a tug firm enough to make my legs weaken in this awkward position. "Is that what you want? For me to track you like an animal and then *consume* you in the snow?"

My heart pumps faster and my breath quickens when I envision him ripping clothes off me and helping himself to my body. "Fuck... That sounds so hot," I whisper as I imagine my hot face in the snow. It would be uncomfortable, but I'd have no choice. I'd be sore after, and soaked, but Saint could carry me back home, straight to a hot bath.

"Does it?" Saint asks with a wolfish smile, and the grip he has on my cock gets even tighter as he grinds against my ass, making the car stir. "Perfect prey. I'm going to consume you many, many times."

I push closer and let out a little moan right next to his ear. "I... yeah. Maybe it's messed up, but it's so hot when you're intense like that. Treat me like you own me and I need to submit." My cheeks heat up when I voice my dirty thoughts, but I want him to know.

His fingers push into my hair and pull my head back, so he can watch me while he jerks me off. And God, the look on his face, so tense and predatory, makes my balls throb for release.

"You are mine. Forever."

A flashlight slaps a white beam straight in my face, and I yelp in panic. I'm dazed as a cop bangs on our window, but Saint pulls me closer to preserve my modesty.

"Are you fucking kidding me? Right in front of the station?" The policeman says. "Get out of the car!"

Saint is still holding on to my dick for a few heartbeats, but then he lets me tuck myself in and raises his hands. "Sorry! It just— happened."

The white beam blinds me again as I open the car door and stumble out into the cold. My knee chooses this moment to erupt with pain. Saint's helping me, but nothing can reduce the awkwardness of the situation as I recognize the cop's face. Todd Chaplain. He was a frequent flier at Chuck's shop.

"Nothing 'just happens'. Seriously, Rowan? I didn't even know you're fucking guys! Way to fucking announce it!"

My face is on *fire*. "I... yeah, but he's my first."

Todd's eyes go wide. "Why do I need to know that?"

He's right. I'm so fucking awkward. As if being kidnapped, beaten and drugged wasn't bad enough for one night, I had to get myself arrested on top of that. To make matters even worse, the lady cop with blemishes on both cheeks, who came over when Saint first broke into my apartment, walks out of the station and rushes our way.

"Everything okay, Todd?" she asks.

"Yes, but turns out we had these lovebirds dogging in front of the building," he says as Saint follows me out of the vehicle.

"What?" She jogs up to us and cocks her head in recognition. "You're the home invasion guy!"

I squirm under her gaze. "Yeah, I—"

Todd squints at Saint. "You're not local." He once more flashes the light in my face. "What are all those bruises?"

The policewoman shakes her head as her expression turns stern. "We've had enough trouble tonight already. Do I need to cuff you, or are you going in on your own?"

Saint steps forward, shaking his head. "I'm so sorry. This has never happened before. You're right, we should have known better," he says, finishing on a soft sigh. "And no, we will not run." With that, he peeks over his shoulder. "You okay?"

Todd rolls his eyes. "Touching. Now lock your car and move it."

"Your first gays?" the female cop asks, and he scowls, watching Saint lock the vehicle.

I can't believe *this* is what I'm getting arrested for.

"I'm not cleaning the other cell for this." Todd shakes his head at me.

"Just put them in with the other guy," The female cop says.

It takes a few seconds, but adrenaline buzzes in my skull when I realize who she means.

The "*other guy.*" Otto Grass.

I lick my lips, not sure if this is a good or bad development, but Saint gives me a wolfish grin.

He pretends he's leaning down to kiss my ear as he whispers, "I have poison."

My heart skips a beat, and I hardly register it when Todd tells us to stop touching.

"I love you," I say to Saint when our eyes meet.

EPILOGUE

SAINT

A YEAR HAS PASSED, and Rosehill Pines hasn't changed a bit. There is the new pop-up bookshop boasting that they sell only Christmas-themed books, but otherwise, the town remains blissfully stagnant. The restaurant where I took Rowan on our first date even features the same seasonal specials. It's as if time here stood still while my life rushed forward, skipping milestones so fast it's difficult to imagine me and Rowan only got together twelve months ago.

It feels like more.

And yet, there's still things I'm finding out about him, like the fact that his family once took a long hike through the Grand Canyon, which he only mentioned when we visited Arizona some weeks back. Or that he really, *really* despises mint tea.

I hope that once we run out of things to find out about one another, we will keep making discoveries together, because I never want to lose the magic sparking between us and the sense of joy I feel in his presence. I used to be lonely, yes, but I didn't understand how empty my life was until he became a part of it.

Now, it's full.

Exciting.

And so damn happy.

I'd cut off my own finger if it made him smile.

And speaking of cutting off body parts, I love that he isn't squeamish about the grisly sides of our work. I have lots of money in savings and wanted to wait until he felt ready to get involved, so we took things slow and cherry-picked two jobs in the summer. We trained a lot beforehand, so he could learn everything from self-defense techniques to using a sniper rifle, and by the time we ventured out, I was certain it would be safe for him to go. Or at least as safe as our job can be.

Coming from a very rich woman, the assignment was so lucrative it would have been difficult to pass on. Her husband, or should I say, *ex*-husband, faked his own death and then started another family all the way down in Paraguay. I was excited to take on the task of disposing of him, because Rowan has never been out of the US before that. Going abroad came with logistical challenges, like the issue of sourcing guns in another country, but we took our sweet time, and I let Rowan make the killing shot once everything was set up.

There's so much innocence in him still, but he recognizes that people and their situations come in all shades of gray, and that makes him perfect for me. In our everyday life, he's sweet and gentle, but there's something wild and magnificent about him when the darkness takes over. A sense of justice that will guide us both in the future.

Human trash needs to be disposed of, plain and simple. That's why I had no moral issues with finishing off Otto Grass in the jail cell, while he was sleeping off his cocaine comedown. He likely passed out as soon as he laid his head down and didn't even wake up when we joined him.

The only regret I have about his death is that Rowan didn't get the satisfaction of cutting the bastard's life short himself, but I'm more experienced with those things, so he did the sensible thing and let me do the honors. I always keep poison in my shoe, for emergencies, and the needle it utilizes is so thin Otto didn't even stir when injected.

Fifteen minutes later, Rowan and I called in the cops when he went into cardiac arrest. Bastard was gone before reaching the hospital, and while both me and Rowan would have liked for him to suffer for all his crimes, what mattered at the end of the day was that he was no longer ruining the world with his rotten life.

Over the next months, Otto was declared the murderer of Miles Brown and the others, since Brown's phone ended up being identified at the murder house, like I predicted. Some of his belongings have also been found in a small utility room in the mall's basement. He'd apparently been sleeping there, so maybe Brown did mean Otto going underground literally. We'll never know. What matters is that the case was closed. When a detective with too much ambition for his own good remembered Rowan's connection to all the dead men and started asking questions, Mrs. Treville once again proved to be an angel in disguise and gave us the perfect alibi.

But our life together is very normal most of the time. Sometimes, we joke around about Rowan belonging to me because I managed to finish the job before the deadline. It's a good way for me to get out of cleaning the kitchen as long as I later also show him he's *mine* in bed.

When we're not traveling, we live together in my apartment in Brooklyn, and while we can't get a cat because of our lifestyle, Rowan has befriended the neighbor's Bengal, so every now and then we get to take care of him. We even took him to a park once, which was all fine and dandy until his leash got tangled in a bush, and I ended up having to crawl between the branches to get him out. Since then, we prefer taking care of the spotty furball at home.

Rowan's presence showed me a new side of my city, since he wanted to see all the landmarks and museums. It's so much more satisfying to explore together than it ever was on my own. Every time we visit a new restaurant or take a day trip, our bond grows, and we get to know each other better. But Rowan is no city rat, so we often visit nature spots and forests, whether it's for a hike or to practice tracking.

Christmas time is also our anniversary, and we decided to spend most of December at the cabin where we made so many memories last year. I admit, some of them not ideal, but Rowan is more than happy about being back, so who am I to complain? Especially when it means we'll be able to visit the Christmas market we missed out on last year, when we got snowed in. We even accidentally bumped into Mrs. Treville the day before, and will get to spend Christmas Eve with the person who brought us together. Talk about happy coincidences...

Gentle snowfall gives the scene in front of us a pinch of magical charm as we walk along stands with local arts and crafts. Mulled wine tastes best in this kind of setting, and as we admire all the decorations, it's impossible to miss that they're even more opulent than last year. Apparently, the current mayor is convinced this might bring in more visitors during the holiday period, and judging by the amount of people crowding the main square, her plan might be working.

As we stop to listen to a choir singing Christmas carols, I stroke Rowan's hand between our bodies, anonymous in the crowd of people eager to join the singing. His knee has been giving him grief today, but he's using the cane I got him last Christmas. It's black, not too flashy, since I didn't want to risk it getting stolen, but has a long knife hidden inside. Perfect for when desperate measures are required. I hope he never has to use it, but he absolutely loves it, so I'm glad I hit the gift-giving jackpot.

"Look, they make taxidermy lamps!" Rowan smiles, pointing out a booth where a man has several unique pieces on offer, including a large deer head with light bulbs built into its antlers.

"Is that of interest?" I ask as we drift away from the singers and enter yet another alley with colorful lights hung between the roofs of small wooden huts, which host all the shops.

"Yeah, I like it. I was actually considering getting into taxidermy at one point."

Ha. Yet another thing I didn't know about him. I immediately give him a gentle nudge toward the booth. "We could get one. The living room is a bit empty right now. We have space for a statement lamp."

I've always kept my apartment elegant and tidy, but I don't mind him bringing in a bit of chaos. After all, it's *our* place now, and I want him to infuse it with his personality.

"You sure? 'Cause I like the really big one!"

How can I say no to him when his eyes light up as if he was stabbing Ted's head all over again?

"Absolutely. We both love nature, why not bring some of it home?" I say, and once again his smile disarms me. Seeing it would be enough of a gift this Christmas, but he's hiding the contents of his luggage from me, so I have no doubt he got me something.

"Rowan?" A female voice speaks up behind us, and we turn around to face Rowan's old therapist. I spied on her for a bit last year and recognize her in the small woman with long blonde hair and a pleasant smile.

Rowan is a bit stiff when he nods. "Mrs. Woken. Nice to see you."

She offers us a smile before focusing on Rowan. "I hope you're faring well."

"He is," I say and rub his shoulder, to make sure she understands he's well taken care of. She never helped Rowan with her talk of forgiveness, but I did.

She blinks. "Oh... I see your friend is looking out for you."

"Yeah, I have a new therapist," Rowan says even though the only therapy sessions he's attending involve my dick, revenge kills, and expensive restaurants. "Though our last session proved to be very useful."

I'm sure he says that for my benefit, because the letter his therapist told him to write during his last ever session with her was what brought us together.

"Well, that's good. If they ever want to discuss your case, do give them my number," Mrs. Woken says before taking another peek at me.

"Merry Christmas," I tell her without embellishing it with a smile.

Rowan says his quick goodbyes, and we move on to the booth where the lamp craftsman is over the moon to sell his biggest piece. We pay and arrange to pick it up later, but Rowan is a bit quiet as we walk among the stalls glittering with Christmas offerings like baubles and light-up garden statues.

"What's on your mind?" I ask, stroking his back.

"I just... I don't know. She would always emphasize that I could only be free if I let go of my anger and resentment. But I only felt released from those feelings after I dealt with my past your way. The pain dulls over time, and I don't regret what we did, but sometimes I wonder if it makes me a bad person."

I sigh, and as we continue our walk between the stalls, I gather my thoughts. "I think it depends on our reasons. I've seen many things doing this job. Some clients are regretful once it's over, but most of them feel content. Unless someone lets revenge overtake their whole life, I think it's more about reestablishing a sense of justice in the world. You are not a bad person. You take such good care of me, and I think you needed those people gone because otherwise you would keep being afraid of them for as long as they lived."

And for good reason, since they were animals. Rowan even told me Otto would sometimes come to his workplace, just to taunt him with his presence. I'm happy about the bastard's death for that reason alone.

Rowan pulls me into a side street, which hasn't been spared the same pizzazz as the Christmas market and has strings of LEDs leading us along the passage.

"It's true. If they got sentenced to prison, I would have still hated them but got on with my life in one way or another. Seeing them act as if nothing happened after destroying my family was so painful, I can't force myself to feel bad about being the one who sent them to their graves." The self-satisfied smirk on his pretty face makes me want to kiss him, and I go for it after taking a brief peek over the shoulder.

I love his new cinnamon toothpaste.

"Where are we headed? You hungry?" I ask, entwining our fingers as we face the exit into the main street.

"I actually have something special planned as part of my Christmas gift to you..." Rowan grins and pulls me to a shop window.

It's a bakery opulently decorated with pink and white. As I stare at the little pastries and cookies behind the glass, I realize this has to be the place where he got me that fancy cheesecake last year.

It's no longer open to customers, but a couple of people are inside, chatting and sipping from stoneware cups.

I glance at him. "Now you have me excited. What is it?"

Rowan gets to his toes to give me a smooch. "I booked us in for a cookie decorating class. So you can really wow me this year."

I look inside, then at him, and take off my hat as excitement heats up my head. "*Really*? Tonight?"

When he nods, I pull him into a bear hug and lean back until his feet leave the pavement.

Rowan laughs as I spin us around. "Yes! Maybe mine will stop looking like they were decorated by a talented child."

I give him another kiss, no longer caring if someone sees us or not. "I love you."

I mean it with all my heart. Rowan filled my life in ways I couldn't have imagined, and every lonely nook within me is only a memory.

With the snow starting to twirl around us out of nowhere and the picturesque bakery as our background, I really do feel like I'm in the prettiest snow globe.

The sweet dark-eyed boy in my arms and the scent of vanilla cookies already hitting my nose will make this the best Christmas yet.

The End

If you'd like to read about Saint and Rowan's first Christmas together, you can find a bonus chapter at https://www.kamerikan.com/freebies or HERE.

Read on to find out about the next book in the series!

If you want to stay in touch with us, follow us on Amazon and join our Facebook group, the **K.A. Merikan Playroom** or join our newsletter at http://kamerikan.com/newsletter .

K.A. MERIKAN
HO HO
HOMICIDAL
MANIAC

HO HO HOMICIDAL MANIAC

MURDER AND MISTLETOE SERIES

"I love Christmas. So every year, I kill someone. As a treat."

Nico

Have you ever fallen in love with a man as he was pointing his gun at you? Well, I have. Tiny problem? I'm in the middle of my murderous Christmas tradition, and he's a witness.

But it's not his fault I got too excited and didn't check if I was alone. I can't just kill him because of my own blunder. Not when he has such dreamy green eyes filled with fear and pent-up rage.

What I can do is take him with me for safekeeping while I work out how to make him understand that while my methods are cruel, my intentions are pure.

Or how to make him fall for me.

Whichever is first.

Blake

My eighteenth birthday was supposed to be the happiest day of my sheltered life. Finally, I would gain independence and inherit half my family fortune. Instead, I ended up kidnapped.

I was about to get carved into pieces when... a Christmas miracle in the form of a beefy homicidal maniac saved me.

Only now I'm trapped in his basement and getting love bombed by a psycho golden retriever. He eats turkey sandwiches for every breakfast, enjoys making festive ornaments out of human teeth, and lets his violent urges shine like a Christmas tree.

I shouldn't find him hot.
I shouldn't want to indulge his murderous tendencies.
And I definitely shouldn't want him to be my first.

But I'm being hunted and might just need a monster to keep me safe.

(And he does actually make really good fruitcake)

"Ho Ho Homicidal Maniac" is a standalone M/M dark romance where a Christmas-obsessed serial killer falls for a poor little rich boy who also happens to be his favorite true crime podcaster.

Themes and tropes: Size difference, serial killer, mistrust, small town, loneliness, possessive hero, grumpy/sunshine, dark humor, abduction, first love, morally gray, sheltered rich boy, psychopath, black cat/golden retriever relationship, stockholm syndrome, betrayal, first time, opposites attract, stuck together, fish out of water, CHRISTMAS, dark secret, dude in distress, wallflower

Warnings: Kidnapping, violence, gore, strong language, and steamy, explicit scenes

Available on Amazon

CRIMINAL DELIGHTS: TAKEN
WRONG
WAY HOME
K.A. MERIKAN

WRONG WAY HOME

K.A. MERIKAN

--- One wrong turn. One right man. ---

Colin. Rule-follower. Future doctor. Witness to murder. Captive.
Taron. Survivalist. Mute. Murderer. Captor.

Like every other weekend, Colin is on his way home from university, but he's taunted by the notion that he never takes risks in life and always follows the beaten path. On impulse, he decides to take a different route.

Just this one time. What he doesn't realize is that it's the last time he has a choice.

He ends up taking a detour into the darkest pit of horror, abducted by a silent, imposing man with a blood-stained axe. But what seems like his worst nightmare might just prove to be a path to the kind of freedom Colin never knew existed.

Taron has lived alone for years. His land, his rules. He'd given up on company long ago. After all, attachment is a liability. He deals with his problems on his own, but the night he needs to dispose of an enemy, he ends up with a witness to his crime.

The last thing Taron needs is a nuisance of a captive. Colin doesn't deserve death for setting foot on Taron's land, but keeping him isn't optimal either. It's only when he finds out the city boy is gay that an altogether different option arises. One that isn't right, yet tempts him every time Colin's pretty eyes glare at him from the cage.

"When Taron looped the heavy metal collar around the slender neck and closed the padlock, his body throbbed with the excitement of knowing he owned this boy.
Was it wrong? Yes, yes it was.
Was it so, so good? Definitely."

Themes: prepping, alternative lifestyles, disability, crime, loneliness, enemies to lovers, forced proximity, fish out of water, opposites attract, abduction, Stockholm syndrome, family issues

Genre: Dark, thriller M/M romance

Erotic content: Scorching hot, emotional, explicit scenes

Length: ~ 70,000 words (Standalone)

This book is part of CRIMINAL DELIGHTS. Each novel can be read as a standalone and will contain a dark M/M romance.

Warning: These books are for adult readers who enjoy stories where lines between right and wrong get blurry. High heat, twisted and tantalizing, these are not for the fainthearted.

This story contains scenes of explicit violence, offensive language, morally ambiguous characters.

Available on Amazon

About the Author

K.A. Merikan is a duo of queer writers who don't believe in following the well-trodden path. In their books you can dip your toe into dangerous romance with mafiosi, outlaw bikers and bad boys, all from the safety of your sofa. They love the weird and wonderful, stepping out of the box, and bending stereotypes both in life and in fiction. Their stories don't shy away from exploring the darker side of M/M romance, and feature a variety of anti-heroes, rebels, misfits, and underdogs who go against the grain.

Be prepared for shocking twists, dark humor, raw emotions, and sizzling hot scenes.

e-mail: **kamerikan@gmail.com**
http://kamerikan.com

More information about works in progress and publishing at:

Facebook: https://www.facebook.com/groups/181754 1075240882

Patreon: https://www.patreon.com/kamerikan